ALL I HAVE TO LOSE

THE SUCCOURI SAGA
BOOK TWO

MERIDITH GIBBENS

STAY INFORMED

Be the first to hear about new releases, including the next book in this series.

Go to: http://meridithgibbens.com

Click "Subscribe to stay informed".

Thank you for your kind support.

CONTENTS

CHAPTER I
THE DREAD

Ben jolted upright out of shallow sleep. Heart pounding in his chest, a familiar feeling of dread shook him, sending adrenaline through his body. For a moment, he was disoriented, unable to recall where he was or focus his vision on the dark surroundings, but soon his mind remembered, and his panic heightened.

He was in the living room of the LeVray home. The previous day Callie's family and friends said a sorrowful goodbye to Callie's father, Ronald LeVray, who had passed away from a severe stroke. Because of Ben's extraordinary Succouri gift, he'd been able to give Callie and her younger brother, Lee, the chance to say a final goodbye, but in the end, they'd had to let him go.

As Ben searched for the source of his sudden panic, his mind replayed his conversation with Police Officer Evans after the funeral. Just over a week ago, Callie was shot on her porch by an evil man whom the police believed to be a fellow gang member and drug dealer of a violent criminal whom Callie's father had been responsible for convicting and putting in prison for life. They hadn't caught the monster yet, and Officer Evans warned Ben that the shooter wouldn't give up until he'd finished the job. Evans advised Ben to take Callie out of town for a while, and Ben had set plans in motion to do just that, but he'd wanted to give her the day to mourn with her friends and family before scaring and saddening her with the reality of the danger they faced.

Since Callie's release from the hospital, Ben had slept on the couch in the LeVrays' living room, unwilling to put his complete faith and trust in the security presence outside the home. Callie had offered him his own bedroom but he felt better sleeping where he could see both entrances to the house and keep tabs on the comings and goings of the provided security.

At this point, the police protection included one patrol car with a team of two cops. They watched the home from the front, occasionally circling the block to check for any signs of trouble. Ben had hired an additional guard to keep a closer eye out, regularly walking the house's perimeter.

Rising from the couch, Ben walked to the nearby window. He could make out the silhouetted figure of the privately hired guard near the back door. It was cold outside in the early February night air, and Ben felt sorry for those assigned this unpleasant yet necessary task.

Despite the guard's presence, the dread continued to plague him. He'd experienced this twice before when he'd first laid eyes on the black Dodge Monaco in Callie's neighborhood and then again when he'd spotted it at the courthouse. Though he'd had no logical reason for the feeling then, the vehicle had unsettled him, but he hadn't followed up on his instincts. That had been a nearly fatal mistake. The occupant of the vehicle turned out to be Callie's shooter.

Ben glanced at his watch. It was just after five a.m. The

house was quiet as Ben scanned each room on the main floor, but nothing was out of place or suspicious.

When he exited the kitchen and rounded the corner, he stood gazing up into the dark stairway. Ben's chest tightened as he heard her name, like it was being screamed, inside his head.

"Callie!" he whispered reflexively into the darkness.

As Lee was asleep in the basement bedroom, Callie was the only one upstairs. Though Ben didn't want to invade her privacy, he had promised himself he would never again ignore his instincts, especially when it came to protecting her. When she'd been shot and he'd had to face the possibility of living without her, the sorrow had nearly crushed him.

For six years, Ben had lived alone, running from what he was. For far longer than that, he hadn't known where he'd gotten his unnatural abilities, and he had no idea what to do with them. Empty and lost after the death of his mother, he'd blamed everything painful in his life on his gift, which, at the time, he thought of as a curse.

But that all changed when he met Callie. She opened his heart, accepted him, and helped him alter his perception of who he was and the power he possessed. That power saved Callie's life and his own heart as well. His identity as Succouri enabled them to share an extraordinary bond, which they were only at the beginning of developing and exploring. As he hesitantly ascended the stairs, he wondered if that connection was involved in prompting his dread as every fiber of his being drew him urgently to her.

Once again, Ben searched the hallways and rooms upstairs, looking for something to justify his rising anxiety, but nothing was amiss. Finally, feeling overtaken by the apprehension that increased with every eliminated potential cause of threat, he approached Callie's bedroom.

Her door was halfway open. Streetlights beamed dim streaks of illumination into the room. Though he'd spent several days in the LeVray home, Ben had never been in Callie's bedroom.

Though there was no doubt of his love and desire, he also possessed an unwavering respect for her. Therefore, he had carefully guarded them both by avoiding placing them in situations that might tempt them beyond their ability to resist. His unique bond with Callie had many wondrous manifestations, but a key consequence was that it intensified attraction and the desire for physical and emotional closeness. They'd had enough experience with this phenomenon to respect its potent power. They wanted to give their relationship time to develop and grow in all ways, believing, ultimately, that the balance would be healthier and more fulfilling. Staying out of her bedroom was assuredly an essential guideline for maintaining their mutually agreed-upon boundaries, but presently, he had no choice. It was a different kind of power that drew him to her now.

Looking around the room, Ben again tried to connect his fear to something tangible. The window was on the right wall and looked out over the front yard. Scanning left, a nightstand was in the corner of the back wall with a lamp on it, and her bed was next to it. The left wall was occupied by a tall dresser and a door, which he presumed to be to a closet. To his immediate left as he stepped just inside her room, was a chair with a robe slung haphazardly over it.

As his eyes circled back to the bed to focus on Callie's sleeping form, he suddenly felt very uncomfortable with how close her bed was to the window. Just a few feet separated her from this point of potential hazard. Impulsively, Ben repositioned himself to fill the gap.

Turning, he looked out the window at the street below. In the early morning darkness, he could only make out shadowy trees, fence lines, and the bulky black shapes of adjacent houses. At the moment, the patrol car was absent, and he guessed it was performing one of its regular neighborhood sweeps.

Slowly, as he sucked in a deep breath, he turned to look at Callie. Sleeping soundly on her right side, she faced away from him, the sheets and blankets tucked up around her just above her waist. The tank top she wore left the healing wound on her left shoulder exposed. Though her back was to him, the dim light fell across the side of her angelic face. Ben had sat by Callie's bedside in the hospital for days and watched her sleep, so he knew well how beautiful she was in this state, but somehow, gazing at her in this intimate setting felt very different.

Before long, he began to regret breaching her privacy without her knowledge or permission. He shouldn't be in here, and he shouldn't be looking at her like this as his desire to lie down beside her and pull her close was swiftly intensifying.

As he turned to leave, Callie shifted and opened her eyes.

"Ben?" She shocked him by whispering into the darkness, which he knew utterly blinded her.

Ben froze, worried that he'd frighten her with his sudden appearance by her bedside, but he quickly realized that it would be far more alarming if he didn't let her know that it was him and explain his presence.

"Yes. It's me, Callie. I'm sorry to intrude. I... I needed to check on you, to be sure you were alright. I..."

Rolling over, she reached out for him, cutting off his explanation. "It's alright," she reassured, with no hint of surprise at his presence.

Returning to stand beside her bed, Ben grasped her outstretched hand. She rose to a sitting position as her vision focused, and her eyes grew wide as she reacted to his expression of concern. As she lifted herself, one of the straps of her tank top slipped off her shoulder, and Ben's pulse quickened.

"Ben, what is it?"

Cautiously, he sat on the edge of her bed and reached to pull up the strap on her shirt so that his eyes would stay firmly focused on her face. "I'm not sure. I just had a bad feeling, like the one I had before when you were in danger. Callie, we need to talk. I wish I didn't have to tell you this, but I can't avoid it. I'm sorry to do it like this, to wake you up, but we need to leave..."

From outside, came the roar of an engine revving up to full power and then the squeal of tires. Without any thought, Ben reacted, throwing himself on top of Callie and pulling her down flat against the bed as he moved.

A heartbeat later, a spray of bullets shattered the glass in Callie's window and ricocheted off the ceiling and walls around them.

A terror-filled scream shook Callie's body as Ben tucked her underneath him, drawing her arms inside his and sheltering her head under his neck. The lamp beside her bed hit the back wall and crashed to the floor, and something grazed his right shoulder, igniting a small flame of pain that quickly burned out.

Outside, voices shouted, and the gunshots ceased for several seconds. Seizing the moment, Ben rolled twice, keeping Callie firmly pressed against him, and dropped onto the floor opposite the window, ensuring that his body hit the ground rather than hers. Then, he swiftly shifted to cover her again. More shots rang out, but now they were well out of the line of fire.

"Ben!" Callie cried as she clung to his T-shirt with both hands.

Her body trembled, and his heart ached for her as he knew the trauma she was experiencing as, once more, she became the target of gunfire.

"You're alright, sweetheart. Everything's alright," he soothed, holding her as close to him as he could without crushing her under his weight. The gunshots ceased, but he continued listening for any further indications of danger.

The dread began to ease when he heard the engine rev again as the car sped away followed by the wail of sirens pursuing. Whoever it was, he was on the run and wouldn't get too far.

As the panic retreated from his immediate focus, the full force of their connecting bond overpowered him, taking control of his senses and thoughts. When he had rolled off of the bed with Callie, they'd dislodged the sheets and blankets, which had twisted around them, wrapping them tightly together. Callie's soft feminine curves pressed against him, and Ben could feel several contact points where their skin touched, drawing a small amount of strength from him which was being overwhelmingly replenished by the intense energy cycling between them. The pleasure of both consumed him.

For several blissful seconds, Ben lost all control, swept away by desire and need. Callie's crying ceased and she audibly inhaled, also abruptly caught inside the tidal wave of passion as the near-constant magnetic pull they felt between them was momentarily satisfied. As he began fiercely kissing her, she responded, letting go of his T-shirt and wrapping her arms around him, drawing him even closer.

Ben possessed only one instinct that was stronger than his yearning for Callie in that moment, and it sobered him long enough to rescue them both. Though they seemed temporarily out of danger, he needed to get her out of this room, away from windows, and secure the house. That penetrating thought broke through his consciousness, allowing him to regain a second of control, and he seized it.

Hastily, Ben rolled away, though his body felt heavy and pained as he did. He struggled to free himself from the tangle of blankets and sheets, but then he scrambled to his feet and lifted Callie into his arms. Keeping his back to the window, he rushed to her bedroom door and out into the hall. When he'd set her down, he reached back, just inside her room, to grab the robe on the chair before closing the door.

As she appeared unsteady, Ben kept his arm around Callie's waist until she adjusted to the disorientation caused by his sudden motions.

"If I let go of you, can you stand on your own?" he asked, still a little out of breath as he watched her focus on his face.

"I... Yes. I think so. What... What's going on? Why are they still trying to kill me?"

She was still trembling, so Ben let go of her and helped her into her robe, both to warm her and to cover her, for Ben's sake as much as those whom he knew would soon be making an appearance. As he placed his hand tenderly on her cheek, he felt the familiar mix of pain and relief at how close he had, once again, come to losing her. Despite the consequences arising from their unavoidable physical closeness, Ben was thankful he'd paid attention to his instincts this time.

Before he could decide how to answer her question, Callie gasped. "Ben! Your shoulder!"

Turning his head, he saw the small stain of blood on his white T-shirt on his shoulder blade. Callie tugged on the short sleeve as he dropped his hand from her face.

Though there was a visible wound, Ben could tell the bullet had only grazed him, as there was no indication of it entering the skin. The wound wasn't bleeding anymore, and it already looked like it had been healing for several days.

Keeping her hand on the skin of his arm, Callie watched in wonder as the wound continued rapidly closing. The healing was progressing more quickly than usual, and Ben had no doubt that the influx of strength from their intimate encounter just a moment ago was the cause.

Amazed, Callie's eyes grew large, and Ben couldn't help but smile, despite their circumstances. Before or apart from Callie, this revelation would have filled him with panic. Peace and contentment settled over him as he relaxed in the truth that he now felt only pleasure at watching the wonder on her face as she saw the evidence of who he was on full display.

The intimate moment was interrupted by Lee's voice and the pounding of approaching footsteps on the stairs. Quickly, she pulled his sleeve down and tied her robe closed, and Ben moved to stand beside her and lean against the wall.

Lee appeared first, and the look of relief on his face as he saw Callie standing there perfectly safe and healthy made Ben smile. Wrapping his big arms around his sister,

Lee lifted her off the floor as Callie gasped for air at the tightness of his embrace.

"Lee! I can't breathe," she complained, though she also smiled at his evident relief.

"I'm just glad you *are* breathing," he panted. "You've gotta stop doing this to me, Sis."

"Trust me, I can think of safer ways to torture you, ways that don't involve me being someone's idea of target practice."

The private security guard also looked relieved as he waited a few feet behind Lee. As Lee and Callie discussed what had happened, Ben approached the guard for a report on the security situation.

"I'm sorry. Can you remind me of your name?" Ben inquired.

The security company that Ben had chosen employed several ex-military specialists. The shifts rotated personnel, so Ben hadn't had a chance to meet and talk with all of them, especially those on night duty.

"Jack Isley," the guard replied as he shook Ben's offered hand. "I'm very relieved that she's alright. That car came out of nowhere and knew its exact target. The patrol car was a block away, and I was just coming around the side of the house when it sprayed the area with bullets. Whoever it was, they obviously weren't trying to kill her. This was just a warning."

Crossing his arms, Ben tilted his head questioningly.

"Your odds of killing someone by firing from a car up into a second-story window are slim," the guard explained. "You might graze them, but most of the bullets will hit the ceiling from that angle."

Ben grimaced at the accuracy of the guard's assessment. "I assume our police officers are in pursuit?" Ben stated more than asked.

"Well, one of them. She will have to simply follow him until backup arrives as there's no way she'll confront him on her own. Her partner took a hit in the arm as he attempted to approach the vehicle. These guys had us at quite a disadvantage since there was no way we would start firing off shots in this neighborhood with the risk of bullets straying into adjacent houses. They knew we wouldn't fire back under these conditions. The officer's in the kitchen with pressure on the wound. I need to get back and attend to him. He'll be okay, but he's bleeding quite a bit, and is in some pain. Help's on the way. Just wanted to be sure you two were secure."

Lee turned to look at Ben, a question in his expression.

"Is the house secure?" Ben inquired, still speaking to the guard while answering Lee's unspoken question with a slight shake of his head. As much as he wanted to go and help the officer, he wouldn't leave Callie unless he knew she was safe.

"No one got out of the car," the guard replied. "They shot up into the window, then at us, and sped off. As soon as I'm freed up, I'll recheck the perimeter."

Lee turned to face Ben. "There are no windows in the kitchen except for the small one over the sink. We'll be fine there, and we can let him check the perimeter while"—Lee cleared his throat—"while we help the officer. I won't leave her side," Lee promised, glancing at Callie.

Ben looked at Callie and she nodded her head, though she still looked shaky.

"We should hurry. After all, he got injured because of me," Callie said with conviction.

The dread had dissipated, and though his priority was

firmly on protecting Callie, Ben couldn't ignore the responsibility he also had to help those in pain. Thanks to Ms. Essie, he had learned more about the purpose behind his abilities, and she'd encouraged him to live out that purpose, taking advantage of any opportunity to help others as only a Succouri can.

Though this life had been forced on him, not freely chosen, this was who he was, and using his gift was the only way to redeem that reality and endure the hardships that also came with the identity. It was challenging, however, to shift his viewpoint so radically in such a short time. He'd spent fifteen years running and hiding from what he didn't understand, but now, though he still needed to be cautious, he was intentionally trying to do the exact opposite. Naturally, he wanted to help anyone in trouble, but he'd suppressed those instincts for so long because of fear and confusion, that the habitual reaction was proving difficult to reverse.

Callie approached and grasped his hand, sensing his struggle. "Let's go help. I'll stay right by you, right where you can see me, and throw yourself on top of me again if you feel the need."

She smiled at him as Lee raised his eyebrows. No doubt, Ben would have some explaining to do later.

CHAPTER 2
THE DEPARTURE

An hour later, Callie hurried to finish getting dressed and ready for the day. She was anxious to return to Ben, knowing he needed her help to recover his strength after giving some of it away to assist the injured officer.

With pride, she'd watched as he calmly aided the man, placing a cloth firmly against his injured arm while allowing several of his fingers to come into contact with his skin as he held it in place. Ben kept him talking, asking him about what he'd seen and then about his family and time on the force. The distraction kept the officer from noticing that the bleeding had stopped entirely, though he was very aware of the cessation of pain.

"Wow!" the officer said with a wrinkle of his brow. "I'm not sure what you're doing differently from that other guy, but it's working."

Lee offered a casual comment about Ben having a lot of recent practice at being a hero. Thanks to the distracting conversation and the relatively short time that Ben had rendered aid before the paramedics arrived, the officer had developed little more than a genuine respect and appreciation for Ben when he left the LeVray home in an ambulance.

One of the medics, however, was the woman who had been a part of the responding team the night Callie had been shot. Observing how healthy and recovered Callie was, she gave Ben several puzzled looks. Attempting to play down the matter, Callie offered a quip about always being a quick healer. Though it didn't eliminate the look of curiosity on the woman's face, it seemed to diminish her suspicion.

Their remaining security guard continued to watch the house's perimeter, but there was no additional suspicious activity. Reinforcements had arrived from the police department so the place was, once again, fully guarded. A team of investigators had also arrived and were inspecting the scene, gathering statements and evidence.

As they were waiting on news from the police headquarters regarding the status of the chase following the shooting into Callie's bedroom, Ben had urged Callie to go ahead and get dressed, promising her that he'd be alright until she could return to help him. Looking questioningly into his eyes, she could see he was sincere, so she obliged his wishes. After all, wandering around in her robe was uncomfortable with all of the male security personnel around.

As she finished combing her hair and applying some makeup, Callie's heart filled with a renewed love for this man whom she'd met only weeks ago. He'd saved her life, not once, but twice now. Without hesitation, he threw himself over her like a shield, willing to sacrifice himself to protect her. He poured his whole being, all his strength, into giving her and Lee a chance to say a final farewell to their dad. The effort had caused him significant exhaustion and weakness, requiring days to recover.

Trusting her with painful memories and a secret that could ruin him if placed in the wrong hands was an enormous risk that required courage. He treated her with respect and honor, even when he had the opportunity and a good excuse to give in to temptation.

Smiling, she recalled how they had lost control for a few seconds that morning, but Ben had been the one to protect them. As they found themselves overtaken by the power of the bond that drew them together, she'd lost all ability to reason. She wanted to stay near him, feeling his body next to hers. Everything else vanished from her world as she became enraptured in the pleasure of being so close to him. The extraordinary sense of belonging and destiny they felt in each other's arms was something only the two of them could understand. Now that she'd tasted the bliss of it, she knew she'd dream of it, long for it, and feel the lack of it much more keenly than she had when she'd been innocently ignorant of its existence.

But she was thankful that Ben protected them from going any further. They'd talked about how they needed to remain in control of the unique bond between them and not the other way around. They'd only known each other for a few weeks, though it felt like a lifetime. There was much more to learn and many beautiful ways to grow together. Callie admired Ben's resolve as he fought hard for the healthy progress of their unique relationship.

In addition, she admired his courage as he faced the responsibilities and burdens that came with the new understanding of his Succouri identity. Nearly overnight, Ben had been confronted with a choice. For very good reason, he'd spent years running from his gift. The burdens it placed on him were nearly as great, if not greater, than the rewards it offered.

But that morning, Callie had watched him sacrificially offer the injured officer his empathy, his compassion, his life-giving strength, all without reservation. The many ways he gave of himself to those in pain were remarkable, and she felt her heart overflowing with joy at the privilege of being a part of it.

That happiness was almost potent enough to let her forget that she'd nearly been killed once more. As she walked past the closed door to her bedroom, a shudder passed through her. She'd used her dad's old room to get ready since hers was the object of investigation, littered with broken glass and now quite cold due to the shattered window. Sleeping in there again without nightmares might prove difficult. She needed some answers. Right before the shots, Ben had said something to her about knowing she was in danger and something about leaving. Her heart pounded as she couldn't fathom that possibility.

As she reached the bottom of the staircase, she smelled eggs and bacon, and her stomach growled. Ben had cooked breakfast for her and Lee nearly every morning since he'd been staying with them. She begged him not to feel oblig-ated to do so, but he seemed to enjoy cooking, and since neither Lee nor she had those skills, it had become his unspoken role in the family. He certainly knew his way around a kitchen, and she teased that Lee might admire Ben more for his cooking skills than his unique gift.

When she entered the kitchen, she saw him standing with his back to her at the stove. Walking up behind him, she startled him by putting her arms around his waist.

"Miss LeVray!" He smiled as he turned to face her, taking her in his arms.

"I'm so, very amazed by you!" she whispered into his ear.

"And I'm so very much in love with you. You take my breath away every time I see you."

Ben leaned wearily against her, so Callie held him as the energy produced by their bond worked its magic. Having something to give him, a way to lighten his burdens, brought joy to her heart. His gifts to her were abundant and generous, both from the part of him that was just Ben and from his touch, and having something to offer in return kept the balance between them beautiful.

Finally, Ben pulled back and placed both hands on the sides of her face, looking deeply into her eyes. "Are you alright?"

She'd never tire of the pleasure she experienced every time she gazed into his eyes. For most of her life, until she met him, she'd been unable to see well enough to read the messages in people's eyes and faces. But now, when Ben touched her, and her visual world came alive in color and detail, she thrilled at the sights around her, each time seeing many things she'd never seen before. Still, her favorite sight by far was his gentle, brilliant blue eyes.

"Yes, I think so. I'm not sure if I'll ever sleep in my room again without nightmares, but thanks to you, I'm alive and breathing. How's your shoulder?"

Ben had also showered and changed, and he now wore a long-sleeve gray shirt. He turned around, and Callie pulled the neck of the shirt out and to the right so she could peer at his wound. Trying to keep her eyes from lingering on his smooth skin and toned muscles, it took her a moment of searching to find anything resembling a wound. There was a small line, remnants of a scar, which looked old and faded.

"Wow! That's a pretty nice perk of this whole Succouri thing."

Ben turned back around to face her. "Yes, it is, and consequently, much better for me to take the hits than you." Cautiously, Ben pulled the neck of Callie's shirt to the side, revealing her scabbed wound for comparison.

"I intend to keep you safe, Miss LeVray, and...That brings us to a conversation I wish I didn't need to have with you, but..." Ben lowered his head, and Callie's heart fell. "Let me get some food in you first," he said as he turned back toward the stove.

Hesitantly, Callie sat on one of the stools at the island, and Ben brought her a plate of delicious-smelling eggs, bacon, and toast, though presently, her stomach was in too many knots for her to eat. After fixing himself a plate as well, Ben settled across from her. Though she had a good idea of what Ben would tell her, she waited patiently for him to speak.

"After the funeral yesterday, Officer Evans spoke with me. He let me know, quite emphatically, that the man that shot you is still out there and isn't giving up. It's some kind of a pride thing, Callie. He can't fail at this, or he loses face and status with the other monsters in his sick and twisted world." Ben paused, contending with the anger rising in him.

He reached across the island to grasp her hand. His warmth helped ease the chill running down Callie's spine.

"I want to protect you; I need to protect you, but, as our experience this morning demonstrated quite effectively, it's going to be impossible to accomplish with him knowing just where to find you and without better security in place. Please, I know that this is a lot to ask – I really do understand – but I need you to trust me. I have to take you away from here, just for a little while, so I can keep you safe." His voice was strained with the urgency of his appeal.

What he was asking of her was certainly significant. To take her away from everything she knew, her brother, her friends, her home, her memories, and right after she'd lost her dad and needed all of that more than ever before, was a huge ask. On top of that, though she could see perfectly when Ben touched her, most of the time, Callie was still nearly completely blind. He was asking her to leave every-thing familiar behind and put her trust wholly in him when he was only beginning to understand that part of her world.

Averting her eyes, Callie felt a tear trickle down her cheek. Ben came to her, lifting her out of her chair and encircling her face with his hands again, forcing her to look at him. "It's so much to ask, I know. I don't want to leave here either. I love this home, Lee, Ms. Essie, all of it too. I have no intention of keeping you away for long. My heart belongs here with you, with this family."

Closing her eyes, she leaned against him, and he put his arms around her. She couldn't speak yet as her emotions threatened to break her down.

After a moment, Ben gently grasped her shoulders and leaned her away so he could look into her eyes again. "And there's more. I want to build a life with you, but I can't do that as long as I'm still completely lost about who I am. I need to move beyond being confused and broken, and to do that, I need answers. I have to figure out who did this to me, who changed me, and why. Why did they abandon me, leaving me lost and afraid? After my mother died, I ran from everything. It's long past time for me to face it, go back home, and put the past to rest. I'm still so mixed up in my head, and I can't move forward like that. I need to set my feet on something solid regarding my past. You've given me the will to do that. But, Callie, I can't…" Ben paused to take a deep and shaky breath. "I can't do it without you. I need your help, your presence with me; to lean on that incredible strength you have that I don't yet possess. I want to take you back with me to where I came from. I want you to know all my secrets, my past, and be there when I hopefully learn the truth. It will be easier for me to keep you safe there. I've already worked out a plan. Those threatening you won't know where we are. Please, I know it's so very much to ask, much more trust than I deserve, but…"

Callie placed her finger over his lips. "Ben, of course I'll go."

Ben exhaled in relief and pulled her to him again as they leaned against each other, feeling their bond growing deeper and broader at the increase of trust between them.

Callie's tears spilled onto Ben's shirt. The tears were a combination of sorrow at having to leave her brother behind, leave her home and memories of her dad, but also at the idea that, after all he'd done, all they'd been through, Ben still somehow felt unworthy of her love and trust.

Ms. Essie's words came back to her. She'd told Callie that pain carried alone for a long time wound itself tightly within someone, like a tangled ball of yarn, and it would take patience and time to unravel. Helping him to uncover his past was undoubtedly important in that process.

Somehow, she needed to help him see himself differently. For so long, he'd believed himself to be poison for others, a cause of pain and loss. Though she'd begun to help him change that, the roots of that perspective still lingered. He'd never be able to fully embrace his gift or move forward with his life until he dug them up.

"What about Lee?"

"I've already spoken to him about this. He's sad and worried, of course, but he agrees with the plan as your safety is the most important thing to him too. He's going to stay with Ms. Essie and Louis. Officer Evans doesn't believe he's in danger, and the events of this morning seem to confirm that, as they were obviously specifically targeting you. They'll continue to provide some protection for him, though, just in case. He'll be safe. I wouldn't leave if I thought otherwise. I promised your father I'd watch out for both of you, and that's a promise I intend to keep."

Though she appreciated his reassurance, the mix of emotions made her suddenly weary. She sat back down, and Ben retreated to his own stool.

"What if... what if they caught him this morning? Maybe it's all over now."

Ben sighed, wishing he could confirm that reality. "Officer Evans will be here to give us a full update in about an hour, but I'm confident that whoever shot at your window this morning wasn't our guy. That was a reckless, bold thing to do, and whoever did it was almost guaranteed to get caught. As the security officer said, that was just a warning, no real chance of success and a great chance of capture. It was likely a minor character sent in some kind of initiation thing or some such evil nonsense to scare us."

Callie slowly nodded, acknowledging a truth she didn't want to accept.

Despite her nerves, Callie took a bite of breakfast. It was delicious, and she marveled at the seemingly endless talents that this incredible man possessed. Though Ben also ate, his concerned gaze never left her face.

"When?" she whispered.

"As soon as possible, by tonight for sure. An old friend, someone I've known since high school, is flying in this morning; should be here by noon. He was a Navy SEAL and now works privately, providing security for those needing protection. His name is Donovan Bradshaw. He's a great man, and I trust him. He'll strategize with us this afternoon before we leave. Then, I want you to have time to say goodbye to Grace and Lobster and let them in on every-thing, if you'd like. I know this is going to be hard for them too. Before we leave, I'd like to stop by and talk with Ms. Essie and Louis once more. I'm hoping they can give us some information on where we might start looking, maybe a contact or another Succouri they know in that part of the country."

Before continuing, Ben huffed frustratedly. "You know, I still don't know much about what I am or how many others like me are out there. I wish we had more time to talk with them, but it will have to be quick."

Callie's head started spinning. In a few short minutes, her whole world had changed, been turned inside out. Despite her own emotional struggle, she reached for Ben's hand and squeezed it. He must have felt the same way, still be feeling the same way, as he was only now beginning to discover a world that he'd unknowingly been a part of for fifteen years.

CALLIE SPENT the next hour packing. Ben encouraged her to bring only the basics and a few days-worth of clothes for the road as he planned to have supplies available in his former home for their use upon arrival. Callie tilted her head in curiosity at the statement, but with all her swirling thoughts and emotions overwhelming her, she simply accepted his instructions and did her best to follow them.

She'd agreed to give him her trust, and she was determined to convince him that he was worthy of it.

Around ten o'clock, they met with Officer Joe Evans. He informed them that they had taken two men into custody. Just as Ben suspected, they didn't believe that either of these men was Callie's original shooter. Likely, they hadn't even had direct contact with the one who had ordered the hit. Young and naïve, they had stupidly believed they'd get away with this and achieve some elevated status in their gang. Still, Officer Evans assured them that they'd do their best to follow every lead offered by whatever they could learn from these suspects through rigorous questioning.

Ben filled him in on their plans to leave, and Evans was pleased that Ben had followed through so quickly on his warning. He promised to stay in touch with them and let them know if and when circumstances changed, allowing them to return home safely.

An hour later, Callie sat in the living room with Grace and Lobster. She'd called them earlier, Grace crying as she sensed the sadness and fear in Callie's voice. Now, tears again ran down her face as Callie explained why they had to go.

"It's only for a little while, Gracie," she promised. "We're coming back. Ben wants that as much as I do."

Though he sat still and quiet, Callie could feel the sadness from Lobster as well.

"Where's he taking you?" Grace asked as she wiped her nose with a tissue.

"I can't say. Only a few know, and it's safer for everyone that way, but Gracie, I'll be safe. Ben has saved my life twice already. He's not going to let anything happen to me. Please, don't worry."

"But you just got shot. You're still recovering, and your dad just…"

Callie put her arms around her friend, amazed that Grace's compassion and sadness were more about her genuine concern for Callie than her own loss. "I know, but as we talked about before my date with Ben, timing on things doesn't always work out very conveniently. I'm sorry that HeartStrings will have to take a hiatus, but I will be back, Gracie, I will."

"I'm not worried about that, and I want you to be safe, but…" Grace looked up, her curious gaze focused on Callie. "There's a lot more going on here than I know about, isn't there?"

Surprised by the question, Callie leaned back and cleared her throat. Ben had given her his blessing to share everything about him with Grace and Lobster if she desired. Her trust in her friends was good enough for him and he understood that Callie might need someone else to talk to about everything she was processing. At this moment, however, the timing didn't feel right. Since they were leaving, all she would do would be to leave Grace and Lobster with many unanswered questions.

"Yes, that's true," she admitted, not wanting to lie to her friend. "I'll share all of it with you both at some point." Callie looked Lobster's way. "Perhaps some of it is already known. Now's not the right time, though. Not when we're leaving. Please, just trust me when I tell you that I'm in good hands and I'll be safe."

Unexpectedly, Lobster put his hand on Callie's shoulder. "You will," he said confidently.

Abruptly, he rose and left the room, and Callie guessed that was his way of saying goodbye. Callie was now certain that she and Ben had underestimated the extent of

Lobster's knowledge concerning Ben's gift, and she admired his considerate discretion on the matter.

As Callie and Grace continued to talk, the doorbell rang, and soon Ben entered the room with his friend Donovan.

Ben approached Callie and took her hand. Her vision focused on a tall, nice-looking man with short blond hair, warm brown eyes, and a very kind smile.

"This is Callie," Ben introduced, and Callie was honored by the pride in his voice.

Donovan reached for her free hand, lifted it, and kissed it softly in an old-fashioned gentleman's greeting. "Ben wasn't exaggerating about how lovely you are. It's very nice to meet you, ma'am. I'm Donovan, and I'm here to help you and Ben escape this horrible nightmare you've been living in."

"Thank you. It's an honor to meet you." Callie immediately liked this man, though she wasn't surprised that she did. Anyone Ben would trust completely and speak of with such high regard had to be a person of the highest integrity.

Ben turned aside, and Grace rose from the couch, wiping her face and sniffling as she tried to compose herself.

"And this is Callie's friend, Grace," Ben introduced.

Donovan offered Grace the same courteous greeting and then turned to Ben. "Wow! How did you get so blessed as to be acquainted with such lovely women?" He chuckled, but Callie noticed his gaze linger on Grace. "Your life has certainly changed since last I saw you, my friend."

Ben nodded, displaying a look of profound gratitude. "Yes, it has. In so many incredible ways."

After a few additional moments of introductory conversation, Callie politely excused herself and Grace and led her friend into the foyer, knowing that Ben needed to talk privately with Donovan without Grace overhearing. Since she also needed to be a part of the conversation, though she was loathe to say goodbye to her dearest friend without knowing how long it would be before she'd see her again, she escorted her out the front door and walked with her to her car.

"Who was that?" Grace inquired when they'd moved well away from the house. "I mean, I obviously know his name and that he's an old friend of Ben's, but... wow! He's... wow!"

Smiling at Grace, Callie sentimentally recalled a similar reaction she'd had when first meeting Ben. She wanted to tell her friend that she'd noticed Donovan also express interest, but Callie hadn't informed her friend about her ability to see when she was holding Ben's hand, so the statement would likely make her confused or suspicious.

"Where's he from?"

"No, sorry," Callie answered, shaking her head. "Still trying to keep you safe by not giving you too much information. If I can, I'll get you his number or give him yours."

Grace giggled. "And here I was worried that you got the last knight in shining armor. Guess there's at least one more out there."

The two women embraced, holding each other for a long moment as Callie's heart ached with the recognition of how much she'd miss her dear friend.

"If I can be in touch, I will. I love you, Gracie. Take good care of Lobster."

A FEW TEARS slid down Callie's cheeks as she re-entered the house to join Ben and Donovan. As she passed through the foyer, Lee met her and, seeing her tears, he quickly embraced her. Callie hadn't seen much of him that morning. Lee wasn't good with difficult emotions and Callie knew that after Ben had told him about their imminent departure, Lee had needed time to process the sad news.

After a moment of holding her, he stepped back, struggling to restrain his tears. "First, you got shot on our porch. Then, I find out Ben's got a superpower. Then, we lose dad. This morning, you get shot at again. And finally, I hear you're leaving." A despairing sigh passed through his lips. "Cal, I don't know how much more I can take, despite being a tough guy." Lee put his fist to his heart.

Tenderly, Callie pulled his fist from his heart, cradling it in her hands. "You're just like Dad, Lee. Tough on the outside but soft and tender on the inside. I'm truly sorry. I don't want to go and neither does Ben. We all need each other, especially right now. There's simply no choice. I'm putting you in danger by staying here. It's me they want, Lee, and I don't want you caught in the crossfire. I'll do anything to keep you safe."

Lee gritted his teeth and his face reddened in anger. "I wish it *were* me, Sis. I mean it!"

Callie touched his cheek, blinking back fresh tears as her heart ached for her brother's genuine desire to protect her and take upon himself the threat that haunted her. "I don't!"

He lowered his chin, taking a deep breath before speaking, this time in a strained whisper. "I wish Dad were here. He'd help us get this..."

Callie put her finger over his lips, cutting off the intended profanity. "The investigators are going through all Dad's files. If there's anything there to find, they'll find it."

Defeated, Lee sighed once more. Callie hated the very idea of leaving him. She would have Ben to comfort her, but

Lee would be left alone to deal with his grief, though she knew Ms. Essie and Louis would do their best to console and care for him.

Leaning close, Lee ensured that Callie could see his candid expression. "Sis, if it were with anyone else but Ben, I'd never let you go."

Callie nodded, returning the same look of sincerity. "If it were with anyone else but Ben, I'd never have the courage to go."

CALLIE AND LEE joined Ben and Donovan in the living room as they strategized security and finalized plans for their departure and travel.

"It looks like driving will be our best option," Ben informed them. "I was hoping to fly us out as it would obviously be quicker and easier, but driving makes us harder to track. Donovan will accompany us out of town to be sure we aren't followed in any way. Then, we should be fine as we'll be continually on the move until we get to Boston."

"Miss LeVray." Donovan turned to Callie. "You'll want to leave your phone behind. They may already be tracking you and Ben through them. I've given Ben a burner phone for the trip, and I'll have new secure phones for you when you arrive at Ben's home."

Callie nodded. "It's just Callie, Donovan, and I understand. Whatever you think is best."

Ben squeezed her hand.

Lee leaned back in his chair and crossed his arms. "Do I get her number?"

"Yes, certainly," Donovan reassured. "When they get their new secure phones. And you're getting one too, as a precaution."

Ben and Donovan continued to fill Lee and her in on the details, but Callie's mind was distracted by emotions and fatigue, making it hard to concentrate. In contrast, Ben was clearheaded and focused, following every word, which left her confident that she could trust him to recall and execute the plan flawlessly.

It was after three when Donovan left. He circled the area checking for anything suspicious ahead of her and Ben's departure. After their brief visit with Louis and Ms. Essie, they would meet up with him again for the drive out of town. Lee still needed to pack and secure the house, so he would wait to go to the Jones' until later that evening.

Ben and Lee packed the Range Rover with their suitcases, and before she was ready, it was time to say goodbye.

Amidst another flood of tears, Callie clung to her brother. She couldn't remember a time when she'd been apart from him for more than a week. Camps and wrestling tournaments occasionally kept him away for a few days, but they'd been together nearly constantly since Lee'd been born.

Holding him now, her heart sorrowed deeply at the unavoidable separation. None of them knew how long they'd need to stay away, and the unknowing made leaving hard to bear. Her sole comfort was knowing he'd be safer with her far away.

"I love you, General Lee," she cried softly into his shoulder. "Don't wear out the Jones' floors with all your pacing."

Releasing her, he stepped back and tried to smile but only one corner of his mouth lifted. "I'll likely gain fifty pounds over there with all her delicious cooking. You probably won't recognize me when you get back." He grimaced and patted her shoulder. "I love you, Callie Flower. Please, come back soon!"

Turning to Ben, Lee held out his hand, but Ben grasped his shoulders affectionately.

"Lee, I'll take care of her. I promise you. And I *will* bring her back soon!"

Lee nodded and swiped his thumb under his eyes. "I wouldn't let her go if I didn't truly believe that. Take care of yourself too, Uncle Ben. I'd like my whole family to come back here in one piece."

As they embraced, Callie smiled, her aching heart warmed by the brotherly love between them.

CHAPTER 3
THE COST

The space inside Ben's Range Rover was quiet on the drive to the Jones' house. When streaks of tears escaped, rolling down Callie's cheeks Ben squeezed her hand, offering comfort, but they both knew nothing could be said to alleviate the pain of leaving, so they waded through the flood of emotions in the comforting silence of each other's presence.

When they were ten minutes from the Jones' house, Ben finally spoke, noticing Callie's tears had ceased. "Did you decide to tell Grace and Lobster?"

Callie wiped her eyes and shook her head. "No. The timing didn't feel right. I didn't want to leave them with many questions that we might be able to more accurately and satisfactorily answer when we return. But I do think Lobster knows more than we thought he did."

Ben quickly nodded. "I think you're right. He stopped to talk with me before he left, and from what he said, I thought you'd decided to tell them."

"What did he say?" Callie asked with sudden alarm.

"He looked right at me and said, he'd be pleased to let

you borrow his Guardian Angel for a while, but that I'd better come back 'cause I was *his* first." Ben briefly glanced at her, offering an amused grin.

Despite her present heartache, Callie laughed at her quirky friend's comment. "Yep. He knows a lot more than we thought."

"Oh, and he left us a souvenir." Ben grasped her hand, lifting it and pointing with his thumb toward the backseat.

Callie turned to look, and there, on top of a pile of coats and blankets, sat the stuffed orange lobster that had graced her and her dad's hospital room for days.

"I guess we can think of it as our good luck charm," Callie said with a soft chuckle.

Ben nodded in agreement.

"Does Donovan know about you?"

"No." Ben's grin faded, and he spoke the word so tentatively that Callie raised her eyebrows, her smile disappearing as well.

Ben shook his head in confusion before explaining his tone, speaking slowly and with grave concern. "The last time I saw him, he was still in the service, and he was strong and healthy, so I wasn't reserved about contact with him. But..."

Ben stopped speaking again, and Callie's heart ached in response to his obvious worry. "What is it?"

"When I shook his hand today, I felt a draw from him, Callie. It totally caught me off guard. I don't understand. He looks fine, and he didn't visibly react to my handshake, but there's something wrong with him. He's been through several tours of duty overseas. I don't know much about what he's been through, but I think he's seen and experienced some rough stuff."

"Was the draw strong? Like, is it serious?"

"Somewhat... Yes." Ben shrugged and his jaw tensed. "I'm still much in the dark about how to manage this whole thing. Shouldn't I tell him if I'm detecting something he doesn't know about? But how? I mean, how do you have that conversation? And, if he already knows but doesn't want anyone else to know, shouldn't I respect his privacy?"

Callie sighed sympathetically. "All good questions for the Jones'. Grace is interested in him," Callie added, now more concerned than excited about the idea.

"I picked up on that and I think it's mutual." There was enthusiasm in his voice despite his lingering concern. "Donovan is a hero, a kind and gracious person, and so is Grace." He paused to chuckle at the way her name paired with the attribute. "They'd probably be a great match."

"She permitted me to give him her number if he's interested. I just hope he's okay. Wouldn't want her heartbroken if..."

Ben patted Callie's hand. "We don't know anything for certain yet, and at the end of the day, the heart will do what the heart will do anyway."

"That's true," Callie agreed, sending Ben a smile filled with the wisdom of personal experience.

Welcoming arms and enticing smells greeted them at the Jones' house. Though it was early for dinner, Ms. Essie had made them a full meal of pork chops, salad, and bread.

The house was as warm and inviting as the people who occupied it. It was modest in size, just a single story with three bedrooms and a small yard, but it was comfortable and charming.

They sat around a circular table in a small dining area off the kitchen. Louis joined them, and Ms. Essie attended to his needs as they conversed. Though he was frail and needed substantial assistance, Louis' smile was full and his mind sharp.

When Ben held her hand, Callie watched Louis and Ms. Essie with interest, noticing how she knew what her husband needed and wanted without him directly asking or indicating. They spoke and moved together seamlessly, and Callie found herself enchanted and inspired by this beautiful example of a mature and healthy bond.

"Miss Callie, I heard 'bout your incident this mornin'. Terrible thing but, with Mr. Sawyer here takin' good care a ya, I was knowin' you'd be alright." Ms. Essie paused to smile nostalgically. "I was sure from the first day he told me 'bout meetin' ya that you two were meant to be together; I just was sure of it."

"Yes, you were." Ben grinned and nodded as he remembered how she had told him that it was too late to reverse course and run away from Callie, even after the first day he'd met her.

"I know you're both havin' to go away for a while, but don't ya be gone too long, ya hear? You two are family now, and I won't wanna be missin' ya for long." She wiped at her eyes with a tissue as she spoke. Callie set her hand on top of Ms. Essie's, touched by her genuine care and concern.

"I don't intend to keep her away for long," Ben assured. "This is my home and, as you told me not many days ago, Ms. Essie, this is my family too."

"Yes, indeed, it is that."

"Part of our purpose in going to Boston is to look for answers. You said that becoming Succouri at such a young age was unusual, especially with no guidance and…"

"Not unusual, Mr. Sawyer," Ms. Essie interrupted, putting up a hand. "It ain't done. There are rules, ways a doin' things that are proper. When one's becomin' a

Succouri he's taught these, and he's agreein' to follow them. As you're knowin', there's great privilege in it, but great burdens too, and it ain't fair to force that on anyone without them well knowin'.'"

Mr. Jones leaned forward and pointed a finger in the air as he spoke. "I was taught about it long before I was choosin' it. I was knowin' for certain what I was choosin', the life, the costs, all a it. And, when I met Essie, I was sure she was knowin' it too since the bondin' means it's all bein' hers as well."

Ben looked at Callie. "I need to know more about what I am before we can move forward. As you're saying, I want her to understand what it means for her as well. I wish I could have given her this information earlier but, it didn't work out that way since I didn't know much of anything when I met her... And still don't really."

Ms. Essie turned to Callie, her voice betraying no hint of doubt. "I wouldn't be changin' anythin'. I'd still be choosin' him with all my heart, no doubtin'. As I was tellin' ya, Miss Callie, marryin' a Succouri is a wonderful adventure full a surprises. And, the bondin' is somethin' so precious, so very sweet. It's makin' any cost well worth the payin'.'"

"I don't doubt that at all." Callie smiled, her short time with Ben already confirming this truth.

"We want to spend time here learning from the two of you," Ben said, leaning back from the table. "There's so much I need to understand, but I'm afraid with Callie's situation, most of that will have to wait a while. I do have a couple of questions I would like to ask you both now though, if that's okay?"

"Go on!" Ms. Essie gestured with an open hand.

"Well, to start, I remember when I first realized that touching people yielded strange results. It wasn't immediately after my marrow transplant, but quite a while later. I think that's why I never connected the two. If the marrow transplant is the only likely source..." Ben let the question hang in the air.

Ms. Essie looked to Louis as this question seemed more suited to his experience. The older man contemplated, folding his arms. "The healin' comes quickly, usually within days. Whatever healin' the body's needin', you get that right away. It can take longer before the rest of it is settin' in, workin' through the body, changin' ya into Succouri. I knew one fella who it took nearly three months before it happened, and we all were thinkin' it didn't work but, in the end, it happened. I've heard sad stories of times when it never did take, but that's mighty rare. For me, it was just a few weeks, but everybody's different."

"But... How is it done?" Ben asked. "As a Succouri doesn't bleed much, wouldn't the doctor notice that and also reject an older donor for a transplant or transfusion?"

Slowly, a sly grin filled Louis' face. "Mr. Sawyer, how many people are knowin' 'bout you now?"

For a moment, Callie thought maybe Louis hadn't heard Ben's question as he seemed off-topic.

Ben cleared his throat and shifted, also puzzled by the question. "Um, well, Callie, Lee, you, and Ms. Essie. Probably Lobster and perhaps soon Grace."

"And I'm assumin' your mama was knowin'," Ms. Essie chimed in, seeming to understand exactly where her husband was going with this line of questioning.

"So, that's seven people we're just now thinkin' of. With all the Succouri out there, if each has a network, a group a folk that is knowin', ain't ya suspectin' that there's some doctors, some facilities, and some networkin' to work that all out?" Louis maintained his sly smile as his eyes twinkled in delight.

Ben placed both hands on the table as he leaned forward, looking at Louis with astonishment. "Are you telling me there's a whole community out there that knows all about this and supports the process?"

"Mm-hm," Ms. Essie confirmed. "It's quiet, of course, and everyone's careful as I'm sure you're also bein' 'bout who you're tellin'. Succouri have a good sense of who they can be trustin'. They're rarely includin' anyone who wants to be doin' harm. Most people are understandin' the beauty in it and wantin' to protect those who are havin' the gift."

Ben blew out a breath and lowered his gaze, taking a moment to accept what he was hearing. Then, with a hopeful expression, he raised his eyes again to Louis. "Can you help me find them, get connected? It might help me when we get to Boston. if I could find some other Succouri or the network, maybe I could discover what happened all those years ago."

Though Callie was encouraged by the possibility as well, she hoped he wasn't setting himself up for disappointment if it didn't work out that way.

"There's kinda an unspoken rule that you can only be tellin' 'bout another Succouri with his permission," Louis said. "If you're givin' me your permission, I'll be passin' the request on to a few I might be knowin' 'bout out that way. If they're wantin', they'll connect with ya. It's needin' to be their choice."

"Of course. I understand. Thank you." Ben dipped his head in gratitude.

Callie looked at Ms. Essie. "How many are there? It sounds like it's not that rare, but it has to be."

A laugh mixed with Ms. Essie's words as she answered.

"It's mighty rare indeed, Miss Callie. But when you're bein' one of um or bein' close to one of um, it doesn't seem as rare 'cause your paths are just kinda crossin'. Maybe it's 'cause once you're knowin' a few, or knowin' yours"—she nodded toward Ben—"you're just recognizin' their way, and your heart's drawn to um, like what happened to me when I met Mr. Sawyer."

"I guess that makes sense." Callie nodded as she wondered if she'd have this ability when given the opportunity. Abruptly smiling, she recognized that, with her limited vision, she was something of a Succouri detector, at least if any happened to touch her.

"It's one big family; everyone lookin' out for everyone else and helpin' to keep it all goin'," Ms. Essie said with a sentimental smile. "You'll be seein'. We'll see 'bout helpin' ya get started since you're needin' a lot a guidance, but just be trustin' me when I'm tellin' ya that now that ya know what ya are, it'll start comin' together."

After they ate, Callie helped Ms. Essie clear away the plates, and Ben and Louis continued to converse for a while longer. As always, Ms. Essie had prepared a delicious dessert, and soon they moved into the Jones' living room to relax and enjoy it, though Callie knew they would need to leave soon to meet Donovan.

When they entered the room, Ben strolled around, studying the extensive collection of photos on the walls. Though she couldn't see them, she noticed he observed each photograph with great interest.

"Who are all these people?" Ben inquired of Ms. Essie after making his way around the room.

"Oh, lots a lives we've been blessed to be a part of. So many, like you two, are family to us now, and we're lovin' um all."

Abruptly halting his examination, Ben turned around to face them. "Are some of these photos of your own children or grandchildren?"

The room fell awkwardly silent.

"I'm so sorry." Ben's regret at the question was clear in his whispered tone as he settled on the sofa next to Callie. "I didn't mean to bring up something painful."

Letting out a slow sigh, Ms. Essie leaned back in her chair. "Mr. Sawyer, I'm feelin' so terrible to be tellin' ya this, 'cause it ain't right or fair that you were so young and never had a choice and ya ain't been taught or told, but you're deservin' to know, you and Miss Callie. Yes, ya are."

Somber and uncharacteristically heavy, Ms. Essie's tone rang alarm bells in Callie's heart.

Ms. Essie took a long, deep breath, hugging her arms around herself as if bracing for the impact she knew her words would have. "Mr. Sawyer, Miss Callie, Succouri can't have children. It's part a what one's understandin' before one's agreein' to it."

No one breathed or moved. Heartbreak pulled the air from Callie's lungs, though she wasn't certain how much of it was her own sorrow and how much was empathy for what she knew Ben was feeling. The silence lingered like thick smoke in the room, clouding every thought and obscuring every hopeful perspective. Each of them wrestled with the impact of the news. Throbbing like an open wound, she felt Ben's heart breaking, and tears filled her eyes.

Shocked and devastated, Ben felt as if his whole world had been turned upside-down and every granule of hope shaken out. Until he met Callie, the idea of having children was far off, though he always knew he wanted to be a father someday. Perhaps because he'd never had a father, Ben dreamed of being the kind of parent he'd wished for, determined to love and care for his own children with all his heart and soul. Since meeting her, building a life and having a family with Callie had become his dream and the focus of his plans for the future. As soon as he felt resolved about his past and could let go of his questions and confusion, he wanted to move forward with those plans. Those dreams kept him going and motivated him as he faced the ghosts from behind him.

Now, the blissful image of that future that he carried in his mind and heart abruptly cracked and shattered, and the sharp pieces from its destruction pierced straight through his soul.

It was already an incredible act of bravery for Callie to embrace this life with him. By doing so, she was walking away from the concept of a normal life.

In addition, he already felt acute regret about obligating her to a future where he likely wouldn't live out a typical lifespan because of the early age at which he'd become Succouri. Now, if she stayed with him, he was dooming her to a future without children too. In addition to contending with his own shattered dreams of parenthood, he had to face that this was all way too much to ask of her, and he wouldn't, couldn't expect her to accept it.

Callie took his hand, but he was numb and lifeless. Since the moment in the recovery room when he'd told her everything, and she'd accepted him, embraced him, and told him she loved him, he'd felt free and light, finally releasing years of emptiness and self-loathing. He'd gained a remarkable purpose and a home. Now, every terrible, lonely, and desolate feeling rushed back at him, like he'd been plunged back into a horrifying nightmare, imprisoned once more inside unyielding bars of isolation and hopelessness. But now that he'd tasted freedom, the return to this hollow existence was unbearable.

"Mr. Sawyer." Ms. Essie grasped his shoulder as she sat down beside him. "You hear me; It's alright. I'm knowin' it's a terrible shock for both a ya. I'm feelin' your heart, but don't be runnin' inside a ya like you used to be doin' on the outside. You were just lookin' at those pictures on the wall. Those are Mr. Jones' and my family. We got plenty of um, lots a love, lots of purpose. It ain't a lonely life in any way; I'm promisin' ya that."

"But why?" Ben whispered, looking up into her eyes. "Why can't Succouri have children?"

Ms. Essie shook her head. "No one's knowin'. Some a our doctors have studied it, and it ain't clear. Of course, some Succouri have already had children before becomin' one, so we're knowin' that they could, but after the change, they can't anymore. Some are just thinkin' it's part a the burden of it. There's so much givin' in bein' one and so much heavy responsibility. Maybe addin' children to it just ain't somethin' prudent. We're not knowin', but it's just the truth of it. We ain't ever known a Succouri who could."

Dropping Callie's hand, Ben covered his face with his hands, trying to hide from his new shattered world. Anger at being robbed and cheated out of any real possibility for happiness overtook him. Only a child, he'd had no real life before this curse was forced on him. He'd been changed against his will before he had a chance to do or be anything else.

Indignation and sorrow rose him to his feet. "We need to go. Thank you for your help and the dinner." Ben barely looked at Ms. Essie and Louis as he spoke.

Ben reached for Callie's hand and rushed them toward the front door, but Callie held him back, stopping to embrace Ms. Essie and Louis. They promised to take care of Lee and look out for him like he was kin. Halfhearted embraces were all Ben could manage as his heart continued to feel twisted and squeezed.

As they headed for their rendezvous with Donovan, they remained quiet. Ben didn't know what to say to Callie, how to apologize for the heartbreak he'd caused her. He'd let her fall in love and bond with him, though he didn't know until it was too late what the bonding was. Though it was the last thing he'd ever wanted to do, Ben knew that her love and acceptance of him would now cause her pain. How foolish he'd been to believe that things were different now, that he wasn't poison for others, leading their hearts to break! Hurting her, this astounding, beautiful woman whom he loved and cherished with all his heart, crushed him with a weight of deep sorrow and regret he'd never recover from.

Initially, he'd been so careful not to tell her his secret until he was relatively sure she could handle it; that she cared enough about him and knew enough about him to process and accept it. If he'd known about this, he would have run away. He wouldn't have placed her in this situation where her heart would inevitably get broken, just as his would.

A part of Ben wanted to turn around and take her home. How could he expect her to help him now? How could he include her in his search for answers to his past when she surely no longer wanted to be a part of his future? Without Callie, it was all empty and meaningless anyway.

But he still needed to protect her. She deserved at least that much after all he'd put her through. He'd never feel any differently about her, never get over her, and he knew without a doubt that Callie would be the only woman he'd ever love for the rest of his life, however long or short that life turned out to be. But that didn't matter. The suffering he'd endure because of being so careless with her heart was well deserved. He'd be sure she was out of danger, keep her safe, wait until her shooter was caught and behind bars, and then, somehow, he'd force himself to let her go, though he knew with all certainty that doing so would destroy him for good.

CHAPTER 4
THE CONFRONTATION

Once again, it was quiet inside Ben's vehicle as they embarked on their eastward journey. They left Donovan behind outside the city limits after he assured them that they weren't being followed and could safely continue. Donovan was headed back to Ben's home to enhance security in preparation for their arrival.

Knowing Ben needed time to process what they'd learned from the Jones', and she did as well, Callie allowed the extended silence.

Ben and she had never talked about children or marriage directly, though they both seemed to understand that they wouldn't be able to withstand the temptations intensified by their Succouri bond for an extended period of time. If they wanted to hold fast to their intentions to do things in the proper order, getting married relatively soon would be necessary. They were already permanently linked by that bond, which was incrementally merging their hearts. According to Ms. Essie, the process was irreversible, and neither of them had any desire to escape it anyway.

Though it was new and at the earliest phases of manifestation, it held them firmly in its welcome grasp.

Now that the bonding had been initiated, Ben needed her to fulfill the purpose of his identity, though, as yet Callie didn't fully understand all that entailed. She possessed no unique gift, at least not like what Ben carried, but she was the only person who could aid in restrengthening him after he'd used his gift. She was like a one-of-a-kind reflecting mirror, capable of giving back to him what flowed out. As she helped him, something in her also grew and flourished. In addition, Callie alone could pull back the veil around his heart, perceiving his burdens and joys. The partnership was complex and beautiful, but that was only a piece of who they'd become as a couple.

Without any of that, if she only had Ben the man, no bond, no magic, she'd still be overcome with love for him. She'd once considered him a good man, but that was a description now proven far inadequate. Ben was a great man. Gentle, kind, selfless, and courageous; all attributes he possessed in abundance. Each day as he moved further away from the self-loathing, fear, and confusion he'd carried for years, like the weight of a dead man, his true nature emerged a little more and began to dominate in his interactions and demeanor. It thrilled her to observe his suppressed nature surface and to become better acquainted with the real Ben Sawyer.

But now, she could feel him retreating. The news from Ms. Essie was causing him to go back into hiding, which shattered her heart.

Though Callie wanted children someday, until she'd fallen in love with Ben, the notion was nothing more than a far-off possibility. The revelation that she and Ben wouldn't be able to have their own biological children saddened her.

With his character and kindness, she knew Ben would be a terrific father, and it would have been elating to see his features and heart pass to their children. But the loss of this opportunity didn't change her feelings for him or her desire to build a life with him.

However, the revelation played into every fear, every insecurity, and every negative definition Ben held about himself, and Callie could feel his heartbreak. She'd just begun to break through all of those insecurities, and now this. How would she convince him that this didn't change anything for her? Even with the costs it extracted, she was committed to their path and purpose. Though she didn't fully understand all that was involved in this life yet, she was unwaveringly sure she was meant to journey next to him in this adventure.

Once she was over the shock of the bad news and had dealt with her own disappointments, her mind began to work hard to figure out how to help Ben in his grief and doubt.

More than an hour into a very quiet and somber drive, Callie turned to face him. "Ben, I need you to pull over, please." She spoke calmly but firmly.

He gave no response and her heart pounded as she thought he might simply ignore her., but at the next off-ramp, he exited the highway and pulled into a parking lot. It was dark outside, so she couldn't see much out her window.

Though he turned off the engine, he didn't speak or look at her.

"Can we walk?"

"Callie, I..."

"Please, Ben. You asked for my trust when you took me from my home. Please, give me yours now; at least try."

Inhaling slowly, he retrieved their coats and a blanket from the backseat. He handed Callie hers and started pulling his on as he opened his door, exited, and approached her side of the car.

As she got out, he offered her his arm, but she reached for his ungloved hand and intertwined her fingers tightly with his. There was no way she would let him go backward and pretend to be just her guide now. Though he didn't resist her grasp, his hand, always unusually warm and gentle, was cold and limp. Their warm connection barely pulsed, and her heart withered painfully at this realization.

Ben led the way, and she silently walked with him for several minutes. As she was consumed with her thoughts, she didn't care much about looking around, but still, she couldn't help but notice how different it was to walk with full sight in the dark. Opportunities to explore her new, wondrous world of sight had been scarce, as her focus had been on her dad's passing and recovering from her physical wounds. Everything around her was bright and open in contrast to the total darkness she experienced without his hand in hers. They were in a small park, and she marveled at the irony. A park near the hospital was where they'd first opened their hearts to one another, and the bond first undeniably manifested.

A biting wind blew, and Callie shivered.

When they were far enough from the car that Ben couldn't quickly retreat and no one else could hear them, Callie stopped walking, turned to face him, and began to speak. "Ben Sawyer, I love you; with all my heart, I love you."

He didn't meet her gaze, so she put her hand under his chin and forced him to look up into her eyes. Shadowed in sorrow, his beautiful blue eyes were dull and lifeless.

"I know exactly what you're thinking. You think you're no good for me, never were. You think you should've run when you had the notion. You think you've ruined my life, hurt me, damaged me. You're worried about the burdens you're placing on me and the ones you have already placed on me. You think this new revelation is an additional burden you can't ask me to carry. I know it all. I feel it all."

Callie put her hand across her chest, though, in truth, right now, she couldn't feel much of anything from him.

"I know you're feeling obligated to help me, and then you're thinking you're going to run.".

"Callie," he whispered, "I'll make sure you're safe. I promise."

"No!" she retorted, letting a moment of anger carry in her response. "Ben, if you're not going to let me in, if you're going to push me away, please take me home. You don't owe me anything; you never have. Everything you've given me, more than I could ever measure, has been given in love, and that's all I want from you. I want nothing given in obligation or duty. That's not who we are to each other. You don't help me because you have to, and I don't help you because I have to. We give because we want to, and because we have something much deeper than a mutual responsibility to one another. Please hear me. I'm in love with you, deeply and irreversibly in love with you. I'm not playing at this, and it's not a fling or a crush. I didn't come on this trip just because I needed your protection or to help you uncover your past. I'm here right now for one reason; because I love you, and I want to be with you."

The warmth between them rose, and a tiny spark of life ignited in Ben's eyes.

"Callie, I.... I love you, and because of that, I can't do this to you." His voice was weak and hoarse, and his gaze fell to the ground once more. "It's too much to ask of you, too much for you to give up. You deserve everything; a full life with children and a man who will live out a long, whole life with you. I can't take that from you."

"Oh, Ben!" Throwing her arms around him, she clung tightly to his neck for a long moment before leaning back to look into his eyes again. "No one's guaranteed any of that ever! Don't you know? I've almost been killed twice. It might be you who doesn't get a full life with me. I know you can protect me and offer me a lot with your gift, but Ben, there *are* limits to that. You can't guarantee I won't get cancer or be hit by a bus or whatever. You're taking risks by loving me too. Did you know my eye condition is likely genetic? If we could have had kids, they might have turned out to be blind like me."

"I don't care..." he interrupted, but Callie wasn't finished.

"I know you don't care. I knew you wouldn't care, that you'd happily accept the risk; that's why I've never talked to you about it. It's the same for me, Ben. I'll gladly take the chance because every day, every moment with you is precious to me! We really don't know for sure about any of this, but even if someone told me for certain that if I stayed with you, I'd only get ten years and then I had to lose you and spend the rest of my life alone, I'd greedily grasp those years. I covet every second, every breath with you. We will figure this out. There's more than one way to have kids if we want them. It's a terrible shock for both of us, I know, but it doesn't change anything. Walk or not walk, see or not see, hear or not hear, remember? Years or no years, children or no children; my love for you will never change. You just told me that the heart will do what the heart will do. My heart is yours, and I know yours is mine. It's done! You can't go back, and running is no longer an option. Whatever we face, whatever happens, whatever new information we learn about who *we* are, it's *us* facing it together. I told you that you wouldn't carry this burden alone anymore, and I meant it. Neither of us can go forward, be who we are meant to be, alone. And Ben, even if we didn't have this miraculous bond that makes it impossible for us to separate, I'd still want you just the same, still need you just as much!"

Tears streamed down Callie's face, and Ben dropped the blanket he was carrying onto the sidewalk and wrapped his arms around her, holding her like he was afraid she might float away. Their warm link grew stronger and brighter.

Leaning his cheek against hers, Ben spoke, his voice strained with raw emotions. "I don't deserve you, Callie LeVray. I'm so very sorry for all I've put on you. When I met you, I swore to myself I'd never add to the heavy burdens you already carry. Now, I'm doing just that, adding more weight. But truly, I can't breathe, can't go on, can't live a moment, not a single one, without you."

Despite her frustration at his insistence that he was somehow unworthy of her or took from her more than he gave, Callie smiled at him. "Does that mean you're staying, not running, literally or emotionally?"

He placed his warm hand on her cheek as a single tear slid down his face. "On our date, I promised you I wouldn't run unless you told me to, remember?"

"Yes, you did!" She laughed in relief, and the full fire of their bond returned in a moment of unmatched joy. "And, in a park much like this one, I told you not to. I set my hand on your knee and begged you not to run, remember?"

"Yes, I do." Life and hope returned to his eyes.

"We're going to face a lot on this journey, hard things

and wonderful things. Ben, I need to know you're not leaving; you're not changing your mind on me again. I need to know you're going to stick around. Please."

Looking directly into her eyes, he placed his other hand on her face. The intensity of the gaze communicated sincerity. "If you want me, I'll be there," Ben answered, quoting another of his promises from their first date.

"I want you, Ben Sawyer. I'll always want you."

LEANING IN, Ben kissed her, slow, powerful kisses, which poured out every emotion in his heart, and she did the same. They'd never kissed like this before. There was passion and desire in it, but those emotions took a backseat this time, yielding to the expression of other beautiful feelings: gratitude, love, and joy. As he continued kissing her, his fingers caressed her shoulders and neck, then tangled in her hair. Moving slowly down her back, his hands enjoyed every touch as he pressed her tightly against him. The thrill of touching her with his uncovered hands still made him soar, and he wanted to memorize the feel of her.

Callie's hands slowly slid from his chest up around his broad shoulders. She stroked the back of his neck under the collar of his coat with her fingertips and then ran her hands up the sides of his face and into his thick hair. Though they remained within boundaries, they allowed themselves to explore each other's bodies in a way they'd never done before, and somehow, the temptation to go too far remained firmly at bay. They needed this moment to reconnect and express their love for one another without the stronger passions threatening to take over, and they lingered long and satisfied in it.

At long last, Callie shivered, and Ben pulled back just

enough to speak to her; his lips lingering less than an inch from hers. "Callie!' he mumbled breathlessly as he brushed his lips against hers. "Are you cold?"

"Yes, but I don't care."

Reaching down, Ben swiftly retrieved the blanket and wrapped it around her. It trapped her hands, and she frowned at him, pouting her lip in disappointment like a sulking child.

Laughing at her playful expression, he opened the front of the blanket, and she grabbed his shirt and yanked him forcefully toward her, kissing him deeply again. Then, she wrapped the blanket around him, cocooning them both inside.

After a few more heavenly minutes of pouring their hearts out to each other in affectionate touches and passionate kisses, Callie shivered again, and Ben reluctantly leaned back, rubbing the sides of her arms to warm her.

"Okay, sweetheart, I could seriously keep kissing you all night, but you're freezing and without that extra heat that our bond usually kicks in with," he paused to grin amusingly. "I need to get you out of the cold. So, can I make a promise, and will you make me a promise that there will be many more opportunities for this at a later date?"

Shivering again as her lip began to quiver, she nodded in response. "It's a deal."

She smiled a radiant smile at him, and the broken pieces of his heart gathered back into place. How he'd gotten so blessed, so outrageously lucky to have found this woman, he didn't know, but he'd treasure her for as long as she wanted him. And Ben, once again, dared to hope that that might be forever.

. . .

Two hours later, Ben pulled into their hotel and glanced at Callie. She slept peacefully, and he regretted keeping them up so late. With the early morning trauma, the emotions of saying goodbye, the shocking revelation from Ms. Essie, and the confrontation in the park, the day had indeed been full, and Ben wasn't surprised that Callie was exhausted.

The hotels he'd reserved had excellent security and service ratings, so as he pulled up to the front entry, a valet met him and asked for his name. After he gave the valet his information and they exchanged keys, Ben got out and went to Callie's side. Lifting her into his arms, Ben carried her through the hotel lobby, up the elevator, and into their room.

Their room arrangements had been discussed before they left. Though they knew sharing a room would invite temptations, after the incident that morning, Ben simply wasn't willing to leave her alone, unguarded. If he stayed in a separate room, he'd be out of sight and earshot, and that wasn't something he could live with. Callie had agreed, also uncomfortable with being alone while her would-be-assassin was at large. In the end, Callie's safety was the priority.

Gently, he set her down on the bed and softly kissed her lips. He tucked a pillow under her head and wrapped a blanket around her. For a long moment, he stared lovingly at her, the gratitude and awe at the unbelievable gift she was to him taking his breath away. He'd told her he needed her strength, and she offered it in spades. Callie had more strength in her tiny body than he had ever possessed, and he was eternally grateful that she used it to hold onto him, even when he caused her pain. Though he was the one with the literal life-giving touch, Callie gave him a life, one worth living.

During that silent hour in the car, Ben had recon-structed every old wall around his heart, knowing he would have to let her go. The thought was unfathomable, and he couldn't breathe as he imagined his lonely, empty world without her, but he'd been sure that was best, especially for her. As he came to grips with that harsh reality, all life, purpose, and joy drained from him. He felt utterly hollow, many times worse than he felt after giving his strength to revive Callie's father. This was deeper, down to his core, like his very soul had been removed from his body.

But, when she spoke to him, she poured hope back in, drenching every dry, desolate space. Though he couldn't have imagined any words would change his mind, she'd found them and spoken them with such genuine conviction that he couldn't doubt their sincerity.

Since the first day he'd met her, she'd always been able to break through his defenses and tear down his walls. Now, Callie also possessed the ability to capture his heart. Somehow, despite his strange abilities and the precarious future that awaited her because of them, she loved him, truly loved him. Seeing past the Succouri in him, she saw him, Ben, and it was that part of him that she wanted most. What she said to him was as life-giving as the strength that poured into him through their precious bond.

Callie was his hero, saving him many more times than he'd saved her, and in more profound ways. The truth in Ms. Essie's words when she told him he wouldn't be able to go forward without Callie in his life, now fully registered. If he'd lost her today, he'd have been finished, as a man and Succouri; resigned to whatever dark fate awaited him.

But unbelievably, she wasn't finished with him. She still wanted him, even with all it cost her to keep him.

He stroked her cheek, not wanting to wake her but unable to pull away.

How I love this extraordinary woman! Ben whispered to himself, his heart nearly bursting as it tried to contain the flood of admiration and gratitude rushing in.

When the bellhop quietly knocked, Ben tipped him and pulled their suitcases inside. Though he wasn't sure if Callie would have wanted to sleep in her clothes, he wouldn't wake her. After brushing his teeth and putting on sweats and a T-shirt, he lay down cautiously beside her, only permitting himself to press lightly against her. Though he wasn't sure if he should allow himself this indulgence, he couldn't abide any distance between them. He needed her, needed to stay connected to her and feel her warmth beside him. As he closed his eyes, he recognized how exhausted yet wholly contented he was. In seconds, he drifted off to sleep as their bond continued to fill him with strength and merge their hearts under its mysterious spell.

In the middle of the night, Callie shifted in her sleep. Ben awoke briefly and smiled as her head now rested on his chest and her arm encircled him. Wrapping his arms around her and kissing the top of her head, he sighed blissfully before fading back into satisfying sleep.

CHAPTER 5
THE PAST

Callie awoke to the feeling of Ben's warm touch on her cheek. Though she smiled contentedly, she was disoriented by the unfamiliar surroundings.

"Good morning, Miss LeVray." Humor mixed with a hint of mischief twinkled in his eyes.

"I'm sorry to wake you, but I was beginning to worry you might sleep the day away and, well, I was missing your lovely, emerald eyes."

Lifting onto her elbows, she looked down at herself, realizing she was still wearing yesterday's clothes. Ben had already showered and dressed. The blue in his shirt made his eyes vivid and striking.

"Where...How?" Callie stammered.

Ben chuckled, and Callie rejoiced at the fullness in the sound. Though she knew it would take time to come to terms with the sad news they'd received from Ms. Essie, Ben seemed recovered from the initial shock, and she rejoiced in the return of his humor.

"We're a couple of hours from Indianapolis. As for the

'how,' you were quite soundly asleep last night, so in the tradition of our first date, I carried you up here." Though he offered a guilty smile, he raised a hand in innocence. "Didn't go any further than that, which is why you're still wearing yesterday's clothes."

Callie tilted her head. "Hm, I didn't even have to wear those slippery shoes or conjure up a snowstorm for the service this time. And, as a bonus, that was the best night's sleep I've ever had." She sent him a suggestive smile, and he grinned back at her.

"Me too," he agreed, kissing her forehead. "Alright," he continued as he leaned back and handed her a cup. "I'm going to step out and let you have the room."

Wanting her to see so she could map out the space around her, Ben took her hand. "Suitcase, bathroom, chai," he said, pointing at each object, including the cup in her hand. "Anything else?"

A wide-eyed stare was her response. The room was enormous and elegant, unlike any hotel room she'd ever been in before. The bed was ornate with an expensive-looking satin bedspread. Chiffon curtains hung from the windows, and the furniture was upscale, mainly leather. A large round table was tucked into its own offset nook in front and to the right of her.

"Wow!" Callie whistled in amazement. "This is fancy!"

"Good hotel, good security," he said with a casual shrug.

"And they have chai tea too?" she asked as she took an indulgent sip.

Ben put up a finger. "Actually, that one was easy this time. I guess fancy hotels like their fancy tea."

"Does that mean I'm fancy?"

A serious expression shifted his features, as he stroked

her cheek with his fingertips. "Fancy, beautiful, and very brave."

Lovingly, she smiled, understanding that the compliment was an expression of gratitude for her words to him in the park the night before. "Well…" She sighed, leaning back and gesturing at the space around her. "Thank you, Ben, for all of this."

Though she had no idea how much this was costing him, she knew it had to be substantial. Repeatedly, she'd offered to help with the cost, but Ben wouldn't hear of it, dismissing her with a smile and often a distracting kiss.

Pulling her into his arms, he whispered into her ear. "No. Thank you, sweetheart."

After a moment, Ben took a deep breath and pulled back. "Alright, I won't be far and breakfast will be here soon, so you'll be okay here?"

She grimaced. "If I don't get lost finding my way around in this enormous room."

"If you do, just call my name. I'll be nearby."

She showered and dressed quickly, glad to put on fresh clothes and brush her teeth. Soon Ben returned, and they enjoyed a delicious breakfast at the round table before checking out and getting back on the road.

Enjoying a time of comfortable silence, Callie's mind began to focus on helping Ben discover more about his past. Because of the trauma of the last weeks, she hadn't had the time or opportunity to follow up on what she knew so far.

She knew about his mom's depression, Ben's leukemia, his marrow transplant, his mom's tragic suicide, and Ben's subsequent lifestyle of running. She knew he didn't know who his father was and that, to Ben's knowledge, his mother and father never had a relationship beyond the one-night stand. Helping him find answers was as important to her as it was to him, so she needed more information.

Just when Callie was about to speak up and ask some questions, she abruptly became aware that Ben was humming and then singing. Low, rich, and very pleasant, the beauty in the sound of his voice gave her goosebumps. Since neither of them had their usual phones and couldn't play from a playlist, Ben had flipped on the radio to a station playing soft ballads. Until she heard him singing, she hadn't paid much attention to it. The Rascal Flatts song was familiar, and as she listened with surprise and pleasure to his voice, she smiled at the words, which recounted the tale of a painful past, a broken road, that had brought the sojourner to a love-filled destiny.

Spellbound, she sat still and silent, not wanting to do or say anything to cause him to stop singing. Like his speaking voice, his singing had a compassionate quality that soothed and quieted the heart.

At last, unable to contain her excitement at learning about this new part of him for another minute, she spoke up. "Ben! You never told me you could sing!"

Smiling, he placed his hand on hers. "It's not anywhere near as beautiful as your cello playing, but I do love music. It actually reminds me of my mother. It was something we sort of shared."

"It's beyond beautiful!" Callie laughed. "Don't let Lee know, or you'll be 'Singing Ben' for sure."

Ben chuckled and nodded.

"Tell me more about your mom," Callie requested, treading lightly as she knew this subject brought both pain and joy. "Did you two perform together or something?"

"Oh no!" he said, putting up a hand. "I'm nowhere near as brave as you are in that regard. She was a big fan of musicals, and she made me sing all of her favorite songs from them. It always cheered her up and eased the depression for a while. She couldn't sing well at all, but she sang with me, nonetheless. I guess maybe I got the skill from my father. Of course, I don't really know."

"How did your parents meet?"

Ben was quiet for a moment as he gathered his thoughts. "My mother was beautiful, truly stunning, movie-star kind of beautiful. She started modeling at an early age and was quite successful at it."

When he paused, Callie smiled, understanding now where Ben's good looks came from.

"By the time she was in her early twenties, she was, let's just say, very well known, but she wandered into some of the darker sides of that world. Part of the reason was probably her battle with depression, which caused her to easily succumb to the temptations of drugs and alcohol, offering her temporary relief from some of the pain. She made a lot of bad choices with partners and the company she kept. My best understanding is that when she was twenty-two, she went to a bar one night, and she wasn't... wasn't all with it, having taken something that inhibited her good judgment as well as drinking a significant amount of alcohol."

As Ben paused to take a deep breath, Callie began to understand why he was so careful to remain firmly in control regarding his affections and actions toward her.

"A man, my father, hit on her as men constantly did because of her beauty and fame, and she slept with him, not even knowing his name. The only thing she ever told me about him was that he was high on something too and, though he initiated the contact, she felt equally to blame because of her own state that night."

Ben sighed, and Callie put her hand on his knee. "Something wonderful, something incredible came of that. Don't forget that." She smiled, and he squeezed her hand in response.

"After discovering she was pregnant, she left that life. It's something I really admire her for. She walked away from all of it to give me a safe life, even if it wasn't necessarily an easy one in many ways. She didn't want me anywhere near the drugs, the fame, the bad influences. She did protect me from that destructive world as best she could, and for that, I'm eternally grateful."

"Did you ever hear from your father? Anything?"

"No. When I was old enough to notice the absence of a father, I asked her about it, but she always changed the subject. I did get the impression that she knew something, maybe at least his name, but again, I think she was trying to protect me from her past associates and mistakes. I can't even be sure my father knew of my existence, though something in me believes he did."

"Do you think there's any way to find him?"

"Well... since I ran immediately after her death, I never went through any of her things. I don't know if she had any files or letters or anything that might be a clue. I... We need to go through all of that when we get there." He shrugged defeatedly. "Of course, I have no reason to believe learning about my father will connect any dots for me regarding becoming Succouri. I used to imagine that my strange abilities came from him somehow, that maybe he was different like me, and passed that along. But now we know this isn't a genetic thing at all, so I have no reason to think finding him will lead to any answers about that mystery."

Callie nodded. "Tell me about your leukemia. What do you remember about it?"

Before answering, Ben again pondered for a moment.

"It's strange. My life before I became Succouri is hazy, like it's another life somehow or like trying to remember something that happened much longer ago than it actually did. I remember being severely ill and losing my hair. I remember my mother's tears, her fear for me near the end. I remember worrying about her spiraling deeper into depression if I died, and I remember some pain, but all of it's like trying to recall a dream. Maybe it's part of the whole thing, the experience of becoming Succouri, or maybe it's just because I was very young, and my life changed so drastically after that. I'm not certain."

"Can you recall if there was anything about the transplant that seemed unusual?"

"Well..." Ben paused, struggling to remember. "I know my mother tried for a long time to find a match. It's nearly impossible to find one, and I remember she seemed like she'd given up hope. Then, out of the blue, one day it just happened. She came into my room and told me they'd found a match and, within a few days, I can't remember the exact timing, I underwent the transplant."

"Hm." Callie ran her thumb across her chin, trying to focus her thoughts. "I suppose they never disclose the donors' names. Privacy laws and such."

"I never asked, but then, I was a kid. Never really had the notion of asking."

"And your mother didn't seem to know who it was?"

"No, I don't think so, but I can't be completely sure of that."

"We might start by trying to find the doctor that did the transplant; maybe he could give us some clues," Callie suggested.

"I wonder if... Could it have been a doctor connected with the Succouri network Ms. Essie and Louis talked about? If I got the marrow from a Succouri, which has to be the case, then how would a normal doctor not become suspicious of the rapid healing, and how would he or she agree to a transplant from an older donor?"

Callie crossed her arms as she thought about his questions. "Was it a normal facility, like a regular hospital?"

"Yes." Ben nodded. "As far as I can remember. I don't recall being moved anywhere." He huffed in frustration before continuing. "I do have a memory of the doctor, though. I remember thinking he was harsh and unkind. I was nervous about the transplant, of course, and I remember thinking he didn't help with the fear, actually made it worse with his sharp demeanor."

"I guess we can rule out that he was Succouri himself then," she said confidently. Though Ben and Louis were the only Succouri Callie had ever known, she was sure that harshness wasn't a characteristic that came with the gift.

Taking a moment to think, Callie stared out the window. She could see enough to determine they were headed through an urban area, likely Indianapolis.

"Ben, will you tell me about the first time you really knew you were different, that something had definitely changed?" she asked, again employing the most compassionate tone she could convey.

"I remember that well," Ben said with a smirk. "A month or so after my transplant, I reconnected with some friends of mine from school. It had been nearly a year since I'd done anything fun, and though I felt strong and completely well almost immediately after the transplant, my mother wouldn't let me leave the house for quite a while. It was summertime, and we all met at the park to hang out and play baseball. There were five of us. I don't remember all of their names, but I remember one, Davey

Lawrence." Ben sighed as he spoke the name. "Everyone took turns pitching and hitting the ball. I'd been up to bat a couple of times, and I remember being excited about how energetic I felt and how great it was to be back to feeling normal again. Davey stepped up to pitch, and the batter hit it hard and straight. The ball smacked into Davey's face with a terrible crack, a sound I still remember to this day." Ben paused to chuckle. "I think that kid went on to play professional ball in later years. Anyway, Davey fell to the ground, writhing and screaming in pain. When I got to him, his face was covered in blood. The hit broke his nose and knocked out a couple of his teeth. I remember grabbing his arm to try to keep him still. After a few seconds, the draw hit me for the first time, and I literally jumped back and let go, not understanding at all what it was. Davey stopped screaming and looked wide-eyed at me as I looked wide-eyed at him in one of those surreal moments. Then he started screaming again, and this time he grabbed ahold of me, and it all happened once again; he stopped screaming, and I felt the strange, frightening draw pulling strength from me. We both fell silent, stunned and confused, as the other boys looked on. He stared at me, and though his writhing calmed, his eyes looked afraid, like he was in a nightmare. I watched the blood stop flowing from his nose, and then I saw the fear and suspicion rising in the other boys' faces as well. I remember jerking away and running."

Ben took a deep breath. "It was horrifying. I had no idea what had happened, what was wrong with me. Because of the sensation of the draw, I knew without a doubt it was me who caused the change in Davey's condition. It wasn't like I could convince myself it was simply coincidence; the feeling of the draw is too exact and direct for that. I didn't understand what he'd experienced from his side, why he'd stopped screaming and become so calm, but I knew I was the cause. As I ran home, I felt weak and exhausted, and I remember wondering if my leukemia was back. Those boys never spoke to me again. I don't know what they decided about what happened, but they were scared, as was I, and it felt that to acknowledge it or talk about it made us all crazy or something."

An ache throbbed in Callie's heart as Ben relayed the memory, and she lowered her head. "That's awful! I'm so sorry."

As he navigated some heavy traffic, Ben had both hands on the wheel, so she placed her hand on his arm, offering comfort and support. Briefly, he covered her hand with his in acknowledgment.

"After it happened a few more times, though not quite as dramatically, I began to understand what caused it, or at least I thought I understood. I began to associate the draw with those who were sick, weak, or hurting, and I became much more careful and guarded, not touching people unless I was sure they were well enough not to take from me. Honestly..." He exhaled, communicating disgust at his behavior. "I hated the feeling of it. I resented the strength others took from me. It made me angry for a long time. It took me even longer to realize the draw was connected to relieving other's pain and suffering and begin to feel differently about it."

Recalling how she'd felt during those final moments with her dad, she nodded empathetically. Through their bond, she'd felt a small portion of the intense draw Ben endured as he transferred his strength. Though it was only a tiny taste, Callie was traumatized by the experience. It felt as if something was yanked from her, pulled out of her; like air being forcefully evacuated from her lungs just as she desperately needed a breath. Shuddering at the recollection, she recalled how, near the end of the struggle, she'd felt Ben slipping away, losing consciousness. She had thought she was losing him forever and that had scared her more than any gunshots in the night ever had. Even when the draw was over, Ben was left weak and diminished, unable to function normally for days. It was certainly easy to understand how the whole thing could be resented, even hated. How he tolerated it, endured it, and even went out of his way to offer himself freely to others was incomprehensible and part of why she had so much admiration for him.

"What about your mother? Did you feel a draw from her when she was depressed? Is that why you thought you were helping her?"

Originally, Ben had believed his touch could help with emotional distress, but Louis had informed him otherwise.

"Yes, but the draw was weak. Besides her depression, my mother did have some physical problems as well. She had asthma and allergies, as well as some chronic pain in her back. Since I didn't know anything about my abilities, I connected everything to her depression. She always appeared happier, better when I held her hand. Now that I know what I do, I think it's likely that the relief of those physical discomforts contributed to her improved mood." Ben sighed and shook his head. "Callie, I just didn't know enough about it, and I was so young, so I just perceived it the best I could with my complete ignorance. Even now, after learning more, it's hard to shift my thinking from all those years retroactively."

"Yes, of course it is." Fifteen years was a long time to spend in the dark, and she empathized with his frustration.

"It wasn't until I helped you and experienced for myself the joy that came from the positive consequences of using it, along with the gratitude I have in sharing this special bond with you, Miss LeVray, that I became able and willing to shift my perspective. When we learned from Ms. Essie the truth of who I am and what the purpose is, that alleviated my fear of being some kind of alien or monster, which obviously also helped me to more easily accept the identity."

She patted his arm again, and then they sat silently for a few moments, considering the impact that Ms. Essie's explanations had had on their perceptions.

Thinking about Ben's mother and Ms. Essie's words brought a question to her mind. "Ben, do you..." She started, but then suddenly felt strange about finishing the question as it seemed almost too personal to ask. Glancing at her, Ben offered an encouraging nod, so she continued. "Do you... Do you still feel a draw when you touch me?"

Though Callie genuinely wanted to know, she was scared to face the truth. It hurt her to think about taking anything from him that way, especially now that she knew more about what the draw felt like.

"Just a weak one," he reassured as he grabbed her hand. As he continued, he spoke hesitantly, trying to avoid upsetting or worrying her. "When we're close to one another, like yesterday morning in your room or last night"—he paused to wink playfully at her—"the strength that's poured into me is much more than what's drawn out. Even when there's more distance between us, I can feel the balance shifting little by little as the draw becomes weaker and the inflow gets stronger. I understand what Ms. Essie was saying as I can certainly tell that, in time, it won't feel like anything is going out as so much more is coming in. Does that make sense?"

"Yes, but..." Turning her body toward him, she focused

on his face, wanting to discern the whole truth. "Right now, with this distance between us, as you're holding my hand, am I drawing from you? I mean, more than I'm filling you?"

There was no immediate answer, and she knew he didn't want her to be pained by his response. "Yes, but Callie, it's fine, really. I'm used to it now, and anyway, you're the one who has to deal with the craziness of seeing and then not seeing, going back and forth all the time. I don't know how you do it, but you do it with grace and patience. The draw is not substantial and..." He flashed her a playful grin. "If you kiss me later it will all even out."

Though she attempted to return his smile, the thought of pulling his strength from him hurt her. She wished that touching her brought him only pleasure, without the cost.

"I can probably arrange that." Though she tried to sound light, the heaviness of her heart broke through in her tone.

"Callie!" Ben exclaimed with alarm. "When I first met you and couldn't touch you because I knew I'd be found out and scare you away, do you know how awful that was? I knew touching you would draw from me, but it was all I wanted. I always had to wear gloves, couldn't feel your hand in mine, couldn't soothe that awful burn I caused, couldn't kiss you without asking you to close your eyes. It was torture, pure torture. The slight draw I feel in touching you is nothing compared to the great pleasure I, Ben, the man, get from touching you like this." He pulled her hand to his lips and kissed it softly. "It's not even close in terms of the trade-off; not close at all. It also can't compare to the joy I feel at you getting to see the world, the whole world. Trust me; it is so worth it, and it's a great privilege and honor to give it."

Callie stretched across the console to kiss his cheek, and

he grinned broadly at her. Her heart filled with love at his unbelievable kindness and generosity toward her, but she still hated that he paid the price for her to see. The idea that her gain was his loss pained her deeply, but she felt trapped knowing neither of them would be satisfied to keep their distance from one another, and indeed the bond would never allow for that.

"When do you think it will fully shift to where I'm not taking from you anymore?"

Traffic was easing as they moved into more rural roads, enabling him to look over at her momentarily. "I'm not sure, but it will happen, and until it does, Callie, it's okay, I promise, more than okay. I'll never take for granted the pleasure and privilege of being free to touch you like this."

His words made her smile, but she quickly averted her gaze. "I wish I had more to give you, Ben. You're doing all this, protecting me, paying for fancy hotels so we're safe, driving me hours and hours, and giving me sight. I just wish I had more to offer you in return."

After a moment of silence, Ben abruptly pulled off the highway onto a dirt road. The SUV bumped and jolted as it came to a stop. Quickly unbuckling his seatbelt, he exited the vehicle, leaving Callie bewildered.

The next thing she knew, he was opening her door and offering his hand. "Miss LeVray," he said in his most charming voice. "You've given me everything. You're the reason I have hope and purpose. I truly wish you understood, but..." Ben's voice shifted to express excitement. "You've given me quite a great idea. Come on."

Callie hesitated, still confused. "Where am I going?"

"Come on," he repeated, his boyish charm on full display in his smile. "I know you're brave. Trust me."

Callie took his hand, and he led her around the car.

"Have a seat."

"Where?" She shook her head, still not understanding what he was proposing.

"You're going to drive, Miss LeVray, so you'll need to sit in the driver's seat."

"Oh no, I'm not!" Callie protested, walking away from him.

Catching her around the waist, he pulled her back to him. "Why not?"

"Because I can't see, remember?"

An expression of mock surprise filled his face. "All this talk about drawing from me, and you mean it's not working? You're gaining nothing from it?"

"No, of course it's working, but..."

Pulling her closer, he spoke near her ear. "You're not always blind anymore, sweetheart. You can see perfectly much of the time, and you should enjoy it and experience some new and wonderful things. Please, humor me."

At his nearness, the fire began to move between them, preventing her from thinking clearly, so she leaned away to focus and look at him. As she gazed into his pleading eyes, a sudden urgency arose; a feeling that what he was asking her to do was important, though she had no idea why.

"I'll never be able to express how thrilled I am with all I've seen but, Ben, I don't have a license. I don't have any experience. What if I get pulled over or crash or something?"

"We'll start here." Ben pointed up the dirt road. "No traffic. I won't let you crash, I promise, and you won't be pulled over unless you're doing something illegal, and I won't let you do that either." His eyes again pleaded irresistibly.

Inexplicably compelled to comply, she hesitantly sat in

the driver's seat. A triumphant smile lit up his face as he closed her door and circled the vehicle to the other side.

First, he helped her adjust her seat so she could reach the pedals and see easily out of the windshield. Then he walked her through the basics of how to shift the car into drive, reverse, and park, and how to switch the lights, turn signals, and wipers on and off. As he guided her through the features of the built-in navigation system, he rested his left hand on her shoulder so his fingers circled the back of her neck, enabling her to see fully. As he finished his instructions, Callie inhaled anxiously, and Ben laughed.

"It's alright. This is an easy car to drive." For a moment, he gazed intently at her. "You're just like me, you know?"

Confused, she raised her eyebrows and met his gaze.

"You also have to change how you've always thought about yourself. I don't plan to spend much time apart from you, so seeing will become more a part of your world than not seeing. You and I both have to work on old perceptions that no longer fit into our current realities." As he finished, he grasped her hand. "I'll try if you will."

Callie laughed and threw up her hands. "Alright, alright. Why are you always trying to make deals with me, Ben Sawyer? I'm terrified but bring on the adventure."

Grinning, he placed his hand back on her shoulder, lovingly rubbing her neck with his thumb.

When several seconds passed and she didn't move or do anything, Ben laughed. "Um, you have to give it some gas. It's a great car, but it won't drive itself."

"I was waiting for you to say 'go' or something," she explained, playfully smacking his knee.

"Go, go go," he said through the laughter as he gestured forward with his free hand.

Her hands shook as she tapped the gas, and the car lurched forward and then stopped.

"Don't worry," he encouraged. "Everyone does that. You have to get used to how much pressure to put on the gas."

They remained motionless as Callie breathed in and out, trying to relax. Ben put a little more pressure on his touch, and somehow, though she knew his gift didn't involve easing nerves, it helped to calm her. As she took a few more breaths, she puzzled at a new, strange sensation emanating from his touch. It was something she'd never felt before, and she had no idea what it was.

"Do you want me to say 'go' again," Ben teased, tapping his fingers on her neck.

"Just give me a second."

"Take your time."

As she took one more deep breath, she felt her heart rate slow down.

When she started driving this time, the car didn't jolt. She eased into a slow speed, and Ben smiled next to her. "Wow! You learn quickly."

Staring straight ahead, she focused on steering and the odd, yet comforting feeling flowing from Ben's fingers. Though she didn't understand how, his touch was clearing her mind, teaching her, helping her to grasp something she'd never known or understood.

"How fast should I go?" she asked, glancing over at Ben.

Surprise mixed with confusion showed in his expression. "Um... Probably no faster than thirty-five or forty; this road's pretty uneven."

Picking up speed, they soon cruised smoothly, despite the jarring caused by the dirt road.

As her heart calmed, she smiled at the powerful feeling of controlling such a large machine. As the pleasure of the new experience registered fully in her mind, she laughed in delight.

Beside her, Ben smiled in response, but soon after, he spoke, and his voice sounded strange. "Okay, stop for a second."

Smooth and steady, she brought the vehicle to a stop and looked over curiously at him. He stared at her with wide-eyed wonder. "Are you sure you've never done this before?"

"No, never." She shrugged in confusion.

"Callie, you drive like you've been doing it for years. I don't understand. I mean, I'm a good teacher and all, but not that good."

Tilting her head, she turned toward him. "I know this will be a weird request, but let me try it again without your touch."

Ben laughed and shook his head. "I'm brave, though not as brave as you, but I'm not suicidal. Plus, I promised not to let you crash, remember?"

"I know, but just like ten seconds. I'll go straight, and you can steer for me. Just let me try something."

Though he shook his head, he removed his hand from her neck and set it on the steering wheel. "Alright, Miss LeVray. Now I'm trusting you."

The world before her went into dark shadows, and she could barely make out the road's edges, but that didn't matter. She tried to remember how it felt a few moments ago. *Just do it like before*, she said to herself.

When she pressed down on the gas pedal, the car lurched and jolted like it had the first time. She tried again, but the same thing happened. She couldn't get it, couldn't catch the same feeling, the feeling of simply knowing exactly what to do.

After throwing them around in the car several more times, she stopped and turned to look at Ben. "It's the bond!" she nearly shouted with joy.

"What?" As he put his hand back on her shoulder, she took in his confounded expression.

"Ben, it's our bond. Remember Ms. Essie said it would manifest in different ways?"

Though he still looked confused, he nodded.

"I don't know why or how, but it's, like, teaching me, showing me what to do. Let's try it again." An excited giggle escaped as she turned back to the wheel.

She began to drive and, once again, it came easily, like an old familiar habit.

"See?" she exclaimed, glancing over at him. "It's easy now, familiar, like something I've done forever. And I know this car too. It's all in my mind, and I could tell you with my eyes closed where everything is."

Shaking his head, Ben blew out a breath in amazement. "Let's put it to the real test," he said excitedly. "Can you turn around?"

"Of course." She offered an exaggerated shrug as if that was a silly question.

Adeptly, she maneuvered the SUV in a three-point turn, and Ben whistled. "Okay, now I'm not sure you're getting this from me as I don't think I could've done that so smoothly."

The miraculous experience made her giddy as she drove back down the road. But when she approached the paved highway, she stopped.

"I'm confident you can do this," Ben assured with a grin. "I think you drive better than I do."

Abruptly turning to face Ben, Callie's smile faded.

Something in his tone was off. He sounded tired, weary. "Ben! Is this drawing more from you? More than before?"

He hesitated, allowing several seconds to pass before answering her. "Let's just say you'll owe me two kisses tonight." He smiled as he held up two fingers.

"Oh no!" she gasped. "Why didn't you tell me?"

"I didn't really realize what was happening until you connected the dots for me. But it's alright. I want to see you do this, at least for a few minutes. Please. Then we'll stop for lunch, and I can take it easy and eat, and it'll be fine."

"No way!" Shaking her head vigorously, she unbuckled her seatbelt and reached for her door handle. "Not worth it to me, not at all."

"Callie!" Before she could rush out, he caught her by the arm. "I'm enjoying watching you. This is wondrous, amazing, and I'll be fine, really. There must be some reason why the bond is working this way right now. There must be a purpose in it."

"Maybe so, but, Ben, I'm here to protect you, help you, make sure you can do what you need to do, be what you need to be. If I'm drawing strength from you, making you weak, I'm not doing what I'm meant to do, and I can't live with that."

"But..." He started to protest, but she leaned over and kissed him, silencing his objection.

When she pulled away, they both struggled to catch their breath. The full fire and magnetism they were now quite familiar with had returned, and its presence made them both rejoice.

"That's one." She put up her finger and sent him a flirtatious grin. "I'll save the other for later as I think I like being a little in your debt. That was seriously fun, Ben, and sort of a dream come true, so thank you. Next time though, please tell me if it's hurting you in any way, as I can't enjoy any experience that does."

A surrendering sigh passed through his lips and he retook her hand. "There's more than one way to fill me, Callie. Watching you do that was incredible. It filled up my heart. I respect your decision, but please consider letting me watch you do that again sometime. I can't imagine our bond would have offered that experience for no reason. There's something to it; I just feel it."

Before they traded places and resumed their eastward journey, she smiled and offered him one more quick kiss in gratitude for the gift of an extraordinary experience she'd never believed possible.

CHAPTER 6
THE FIRE

After enjoying a leisurely lunch at a friendly country restaurant just over the border into Ohio, Callie and Ben settled into easy conversation and comfortable moments of reflective silence as they continued their trek toward Boston. They ate dinner near Akron, and afterward, Ben let Callie know they were not far from their stop for the night.

For much of the day, Callie had enjoyed staring out the window, taking in the beauty of the landscape from a whole new perspective as Ben smiled and held her hand. Now that it was dark, there wasn't as much to see, though there was still a great deal more than she'd been able to take in before meeting Ben and benefiting from his gift.

"You know," Ben said, as he reveled in the wonder on her face. "I'm glad we decided to drive instead of fly. It's taking longer, but I would have missed all this; your first venture behind the wheel and watching your face as you take in the sites with new eyes. I feel a little sad for Lee, though, as I know he would have loved being here to see it too."

Ben thought about what it must have been like to grow up with Callie, watch her for years as she navigated a world not designed to be easy for someone with almost no sight. All of that history and shared difficulty would make moments like these even sweeter.

At the mention of her brother, Callie smiled warmly. "I'll be sure to show equal enthusiasm when I get the chance to share some of this with him around. He deserves that, as he's always been so supportive and kind."

"I always wished I had siblings," Ben admitted wistfully. "Donovan was the closest thing I ever had to one."

"How did you meet him?"

"We met in high school. I loved sports and was athletic, but with my issue with contact, not many sports were available to me. I joined the cross-country team as I figured running would be pretty safe. Donovan was a year older, but we became friends almost immediately and eventually ran together outside of school as well as with the team. He came from a wealthy family with high expectations and ambitions for him. They wanted him to be a doctor or lawyer or something else that they deemed big and impor- tant, but he had a passion to serve." A proud smile lingered as he spoke of his friend's admirable qualities.

"When he told his family that he wanted to join the military, well, let's just say they were not pleased or supportive. He tried to make them understand his passion, but they pretty much disowned him when he insisted on sticking to his goals."

"That's unbelievable!" Callie said with a sad sigh and a shake of her head.

"He actually stayed at my house for a while just before he left for basic. He was heartbroken over his parents' rejec- tion. I've never heard the end of that story, as we've only had intermittent contact over the years because of his deployments overseas and, my continual running. I hope his parents appreciate the hero he has become."

"I hope so too," Callie agreed. "Does Donovan know about your mom?"

"Yes. A few years ago, I met up with him for a brief visit. He had obviously heard about my mother, probably from mutual family friends in Boston. He didn't mention her death directly, and I was certainly not interested in talking about it, but he let me know he knew I was troubled by the past and offered to help me. It was really kind, and if I'd been in a sane and rational place, I would have accepted his generous offer. I just kept thinking that I'd inevitably have to run again and, if I accepted his help, I'd end up hurting him when I suddenly disappeared one day. Needless to say, he was quite shocked when I called him several days ago." Ben chuckled as he recollected the phone call.

"What do you know about his time as a Navy SEAL?"

"Um..." Though he heard Callie's question, his attention had shifted to focus on a dark plume of smoke rising in the distance. It was difficult to see against the dark background of the night sky, but Ben's perfect eyesight fixed on it.

"Ben?" Callie inquired, concern in her voice.

Letting go of her hand and gripping the wheel, he tried to pinpoint the smoke's source. Something in his gut registered alarm and urgency. It wasn't the same dread he'd felt when Callie was in danger, but it still made his heart pound.

"I'm sorry," he said distractedly. "Just a minute."

As they approached the plume of smoke, Ben began to see the dark form of a structure beneath it, and he warned Callie to hang on before jerking the wheel and exiting the highway.

"What's going on?" Callie gasped as she braced herself by pushing against the dashboard.

"I think there's a house fire. It looks like maybe a farmhouse, and there's not much around here, so they may not have help."

Her eyes grew wide with concern.

Following a winding paved road, he kept the trail of smoke firmly in sight. The road soon veered right, and the smoke was left, so he turned onto a long dirt driveway lined with trees. The branches obscured his view momentarily, but when the canopy lifted, he saw the fire.

Not far ahead of them was a large house, the left side of which was ablaze. The orange flames danced in the windows and the black smoke hovered like a shroud over the house. No emergency vehicles were in sight and he heard no sirens.

Ben hit the gas, speeding their approach, and within a few seconds, they stopped in front of the house. Moving swiftly, Ben exited and jogged to Callie's side, flinging open her door.

As he took her hand and they advanced toward the house, Callie let out a cry, now fully able to take in the scene in front of them. "Ben! Do you think there are people in there?"

"I hope not!" he answered, his voice carrying his alarm.

The smell of smoke hung thick and heavy in the air, and the roar of the fire fueled his sense of urgency.

In front of the house, a woman stood alone, wringing her hands and crying as she scanned the billowing smoke, looking for something or someone. Shorter than Callie and unusually thin, she rocked unsteadily, shifting her weight like she might take off running at any moment.

"Ma'am." Ben approached and put his hand on her

shoulder to prevent her from running toward the fire, but she didn't respond, keeping her eyes focused on the house.

Dropping Ben's hand, Callie moved directly in front of the woman, blocking her view. The tactic worked as the woman stopped rocking and stared at them.

"I'm Callie and this is Ben. Is there anyone inside? Are you alone?"

Releasing the woman's shoulder, Ben marveled with pride at Callie's composure and how she'd said exactly what he'd been about to say.

"My husband, my son," the woman muttered as she pointed at the house.

"Are they both still inside?" Callie asked urgently but calmly.

"My baby's upstairs. Nathan went in for him, but he hasn't come out." The woman's voice shook with anxiety and fear.

"Where's your baby's room?" Ben asked, moving to stand beside Callie.

"There." She pointed to the upper right side of the house, and Ben felt a spark of hope ignite as that side wasn't on fire yet.

Ben turned to Callie. "Callie, I..."

"Go!" she said, standing on her tiptoes and kissing him swiftly. "But, Ben, be sure to come back!"

He brushed his fingers across her cheek and pressed their shared cell phone into her hand before turning to run toward the front door. As he did, he shook his head, overcome with love and admiration for Callie. They'd never done this kind of thing together before, not like this. He thought he'd have to explain, convince her to let him go. He'd been prepared to offer a brief but passionate plea for her not to worry and to let him do what he was meant to do, but none of that was necessary. Without a word of explanation, she understood. He knew she'd summon help and comfort the distraught woman, so he was freed up to do what he needed to do, was meant to do. He abruptly understood why this life required a special kind of partnership. More than that, he knew with certainty he'd found the perfect partner, or maybe she'd found him.

When Ben reached the front door, the heat from the blazing fire intensified. When he opened it, he stepped back, allowing a blast of smoke and heat to stream out and settle. Though the smoke filled his nose and mouth and stung his eyes, he could breathe without coughing, though he doubted anyone who wasn't Succouri could last long in these conditions. Truthfully, he'd never faced smoke and fire like this before, and he had no idea what he could or couldn't withstand in this situation.

"Succouri ain't immortal or invincible." Ms. Essie's words rang in his head.

Ben's body could repair and heal rapidly. Still, rapid healing didn't mean invulnerability, and he certainly didn't want to put his gift to an unnecessary and uninformed test that might prove fatal. But there was a man and a baby in this house, and presently he was the only one who could help them.

As he entered the foyer, thick darkness pressed in around him. Inching forward, he followed a wall on his left until it ended, and he could peer into what looked like a kitchen, though he couldn't be sure as his vision was limited through the heavy smoke and lapping flames that covered the back of the room. The heat was intense, and Ben took off his shirt and tossed it to the side, leaving him wearing his white undershirt. It didn't cool him off much, but he figured the less loose clothing, the better. The fire was still contained inside the kitchen, but he didn't think it would take long to spread into the foyer, so he wasn't confident the same route would be available for his exit upon his return.

Turning right, he moved away from the inferno, and again followed the wall for guidance as visibility was extremely limited. After a few steps, the space on his right opened into a room, and he could make out the back of a dining room chair through the haze. Passing by the room, Ben continued following the wall as he searched for the staircase.

As he breathed in more of the thin air, his lungs began to burn, and he coughed several times, suddenly short of breath. Sweat ran into his eyes, and as he looked at his arms, he saw that they were covered in a layer of ashy dust.

When he reached the end of the wall he was trailing, he realized he must have missed the stairway, so he doubled back, following the wall on the opposite side of the hallway. Relief eased the panic as, after a few steps forward, he found what he was looking for.

The burning in his lungs intensified and he coughed again. Breathing this air no longer adequately supplied him with the oxygen that even his Succouri lungs required. At this realization, Ben's sense of urgency rose, and he turned quickly to rush up the stairs, but after a few steps, he nearly tripped on a man, passed out or dead, his body awkwardly slumped over several stairs.

"Nathan!" Shouting, Ben knelt and gripped the man's arm firmly.

How Nathan had made it this far in the smoke and heat, Ben couldn't comprehend, though Nathan was certainly familiar with the layout of the house, which would speed his advance, whereas Ben was wandering in the dark unknown.

Nathan's face and clothing were also covered with ash and soot, preventing Ben from getting a visual reading of his condition, but when the draw hit him, powerful and greedy, Ben was relieved at the confirmation that he was still alive.

A second later, Nathan opened his eyes and began coughing violently.

"Nathan!" Ben shouted again, trying to get the man's attention focused quickly.

As he waited for him to respond, Ben contended with how he would get this man out and still have time to return for the child upstairs. Without knowing his way around and with the smoke and darkness obscuring his sight, it was slow going, and time was not on his side as he knew that the foyer would erupt in flames at any minute.

Coughing, Nathan at last looked up at Ben in confusion. "It's okay. Take some deep breaths. I'm Ben. I can't explain this, no time, but you need to hold on to my arm or let me hold onto yours, and I'll get you out of here. You can't let go. Do you understand?"

Bewildered and disoriented, Nathan froze momentarily, but then jerked away and turned to bolt up the stairs. After ascending three steps, he dropped to his knees, clinging to the railing, before collapsing into a fit of fierce coughing.

Rushing to his side, Ben again grasped his arm. "Listen! You must hang on," he pleaded. "You won't be able to breathe the air on your own."

Putting the large man's arm around his shoulders, Ben tried to lead him back down the stairs, but Nathan wouldn't cooperate.

"My son!" he cried out. "I'm not leaving without my son!"

Trying to focus his thoughts through the panic and urgency, Ben struggled to fix on a course of action. He needed to get him out of the house as he may have already breathed in too much smoke at this point, causing permanent damage to his lungs. Even for Ben, the knives in his chest were intolerable now, and Nathan had been in here much longer and, of course, he wasn't Succouri.

But if he took the time to argue with him and eventually take him back out, it would likely be too late for the baby. Nathan knew exactly where the child's room was, so he could lead the way in the thick smoke and darkness, speeding up the rescue, but keeping him alive up and down again with Ben's strength already thin due to his own physical demands was going to be an immense battle. As both of their bodies weakened, the draw pulled from him, like a hungry beast that wouldn't be satisfied. Supplying strength and wholeness for two grown men would inevitably result in a rapid drain of his remaining energy.

Looking into Nathan's hazel eyes, Ben saw his determination. This father was not leaving without his child. His sacrificial love moved Ben's heart, and he felt again the sharp sting of knowing he'd never have the chance to love a child of his own.

"Alright." Ben relented. "You lead the way, but Nathan, hear me! You must hold onto me to keep going."

Though Ben still held his arm, Nathan reached out with his free hand and clamped down on Ben's wrist, finally understanding the necessity of the contact. Ben let go and allowed Nathan, with his fear and love for his boy driving him, to rush them forward, struggling in his weakened state to keep from being dragged by the man.

Another round of coughing hit Ben, and each breath felt like sucking air through a straw. The draw of strength passing from him into Nathan surged, dizzying him and decreasing his own body's ability to stay unharmed by the thickening smoke.

When they reached the top of the stairway, Nathan turned right, and Ben was grateful they were headed in a direction where the blackness was less oppressive. As they progressed and Ben's strength lagged, he became increasingly dependent on the large man's firm grip on him as each step became more arduous. His lungs burned as, no matter how many breaths he took, he couldn't get enough oxygen. The force of the draw continued to swell as more and more was required to keep Nathan whole as he also inhaled the toxic air around them.

At the end of the hall, Nathan swung open a bedroom door, dragging Ben into the room behind him. The smoke was noticeably thinner inside, allowing Ben a critical moment of reprieve as both men breathed easier. But then, they heard the soft cough of a child.

Instinctively, Nathan released Ben and rushed to a crib along the back wall. He lasted long enough to lift his son, a baby who looked to be about a year old, into his arms and secure him tightly against his chest.

"Alex!" Nathan managed before collapsing to the floor in a fit of uncontrollable coughing.

Kneeling, Ben placed one hand on Nathan and the other on the head of the baby, now precariously rocking in his father's arms as he choked and sputtered. The child's eyes were open, and he stared at Ben in confusion, but without a hint of fear. As he looked at his sweet face, Ben's heart ached and a renewed fervent need to save this young family rose within him.

But now, the draw overtook him. The appetite of the ravenous beast drew strength from every part of his body. Lifting himself from the floor felt impossible, much less walking. The forceful pull grabbed at his chest, taking his already meager breath away. He'd never done this before, never tried to help two people while struggling to keep his own body whole. What little strength remained was being siphoned three ways, and he didn't have enough to go around. Though he was Succouri, he was still just one man with one man's strength.

There was one thing he knew for sure; they had to hurry. If they didn't get out of this house before he ran dry, they'd all die in this fire, including him.

In a quick motion, Ben grabbed the baby from Nathan's loose grasp and locked his arm in place as he held him firmly against his chest. Then he shook Nathan with his free hand, rousing him.

Looking him directly in the eye, Ben spoke through the tightness in his throat, urgently articulating each word. "Nathan, we have to get out of here. Now! I'll do my best to help you both, but I can't hold out for much longer. We must move quickly. You hold onto me and lead the way and just keep going. I've got Alex. I'll hold on to him with all my strength, I promise, and he'll be safe and breathe easy here. Let's go!"

Nathan's eyes communicated comprehension, and he grabbed Ben's wrist tightly and rose to his feet, lifting Ben and Alex with him off the floor.

"Please, just be sure my son is safe," Nathan pleaded as he moved for the door.

"We're all getting out of here," Ben encouraged as Nathan dragged them into the hallway. In a strange twist of irony, Nathan presently possessed the most available strength, though, in reality, it was wholly Ben's extracted healing energy that kept him well enough to stay conscious and advance.

Stumbling and coughing, Ben kept up with Nathan, holding Alex secure with a determined grip. The child stared at Ben's face, surprisingly calm, and Ben could feel his steady breath on his neck. Though Ben was a complete stranger, Alex appeared comfortable and relaxed in his arms, even offering sweet smiles when Ben made eye contact. The trust in his eyes drove Ben on as he couldn't bear the thought of this child perishing because he was too weak to carry him out.

When they rounded the corner to descend the stairs, they stumbled as an explosion shook the ground under their feet. It knocked Ben's weak body off balance, and he steadied himself against the wall to keep from falling.

"It's okay. Just keep going!" Ben shouted as soon as he regained his equilibrium. Panic raged in him as he felt his strength reaching its end, and it forced every ounce of adrenaline into his muscles, temporarily boosting his scant supply. Nathan descended the stairs and Ben struggled to keep step with him so he wouldn't tumble down behind him. His body shook furiously, which threw off his balance. Without a hand to steady himself, stable maneuvering was impossible as Nathan's pull lurched him forward unevenly.

Halfway down the stairs, the smoke grew so thick that Ben could barely see Nathan right in front of him, and the heat enveloped them like walking into a furnace. But Nathan kept going, keeping a firm grip on Ben.

When they reached the bottom of the stairs, Ben looked to his right, coming nearly face to face with the hungry red and orange flames. It was impossible to judge distance through the blinding smoke, but he was confident the fire had breached the foyer and was licking into the hallway they were standing in.

"Dining room!" Ben yelled, but his voice was hoarse, and he coughed continually. Nathan pulled him forward and then to the left, entering the room mere yards from the advancing flames that soon engulfed everything beyond the threshold of the room. Ben hoped they could get out through a window, but regardless, this path had been their only option.

Violent coughing seized both men as exhaustion, heat, and suffocation overtook them. He desperately hoped Nathan would keep a firm hold on him, confident that no normal person could survive for more than a few seconds in this environment. If Ben lost contact with either of them, they'd be dead before he could grip them again.

But Ben couldn't hold onto consciousness. His world spun, twisting in a swirl of flashes and fog as his thoughts drifted, like scattering dust in the wind. As uncontrollable trembling brought him to his knees, he rallied the last ounce of strength and focus to hold firm to the child in his grasp. Someone grabbed him, lifting him somewhere, forward maybe; he wasn't sure.

It was over; he had nothing left to give. The last second of consciousness began to fade and he saw Callie's angelic face, smiling and calling his name.

The sound of shattering glass roused him, and cold air rushed in, granting him a long-overdue intake of oxygen. Strong arms lifted him and carried him outside, setting him back on his feet. A mask was placed on his face and someone tugged at his arm.

"Sir, we've got the baby. You can let go. It's alright."

The words were gibberish but he understood that he needed to release the child. It took Ben several seconds to unlock his muscles as he'd been so determined to keep that grip no matter what happened that his body was slow to relent.

When he let go of the child, his mind went blank. Where was he? What had happened? Every thought, slippery and amorphous, passed in and then out of his mind before he could grasp it. Only one word held its substance, kept him upright, and moved him forward. Callie!

Without rational thought, simply following a familiar magnetic pull, Ben removed the mask from his face, dropping it on the ground as he began to walk. Like a rope encircled his body, and someone held the other end, slowly drawing him to them, Ben moved involuntarily, yielding to the tugging.

"Sir, you need to come with us; we need to get you to the hospital."

But Ben could no longer hear them or comprehend the words. He just kept walking.

CHAPTER 7
THE RETREAT

Tears streamed down Callie's face as she stood surrounded by flashing lights and chaotic motion. It felt like hours had passed since Ben had entered the burning house and her heart pounded in fear as she waited in unbearable anticipation.

She knew he had to go. This was what he was and part of the life she'd chosen to share with him, but that didn't prevent the anxiety from overwhelming her. Ben's Succouri gift was powerful, but neither of them had any idea what that gift would offer him in the way of protection in this dangerous situation.

As she'd stood with her arms around the distraught woman, trying to reassure her, her mind filled with questions she couldn't answer. How would his body manage the smoke and heat? How was he going to help others when he would need his strength to keep himself from harm?

For a while, she'd been able to distract herself from the panic by focusing on getting help, calling 911, and coaxing the upset woman into offering the dispatcher their exact location. But after that was done, Callie's mind gave her no peace as it cycled questions and fears around in circles with no resolutions.

She tried tuning into anything she could pick up from Ben through their bond, as she'd been able to do in the hospital when he'd struggled to keep her dad alive, but for a long time, she couldn't sense anything. But when the explosion shook the ground beneath her, causing her and the woman to cry out in fear, everything changed.

As the sound of sirens echoed in the night, Callie stood with her hand over her heart, feeling Ben's battle and sobbing uncontrollably as she felt his consciousness slipping away. When a fireman approached and asked if anyone was inside, Callie did her best to calm down long enough to give clear and detailed information. "Hurry!" she'd begged them. "They're trapped in a room near the front of the house."

How she'd known that was a mystery. The words were spoken without the thought first forming in her mind. The man rushed off, and though she couldn't see in the darkness, she heard the breaking of glass and the shouts of the emergency personnel as they ran past her. The woman she'd been comforting also ran off, leaving Callie standing alone.

Taking a deep breath, she closed her eyes, whispering his name as she tried to find their connection, desperate for him to be alive and conscious. Then she began to walk.

The motion was inexplicable as she simply yielded to a well-acquainted pulling. In the past, when Callie had tried to understand the strange magnetism between her and Ben, she'd described it as two people headed toward the same location, and that was exactly how it felt now. Completely blinded by the darkness, she nevertheless moved forward following a drive to reach him that had no basis in logic at all but relied exclusively on the connection to his heart. As she surrendered to the pull and approached the house, she heard the bewildered voices around her.

"Where's he going? Sir, you really need to come with us."

When his dark form appeared within her limited field of sight, Callie immediately knew it was Ben. Running to close the gap between them, she threw her arms around him, nearly knocking him over as his body had no strength to counter her force. Quickly retreating, she grabbed him firmly by the arms to keep him from falling backward.

"Ben!" Her cry of pure joy hung sweetly in the smoky air.

As she steadied him, holding tightly to his bare arms, alarm rose at the extreme heat emanating from his skin. When her eyes focused, she gasped in shock. Ben's whole body: his hair, his face, his arms, and his clothes were covered in black grime.

"Oh, Ben!" She wept as she reached to touch his face. Even with full sight, without their bond, she wouldn't have known it was him as his features were hidden by the black residue.

As she continued to hold tightly to him, she felt his body trembling and she knew from experience that this meant he was close to unconsciousness. His eyes were closed and his breathing labored and raspy.

Standing stunned, stroking his feverish face, she felt a tug on her arm.

"Ma'am. Ma'am!" A paramedic tried to get her attention, nearly shouting in urgency. "We need to get him to the hospital. This man just rescued a baby and another man from a house that was so dangerous I'm not sure even a firefighter in full gear would have attempted it. I don't understand how he's still standing. The other man's alive but in rough shape, but the baby's not even coughing and seems normal. We need to take him now, please; he might be in real trouble."

Callie tried to focus on what she needed to do. Ben *was* in real trouble; that much was certain. He appeared catatonic, standing but not looking or speaking. Though he had been walking toward her, she wondered if he was functioning solely from his Succouri instincts, as he seemed incapable of processing much beyond that.

For a split second, she thought maybe the paramedic was right; perhaps he should go to the hospital, but, in the next second, her thoughts began to clear.

Turning to the man, she spoke with a tone of authority and finality that left him speechless. "I understand. I know he needs help, and I promise I will get him exactly what he needs."

Staring at the medic only long enough to observe his confounded expression, she quickly turned back to Ben, grasped his hand, wrapped his arm around her shoulders, and walked away from the house. To her relief, Ben moved with her, and now she was sure that he was reacting to the pull of their bond, staying as close to her as he could as the Succouri in him craved the strength flowing from her.

Knowing it wouldn't take long for the chaos to settle and more well-intended emergency workers to come after them, she moved them as swiftly as she could toward Ben's SUV. She needed to get Ben out of there. The man he'd saved certainly already knew Ben's secret, and obviously, there was some suspicion regarding his extraordinary rescue. Before anyone got organized enough to begin inquiring seriously, they needed to disappear.

As she approached the SUV and maneuvered Ben

toward the passenger side, she shook her head in amaze-ment as she now understood why their bond had mani-fested itself in the way it had earlier in the day. Without the experience of already having driven and knowing she could, they'd be in serious danger.

With her free hand, Callie opened the door and guided Ben into the seat. His eyes were still closed, but she noticed that his breathing sounded less labored, though his body still shook. He slumped forward, but she crossed the seat-belt over him and buckled it. Callie touched his face again, and it still burned with heat. Though she was desperate to clean his face and get him some water, the priority was retreat, so, still weeping, she kissed his forehead and withdrew.

When she opened the driver's side door, she sighed in relief when she found that Ben had left the keys on the seat. After she started the engine, she stared out of the wind-shield for a moment, taking deep breaths, trying to draw out her courage from a place deep within her.

As she was growing up, trying to manage school and life as a child with blindness, she'd had to overcome countless struggles and obstacles. Her dad had helped her, given her strength, and taught her to persevere and find a way. Now, Ben needed her to be strong, to take care of them both. She sucked in one more deep breath as she summoned all her courage.

Her heart broke, and fresh tears dripped as she reached for Ben's arm and placed his hand against her neck, tucking it into the collar of her coat to hold it in place. Though Ben had almost nothing left to give, and this would draw what little remained, she presently had no other choice.

"Ben," she cried out, looking in agony at his slumped form. "I'm so sorry!"

Despite his emptiness, her vision focused, and her mind filled with the needed knowledge. As quickly as she could manage, she backed up and turned the vehicle around, moving them away from the burning, chaotic scene and the danger of discovery.

As she drove under the canopy of trees and the noise of the sirens faded, Callie looked at the navigation system. It was already set to a destination about fifteen miles away. Since she didn't want to wait that long to get Ben some water and clean his face, when she reached the end of the dirt driveway, she turned left instead of right, which would have led her back to the highway. The emergency vehicles were coming from that direction as well, so by going the opposite way, she could find a spot to pull over out of the path of any potential scrutiny. After driving for about a mile, she pulled into another dirt driveway and came to a stop.

Leaving the SUV running, she removed Ben's arm from her shoulder and reached into the back, retrieving a box of tissue. After extracting a handful of tissues and placing the box on the center console, she hurried to Ben's side and opened the door. In the darkness, she blindly grabbed for the water bottle from her cupholder and wetted the wad of tissues with it. Touching Ben's hand so she could see what she was doing, she gently wiped his face, first cleaning around his eyes.

When the cold water contacted his burning skin, Ben sighed, and his eyelids fluttered, making Callie's heart relax with relief and sending a fresh stream of tears down her face. It took several additional wads of wet tissue before the grime was cleared enough to reveal Ben's familiar, handsome features, and the sight overwhelmed her with joy.

She placed her hands on the sides of his face and kissed

him repeatedly on the lips, and his stunning blue eyes opened, focused on her face and began to shine with a flicker of life.

When she sensed he was revived enough to understand her, she placed the water bottle in his hand. "Ben, please, please drink."

Though he moved robotically and Callie still wasn't sure if his mind was fully aware of what was happening, Ben lifted the bottle to his lips and drank vigorously, causing her to let out a relieved breath that was almost a laugh. Touching his forehead, though he was still extraordinarily hot, she thought he felt slightly cooler than when they'd left the house.

The cold night air filled the car. Though Ben was unusually hot, Callie was freezing. The temperature had dropped, and the chill, along with her frayed nerves, had left her shivering most of the time that Ben had been inside the burning house. Her face was red with cold, so she pressed it against his in an attempt to cool him further. In addition, she hoped the contact would return some essential strength to him before she had to withdraw it again to get them out of there.

His eager response came quickly as he also pressed against her, telling her that the contact was working, and Ben was leaning into the inflow of strength. The heat radiating from him calmed her shivering, and she gladly remained still for a long moment, breathing deeply and wishing she could somehow measure the strength he was regaining. If she felt safe staying where they were, she'd happily remain there as long as he needed her. The pain in her heart for him, as weakness and unconsciousness, weighed him down, was unbearable. Though there were many wonderful aspects of partnering with Ben in this incredible life, watching him struggle and feeling him empty himself to the point of blacking out was excruciating.

"Callie." Ben's unrecognizable voice broke the silence, startling her. The sound was raspy and strained, and Callie's heart churned again in worry, even in her relief.

"Yes, Ben, I'm here!" Laughing joyfully at his awakening, she pulled back to look at him, but he leaned forward and pressed his cheek against hers again.

"Are you okay?" he whispered.

Callie exhaled in amazement. He was the one who'd rushed into a burning house, but he was worried about her.

"Ben!" She spoke his name through tears of love and admiration. "I'll be okay when you're okay. What you did... I have no words. I continue to be so amazed by you!"

She tenderly kissed his lips several times before returning her cheek to his.

"Are they... Are they alive?" Though his voice was tired and weak, it was like beautiful music to her ears.

"Yes!" she exclaimed. "Ben, yes! They are alive. They said the baby seemed totally normal. You saved them! Do you hear me? You saved both of their lives!" His whole body relaxed at her words.

"I love you, Ben Sawyer! You scared me to death, but I love you with all my heart."

As she leaned back again to look at him, the corners of his mouth turned up in a weak smile. "I want to marry you, Miss LeVray. Very soon, I want to marry you."

Staring at him in surprise, Callie stopped breathing. "Ben?"

He didn't respond, and she wondered if she'd heard him correctly. Soft and strained, his voice was hard to hear and now his eyes were closed again.

"Ben?"

Again, no response came, so she leaned in and put her ear near his mouth. He was breathing, maybe asleep or slipped back into shallow unconsciousness.

As Callie gently kissed him one last time and closed his door, moving back to her side of the car, her heart overflowed with emotions. Maybe he hadn't meant to say it, and likely he wouldn't remember that he had, but now she knew what was in his heart, and the truth of it filled her heart so full of love that she could barely breathe.

Though Callie drove the entire fifteen miles to the hotel with ease, she wept bitterly as she felt Ben's hand on her neck. Drawing from him now in his already utterly depleted state was like willfully holding his head underwater, knowing he was already drowning. Worse still, she could feel him slipping deeper and deeper into the abyss of unconsciousness and the pain and fear in that made her whole body shake with desperate agony. How much his body could take before the draw caused permanent damage or worse, she didn't know. It was shocking to her that he could give her anything at all as he was so empty. Nevertheless, Ben gave her what she needed. Several times, she placed her hand on his knee and pleaded with him to hold on just a few minutes longer, and she almost pulled off the road to boost his strength temporarily again, but in the end, getting him to the hotel as quickly as possible where he could rest and recuperate fully seemed the wiser choice.

When she finally pulled into the upscale hotel Ben had reserved for the night, Callie was a mess of tears and nerves. There was no valet at this hotel, so she parked in the nearest parking spot as she tried to figure out how to get Ben inside and get them checked in without questions or suspicions. Relieved to remove his hand from her neck, she looked over lovingly at him, wishing he'd open his eyes and ease her aching heart. She felt nothing from him through their bond now, which worried her to the point of feeling sick to her stomach.

Still having no clue what she would do, Callie grabbed Ben's wallet from the center console and shoved it, along with the keys and cell phone, into her coat pockets. When she tried to get Ben out of his seat, he was nearly a dead weight, and it took all she had to lift him and encircle his arm around her neck. Panic set in when she tried to move with him, but now he didn't have the same ability to cooperate and walk with her, so she leaned him against the side of the SUV for a moment to figure out what to do.

"Ben, please. You have to walk with me. I can't carry you," she whispered as she stroked his lifeless face. The additional drain from him as he gave her the ability to drive had pushed him into a state of total helplessness. Even his Succouri instincts weren't functioning now.

"Let us help you."

Startled by the gentle voice behind her, she turned her head and saw a man and woman were approaching. They looked to be in their thirties, both with dark hair and eyes. Their faces were kind, and though her heart raced with fear of discovery, she found herself staring at them intently as something about them was reassuring.

The man didn't wait for Callie to respond but came up on Ben's opposite side and encircled Ben's free arm around his shoulders.

"It's alright," he said with a sympathetic smile. "I've got him."

Callie remained frozen in place, glad for the offer of help but conscious that if she let go of Ben, she wouldn't be able to see where she was going. How would she explain that to this couple as she'd just exited the driver's seat?

"Um, thank you, but..." she stammered as she searched for words.

Though she unquestionably needed their assistance, she couldn't take it without risking exposing Ben's secret, and protecting him was her highest priority.

Still staring, trying to come up with a response, Callie noted something in the man's expression that put her at ease. He had a look, a gentle smile, a tone in his voice, something she recognized.

Then, she remembered Ms. Essie's words. She'd told them that now that they knew about the Succouri and especially now that Callie knew Ben specifically, they'd be able to identify others when they met them. This man had a way, a quality, a look that was like Ben's. Though she wasn't confident enough in her assessment to come out and directly ask, she was sure enough to release Ben and allow this man to help her.

"Thank you." She sighed in gratitude as she turned to the woman. "May I have your arm? I don't see very well."

"Of course!" The woman's voice revealed surprise, but it was warm and compassionate, and she quickly approached to offer Callie her assistance.

The four of them moved toward the front of the hotel, the man nearly carrying Ben's full weight making progress slow going. Callie was glad for the darkness as it made it harder to see Ben's filthy clothes and skin and his lifeless face. Once they got inside, that advantage would be lost.

"I'm Elena," the woman offered, "and this is my husband, Raul."

"I'm Callie and this is Ben."

"Your husband?" Elena questioned.

Smiling at the memory of Ben's earlier dazed proposal, she struggled for an answer. "No, but..."

She could find no word to define her relationship with Ben, as 'boyfriend' certainly seemed ridiculously inadequate.

"Well..."

Laughing, Elena patted Callie's hand. "How long have you two been bonded?"

Callie sighed in relief. Elena was obviously much more practiced at readily identifying other Succouri. Her heart stopped racing, and she smiled freely as a wave of peace and gratitude washed over her.

"Not very long, but... How did you know?"

"It gets pretty easy to recognize. Plus, you told me you couldn't see, but you were driving, and then there's the fact that Ben here definitely stands out. Fire?"

"Yes. He rescued a man and his infant son." Callie spoke with unrestrained pride.

"Wow!" Raul spoke up. "That's fantastic, but that's one of the toughest rescues. Fighting the smoke and heat yourself while helping another, that's very hard. I'm surprised someone so new to this life would attempt it." Raul's voice carried the deep empathy of personal experience.

She smiled at Raul's assumption that Ben's young age meant he was new to his Succouri life, knowing that, in truth, Ben had likely been one for several years longer than Raul.

"Can you help him?" Callie asked hopefully.

Raul and Elena laughed, but the sound conveyed confusion about Callie's question more than any real humor. "I can get him to the room for you," Raul replied, "but the rest is something only you can do for him. As deep as Ben here is in unconsciousness, he'll only be able to respond to the pull of your bond, for a while anyway. He's likely not understanding anything else right now."

"But can't your touch help him?" Callie pleaded.

Elena patted Callie's hand again. "I guess you're new at this, and he hasn't told you everything yet. A Succouri can't help another Succouri. Not like that anyway. Only the bonded partner can provide what's needed in this situation."

As she knew Ben's touch had strengthened Louis when they shook hands, Callie felt confused at Elena's statement. But then, Louis had already passed along his gift and could no longer give out as an active Succouri, so maybe that was the difference.

"He needs *you*, Callie," Elena continued. "He saved them; now you save him. That's how this works. You have something that no one, not even another Succouri, can give him, and it works the other way around too. For the next few hours, until some of his strength returns, you're the only one who can reach him because you can connect with his heart."

Already having experienced this when she and Ben had somehow found each other in the dark, she nodded in understanding.

Before they moved inside, Callie stopped and turned to Elena. "How are we going to do this? I mean, the room isn't in my name, and I don't want to make anyone suspicious."

Raul halted and turned around. "I'll hang back with Ben here so they can see him, but not too well. You go with Elena. As long as you have his ID, they'll let you check in. When we get you two settled, I'll come back for your suitcases. It's going to take Ben several days to fully recover from this, especially if you two are only newly bonded. Make sure he drinks plenty of water; we'll bring you some. I think it's going to snow tonight, so we'd planned on sticking around for a day or so anyway to avoid traveling in it. We can help you; you just help him."

"Thank you!" Callie whispered, her heart full of genuine appreciation.

As Raul had predicted, the hotel gave her the room key without too many questions when she presented Ben's driver's license and credit card. Raul stood at a distance, holding up Ben in the shadows of the dimly lit lobby and Callie caught from the clerk's annoyed tone that he believed Ben was intoxicated. Besides the staff, there was no one else around as it was after eleven o'clock. Getting Ben to the room was a slow and difficult undertaking, but eventually they made it, and Raul lowered Ben to the couch before going out again to retrieve their suitcases. Elena brought them several bottles of water which she set down on the coffee table in front of the couch.

"Will he be alright?" Callie asked anxiously. Though she'd helped Ben before, she felt nervous now as he was so completely lifeless this time.

Offering a quick reassuring embrace, Elena nodded, and Callie was astonished at how she and Raul already felt like old friends. "Yes, he will. You'll know what to do, Callie. Just trust your instincts. We'll check on you tomorrow and bring you some breakfast and I bet he'll be able to talk with us by then."

"How do you do this?" Callie asked, lowering her head as tears slid down her face. "How can you stand to watch Raul go through this over and over again?"

Sighing sympathetically, Elena put a hand on Callie's shoulder. "It doesn't get easier. I wish I could tell you it does, but it doesn't. Actually, it gets harder as you grow to love him more. But it does get easier to help him. You'll learn how to best revive him and even how to help him while he's helping others. You'll see."

The vague statements offered by both Ms. Essie and now Elena regarding how the bond worked and how to best render aid, frustrated Callie as she felt an urgency to help Ben now in the most efficient way possible. For reasons Callie couldn't understand, those with the knowledge didn't feel it was appropriate to share the details that seemed crucial to her right now as she stood looking at Ben's lifeless face.

As soon as Raul returned with the suitcases, they said goodbye to Callie and hurried out.

After removing her coat, Callie sat down next to Ben, pulling him to her. Last time, when she'd helped him, she'd simply held him against her and that had been enough to revive him, so she started there, trying to follow Elena's advice and go where her heart led her. As she pulled him close, his head fell against her neck, and she held it in place with her hand as she stroked his face. He was still feverish, and the pungent smell of smoke lingered in his hair. She needed to cool him off, get him out of his filthy clothes, and wash off all the grime, but he needed to regain some strength so he could walk with her as there was no way she could drag him or carry him.

Content to simply wait until enough strength returned that she could offer him more, Callie leaned her head against his and caressed his face. Closing her eyes, she tuned into the life-giving sound of his steady breathing. He was alive, he was here with her, they were safe, and right now, that was all that mattered and more than enough for her.

CHAPTER 8

THE RECUPERATION

An hour passed as Callie waited for any sign of renewed life from Ben. Though she was exhausted, she couldn't sleep as the ache in her heart to hear his voice, look into his eyes, or feel anything from him indicating he was coming back to her throbbed as a gnawing need that wouldn't relent.

At long last, she felt him shift, pressing his forehead against her neck, and sighing contentedly. Whispering his name, she kissed his smoky, matted hair before leaning away to look at his face.

A single lamp cast dim light around the room, offering her just enough illumination to see him blink his eyes several times, the small sign of life calming the raging storm of anxiety inside her.

Leaning him back against the couch, she reached for a water bottle, removed the lid, and offered it. At first, he only blinked, looking like he was unaware of her presence and the offering, so she reached for his hand and placed it first against her cheek and then around the bottle, trying to anchor him to reality. After a few additional seconds of vacant staring, Ben grasped the bottle and lifted it, drinking heartily and making Callie sigh in relief. He drank the entire bottle before lowering it from his lips and leaning back against the couch.

Callie placed the empty bottle on the coffee table and turned to stroke his face with the back of her fingers.

"Ben," she whispered. "Do you think you can walk with me for a minute?"

Kissing his lips, she was pleased they were now much more moist and soft.

He looked at her then, his eyes registering recognition, and his lips formed a weak smile. Though she wasn't sure whether he understood her question or simply recognized her face, she returned his smile, grateful for the small communication.

"Alright then, I'll be right back. I'm not going far," she promised as she rose from the couch and crossed to the bathroom.

The luxurious hotel had a large bathtub, which Callie was grateful for as she filled it with warm water, careful not to let it get too hot. Ben still felt feverish, and she wanted to bring his temperature down while ensuring he was comfortable.

When she returned to him and touched his hand, she was happy to see that his eyes still blinked, though he remained silent even as she sat next to him and put his arm around her shoulders. When she stood and pulled at him, he cooperated with her, though his movements were slow and labored. Once again, she could feel the magnetism of their bond working, compelling Ben, even in his otherwise unresponsive state, to stay close to her. Until today, she hadn't understood the purpose of the powerful pull they experienced, but now it all made sense.

When they were standing in front of the tub, Callie took a deep breath. She knew she had to help Ben out of his dirty clothes, but though she felt no sense of guilt or shame in taking care of him in this way, she hated breaching his privacy while he could not understand what was happening or offer his consent. She wasn't sure how he'd feel about it later when he became aware of what had transpired. Her intense attraction for him complicated matters, leaving her heart and nerves racing.

Since she was the only one who could coax a response from him, and right now, this was the help he needed, she had no choice but to proceed, but Callie determined to do her best to show the highest respect for him, treating him as she knew he would treat her if the situation were reversed.

As she removed his arm from her shoulders, Callie momentarily steadied him by grasping around his waist until he seemed balanced enough to stand alone. Looking into his eyes, she tried to communicate her love for him before reaching to lift his white T-shirt, which was streaked with black grime, over his head. To her profound relief, Ben cooperated with her as she removed the rest of his clothes, doing her best to divert her gaze to afford him as much privacy as possible despite the unavoidable demands of the circumstance. Focusing on his face, she helped him into the bathtub and supported him as he lowered into the water. Though he still didn't speak, he maintained a look of peace and satisfaction as he leaned back and relaxed. When he was settled, he closed his eyes.

In short order, the water in the tub turned black as the grime from Ben's body washed off, and Callie had to drain and refill the tub twice before the water was clear enough to wash him with it.

As she leaned over him, lovingly wiping the evidence of his dangerous rescue off his body with a soapy washcloth, she was again overcome by a wave of deep love for him. Ben had rushed into an inferno without a thought or concern for himself. He'd selflessly saved a man and baby he didn't know, fully mindful that he might not make it out, and that, even if he did, he'd suffer for a long time just as he was suffering now from the effort. When he spotted the fire, he instantly reacted by rushing to help, demonstrating that he was fully embracing his new identity and life even though he'd never asked for it or been given a choice. He was protecting and caring for her with every resource and ability, willing even, without hesitation, to give up his life for her if necessary. No words could describe the courage of such an extraordinary man, and her heart couldn't contain her gratitude at knowing that his heart belonged to her.

Covering his eyes with her hand, Callie poured warm water from a cup over his hair, and then worked shampoo into the matted tangles, causing another smile to cross his face, filling up her heart. Though she was careful with her gaze, Callie's stomach fluttered, and her heart pounded as she touched him. Like his soul, Ben's body was extraordinarily beautiful, in the most masculine sense of the word, lean and solidly muscular. His skin was smooth and flawless, not a scar or blemish to be found. Callie had expected that, as she knew his Succouri gift would heal any wound or mark, but the impact of seeing him like this for the first time left her awestruck and breathless.

As she cautiously rinsed his hair and tried to control her thoughts, even as the fire moved stronger than ever between them, she began to ask herself some questions that she hadn't previously considered.

Becoming a Succouri at the age of twelve was unprecedented, and Ms. Essie had said she'd never known or even heard of anyone like Ben. Typically, a person would have had a chance to develop fully, both physically and mentally, maturing into their own distinct identity and sense of self before taking on the additional Succouri persona, like putting on a uniform to fulfill a role. Since those who chose the role were typically at least thirty, they would possess established personality traits, preferences, and habits.

But Ben had been too young for that. He wasn't even physically mature when this new and powerful identity was thrust on him, and his distinctive personality was only in the earliest stages of asserting itself. Therefore, the Succouri blood that now ran through his veins and powered his touch would have had a much more profound impact on him, likely merging with rather than simply adding to his developing attributes.

Indeed, even in her brief encounters with Raul and Louis, Callie had noted a difference between them and Ben. It wasn't easy to define, but she could perceive in them a slight separation or border between the Succouri nature and their natural look and manner. The two identities worked side by side beautifully but maintained some autonomy. But with Ben, who he was as a man and who he was as a Succouri seemed intertwined or fused together. Ironically, though Ben had never heard the word and had no idea what he was for fifteen years, he was likely more purely Succouri in nature, both in his physical being as well as his personality, than anyone who had ever claimed that identity.

She had the distinct feeling that no matter how much they learned about this life, Ben and her journey would be unique because of this fact. How that would all play out was unknown. Until they knew more about what normal was in this life, they wouldn't be able to determine how their experience strayed from that reference point.

When Callie was satisfied that she'd done her best to clean him, she let out the water in the tub and grabbed a towel, tossing it over her shoulder. Though he worked with her as best he could, it was difficult to get him up and out of the tub in his weakened state, and her heart continued to break for the high price he paid, the hardships he took completely upon himself without those he saved even being aware of the depths of his sacrifice. They benefitted as his strength poured into them and gave them what they needed, but the man and child he rescued would likely never know what it cost.

Still doing her best to restrict her gaze, Callie dried him off and wrapped the towel around his waist. She put her arm around his back this time, guiding him back into the room, noticing that he walked more steadily now and didn't seem to need to lean on her. The bath had helped him, or maybe it was her contact with him as she washed him and cleaned his hair; she wasn't sure, but she was glad for the progress. Pulling back the sheets and blankets, she helped him to settle comfortably in bed, and then covered him up, tucking the blankets tightly around him.

"I love you," she reminded him as she leaned over to kiss him, and he rewarded her with a full smile.

He closed his eyes, and a look of contentment fixed on his face, making Callie finally fully relax in the truth that Ben would eventually be himself again.

She took a moment to change her clothes, as she'd gotten quite dirty from all of her contact with him. After putting on a T-shirt and sweats, she retrieved her hairbrush. As she climbed into bed and lifted Ben's head into her lap to gently brush out his tangled hair, she wondered how late it was. Not presently having a watch or their one phone nearby, she could only guess that it was probably after two a.m.

For a long time, she sat cradling his head on a pillow in her lap, brushing slow, gentle strokes through his hair. He smiled several times, each time a little broader, seeming to enjoy the experience, so she continued the action even after the task of untangling his hair was accomplished, as it appeared to be bringing him a measure of comfort that Callie rejoiced in.

At long last, weariness overtook her, and she lay down next to Ben, wrapping herself in a separate blanket but staying tucked up close beside him so their bond could continue to fill him with strength.

Just before drifting off to sleep, she was surprised to feel Ben shift toward her and wrap his arms around her, pulling her tighter against him. His bare chest was warm, but she was pleased he no longer felt feverish. In Ben's fully conscious state, she didn't think he would act so boldly, but presently, he was behaving more out of instinct than rational thought.

Her face now pressed against the defined muscles of his chest, and she could hear his heart beating steadily. Abruptly, she was consumed with desire for him as the familiar fire of their bond worked to magnify every natural attraction already raging in her. Breathing unsteadily as her heart pounded, she willfully restrained the powerful urge to touch and kiss him, even as she smiled, knowing that if she was feeling this way, it meant that a great deal of energy was working its magic to heal him.

Allowing herself to indulge in a moment of longing, she imagined what it would be like to be his, completely his, but she soon refocused on how he currently needed her and her responsibility to protect him. Right now, Ben was incapable of rationally choosing or rejecting any course of action. If she propositioned him, he might respond, but it wouldn't be a conscious choice, and she would never disrespect him that way. Repeatedly, he'd protected them from crossing boundaries they'd already decided not to breach. Now it was her turn to do the same.

Closing her eyes, she relaxed against him, letting herself drift into an exhausted sleep, though her dreams were not as easily dissuaded.

It felt like no time at all had passed when Callie awoke to the welcome sight of Ben's loving gaze focused on her as he sat on the edge of the bed. Smiling at her, his expression was playful and amused. A surprised inhale sounded from her as she sat up quickly, her head spinning, and he laughed even as he placed a hand on her shoulder to steady her.

"Ben!" she exclaimed as she flung her arms around him. He embraced her enthusiastically, though she could feel weakness lightening his hold.

Laughing together, Callie grabbed his face, kissing him repeatedly as he affectionately played with her curls.

After laughing, kissing, and embracing for several joy-filled minutes, Ben pulled back to look her in the eyes, humor still playing at the corners of his mouth.

"Good morning, Miss LeVray. While I definitely want to continue this affectionate reunion, I do have two important questions for you." As he continued, he put up corresponding fingers to demonstrate. "First, though I can't imagine waking up in a more pleasant circumstance; how in the world did you get us here? And second, hm..." He tilted his head, unsure how to word his second question. "Why is it when I take care of you, you wake up fully clothed, but when you're in charge I wake up, well, considerably less than fully clothed?"

Callie laughed, knowing the second question wasn't really a question but a way of defusing some of the awkwardness caused by the unavoidable situation she'd faced. Looking at him, she realized Ben had dressed, and she wondered how he'd managed that on his own.

Holding a coy smile, she replied. "Would it help if I told you I did my best not to look?"

Ben grinned suspiciously back at her as he studied her expression. "Hm... Well, then, can you also reassure me you'll forget what you did see?"

Sucking in a breath, she slowly shook her head. Though she still wanted to alleviate the awkwardness by holding onto some humor, she had to tell him the truth. "Sorry, Ben. I can't promise you that."

A revealing moment passed between them as she allowed her face and eyes to carry the honesty of her experience and emotions, and Ben read the message clearly.

At last, softly chuckling, he pulled her into an embrace as they relaxed in the knowledge that what was done had to be done, and it was alright on both sides, though it did forge a new depth of intimacy that couldn't be ignored.

"Fair enough," he said as he pulled away and slowly stood. "Come have breakfast with me," he offered, extending his hand.

"Breakfast?" she questioned, taking his hand and rising to her feet.

Walking with him to the couch, she noticed how difficult it still was for him to move around. He'd likely expended much of his small supply of energy getting himself up and dressed. As she sat down beside him, she made sure to keep close contact, knowing her job in aiding his recovery was far from over. At least now Ben could tell her how he felt and what he needed.

"Yes," he said, tilting his head in confusion. "I woke up to a soft knock on the door. By the time I... put some clothes on and got to the door, there was no one there, but there was a tray of food waiting."

Callie smiled and placed one hand over her heart. "Bless Raul and Elena!"

She picked up a banana and started peeling it.

Staring blankly at her, Ben squinted in confusion. "Um... Information, please."

Ben grabbed a full bottle of water and a muffin.

As they ate, Callie filled him in on how she found him after the fire, the drive back to the hotel, meeting Raul and Elena, discovering they were Succouri, and describing how they'd helped them. She left out the part about giving him a bath and his confession of wanting to marry her. He listened with stunned amazement.

"Callie!" He exhaled slowly. "That's incredible! I guess I did promise you adventure. I knew the bond was working that way for a reason yesterday, but that's still extraordinary. And, I guess we finally fully understand the purpose behind the magnetism thing as well." He leaned back against the couch and crossed his arms, shaking his head several times as he tried to take it all in.

Turning her body to face him and tucking her legs underneath her, she looked questioningly into his eyes. "Do you remember any of it; the fire, the rescue, afterward, anything?" she asked softly, not wanting to make him relive anything painful but desiring to hear his side of the story.

He shared what he remembered after he'd entered the

house. When he spoke of holding the baby, Callie felt the sadness in his heart, and she knew he was thinking of their recent difficult news from Ms. Essie.

"The last thing I remember clearly is the sound of glass breaking and hearing you call my name in my head, but everything after that is a blur and feels more like a disjointed dream than reality." Ben stared unfocused at the space in front of him.

She nodded, though she wished he'd share more of what he recalled, even if he wasn't sure if it was real.

Ben rested his head wearily against the back of the couch but turned his face her way. "Yesterday, you told me you wished you could give more, do more." He paused to chuckle and raise his eyebrows. "Callie LeVray, thank you! You saved my life, protected my secret, and cared for me when I was completely helpless. You're the hero here. I've always needed you since the first day I met you as the woman I love and the one who holds my heart. But now, you can't possibly question how essential you are as my partner in this new life we're figuring out together. You're amazing, sweetheart, and I owe you a debt I can't ever pay."

Though his words were kind and generous, Callie shifted, turning her body to face forward and lowering her head into her hands. Ben put his hand on her back and leaned forward, confusion and concern wrinkling the corners of his eyes.

"Ben!" Callie's voice was a sorrowful whisper. "Don't say that. I... I don't deserve that. I had to take from you, when you were weakest, most vulnerable. To get us out of there, to be able to drive us away, I had to take from you, hurt you, and... it broke my heart. You'd have a far easier recovery if I hadn't needed to do that. If you'd chosen someone who... who didn't need your help that way, that wouldn't have been necessary." A tear traced down Callie's face.

"Oh, Callie!" Ben gently grasped her hands, pulling them away from her face, and then reached to lift her chin with his finger. Gazing at her for a long moment, his expression was pained, and Callie saw tears welling up in his eyes as well. Then, he wrapped his arms around her and leaned back again, pulling her with him as he did his best to hold her tightly.

He stroked her hair as he continued. "First of all, I don't want anyone else, and I never will. I love you and only you for the rest of my days. I'm so sorry you faced that difficult dilemma, but you made the right choice as you did what you had to do to protect us. Second, no one else could have done what you did last night. The strength you've gained because of your challenges prepared you to endure the difficulties of this crazy life with me. This is hard, really hard, and there's so much to lose, so much we've already lost. Not many people have the inner fortitude to stay strong and clearheaded in a chaotic situation like that one. And Callie, yesterday, we saved a baby and a father and husband. We did that together, you and me. You were right when you said this was a shared gift and burden and that whatever happens now happens to both of us. You were exactly the person I needed last night and will always need. Lastly, sweetheart, I'll be just fine. You don't need to worry. You haven't hurt me. In fact, you took exceptionally good care of me. And, without a doubt, I'm here, talking to you right this minute, safe and sound, because you accomplished, well, frankly, a miracle in an unbelievably impossible situation."

Callie pulled away, offering him a weak smile as she looked him in the eyes. "How are you feeling? Truthfully."

Sighing, he shrugged his shoulders. "That was the

toughest rescue I've ever attempted, harder than the situation with your father. Without your help last night, I'm sure I'd still be out of it. I'll be okay, but I'm not going to run any marathons for a while. It feels a little like having the flu. At least what I can vaguely remember of how that felt. Everything aches."

Callie nodded. "We definitely need to stay here for a couple of days and let you rest," she said, but Ben shook his head.

"We can't stay too long in any one place, especially without good security. That monster is looking for you, and being on the move keeps you safe on this trip. We'll stay tonight, but we have to go tomorrow. We only have one more day of driving, and then we'll be at my former home, and it'll be much safer there."

"But you can't..."

Ben put his hand on her cheek. "With your help, I'll be okay by tomorrow. I'll just be tired, but it's just one day of driving, and I'll drink lots of coffee."

"Ben, I..."

Interrupting her protest, he surprised her with a kiss that swept her heart away with its honest expression of love and gratitude. When she got over the shock, Callie returned the kiss, expressing her own relief and joy at his return to her.

When they finally pulled away, they clung to each other for a long while, not needing words to say what had already been beautifully communicated.

"We've lost a lot in the last couple of days," Ben finally whispered against her hair. "But I can't lose you, Callie. You're the one thing I can't ever lose."

· · ·

BEN HAD the chance to meet Raul and Elena for himself when they brought lunch, and they all sat eating it together around the table in their hotel room. Raul offered Ben a friendly smile and a firm handshake in greeting. Ben was perplexed when he didn't feel an inflow of strength from him as his body continued to ache, and he fought the weariness that weighed him down. Still, he was glad for the opportunity to meet another like him and learn from his experience.

"I've helped in a couple of fires and"—Raul paused to shake his head in empathy—"they're really tough. I'm not sure I've ever pulled two people out simultaneously, though. I feel your pain, man." Raul grimaced as he empathized.

"Thank you for helping us last night. From what Callie's told me, she couldn't have managed without your help."

Raul and Elena nodded in response and Elena patted Callie on the shoulder. "She told us you two are new at this," Elena said. "You're very young for a Succouri, Ben. Do you mind if I ask how long you've been one?"

An awkward silence lingered as Ben considered how to answer the question. The reality of his early transformation had shocked and dismayed Ms. Essie, and he wasn't sure how other Succouri might react to his unusual situation.

"Well," Ben started hesitantly. "That's a long story. I've actually been one for quite some time. My situation is a bit unusual."

Though they stared at him with surprise, they didn't look alarmed, so he inhaled slowly and continued. "When Callie says we're new at this, she means the bonding and also knowing what I am. I've had these abilities since I was young, twelve years old. I had a marrow transplant back then, but I've only recently understood that the gift came from it. I spent fifteen years completely ignorant about all of it."

Stunned, Raul and Elena sat speechless, and Ben worried that maybe he shouldn't have told them after all.

After a moment, Raul set down his cup of coffee and leaned toward Ben, whistling out a long breath of air. "That's horrifying, and I would've thought impossible if you weren't sitting right here in front of me. I understood it couldn't be done in someone that young."

"But," Elena protested, "if you and Callie only met recently, how did you survive that long, not go crazy, without the bonding?"

Ben made a mental note of the 'go crazy' reference, which provided him with more detail than Ms. Essie's vague suggestion of what happens to a Succouri who doesn't bond. He felt again the acute gratitude in meeting Callie before it was too late for him.

"I didn't use it much until very recently. Because I didn't know what it was, I ran from it," Ben explained.

"Plus," Raul interjected, "you wouldn't have been able to bond anyway until you were an adult. I mean, it's not for kids, if you don't mind the frankness."

All heads nodded in complete understanding and agreement.

"Still," Elena continued, "I've never heard of a Succouri lasting more than two years alone, much less fifteen. And I agree with Raul; what you're saying shouldn't be possible. No doctor working with the Succouri would do it. So, how in the world did you end up with Succouri marrow?"

"That's what we're headed to Boston to find out."

"Boston?" Elena asked as she and Raul exchanged a look that Ben didn't understand. There was a moment of silence, and then Elena returned her gaze to Ben.

"Ben, I wonder if, and it's totally your choice, of course, but my father is a retired doctor. Well, at least he retired from regular practice. He works with the Succouri and helps with transferring the gift as well as other services. He's not far from Cape Cod. He also researches and studies how this all works." She paused to laugh. "Not that he's had a lot of success figuring it out. I wonder if you might be willing or interested in seeing him. I doubt that he, or anyone else in the network, has ever known anyone like you, so I don't know if he'll be able to answer your questions or discover anything helpful, but it might be worth a try."

Leaning back in his chair, Ben stroked his chin as he considered the offer. He needed answers, and he certainly wanted to connect with the network, but he didn't want to become a science experiment of sorts or have his name gossiped about because of being so unusual.

Before he could answer, Callie spoke up, and he grinned at how apropos her question was, though he wasn't surprised. "Could your father keep Ben's situation private?"

"Yes, certainly!" Elena said without hesitation. "We don't gossip in the network, and we don't share secrets or identities without permission."

Ben nodded and stopped stroking his chin. "Alright then. If you give me his information, I'll connect with him when we get to Boston. We're heading out tomorrow and should be there late evening."

Raul's eyes grew wide with surprise. "Wow! That will be rough, Ben. But, given your celebrity, it's probably a good idea."

Callie and Ben turned their heads at the same time to look questioningly at Raul.

"Celebrity?" Callie spoke up first.

Raul tossed a newspaper that had been on the table in front of him to Ben, and Ben flipped it around, his face registering shock and then panic as his eyes focused on the headline.

Local Farmer and His Infant Son Saved By Mysterious Guardian Angel

"Ben?" Callie inquired with concern, and he read her the headline in a strained voice.

Gasping, she put her hand over her mouth as Ben scanned the article for details about him. He cringed when he found a mention of his vehicle. Someone reported seeing a gray Range Rover one minute, and then it was gone.

Nathan had given a vague description of him, brown hair and vivid blue eyes. He told the reporter that, "...the miraculous stranger had touched him, enabling him to breathe the toxic air," and he expressed exuberant praise and gratitude for, "...the brave, compassionate hero, who looked like an angel, and saved him and his son from certain death."

Continuing to scan, he looked for any direct mention of their names but didn't see that Nathan had revealed that, not yet anyway. They'd introduced themselves to Nathan's wife as well, so Ben guessed it was only a matter of time before that information would come out. In their haste to help and comfort, neither of them thought wiser of giving out this information, and Ben regretted the oversight. They had much to learn about protecting themselves while still fulfilling their purpose.

Pushing back from the table, he abruptly rose, the sudden motion causing him to nearly lose his balance.

"Callie, we have to go, now," he said with urgency.

Understanding the reason for his alarm, she stood and came to offer him her shoulder to lean on.

Raul and Elena stood as well, confused even as they tried to reassure them.

"There's no need to panic," Raul encouraged. "No name was given, and if you lay low and leave tomorrow, it's unlikely anyone will connect you to this article."

Ben turned away, and he and Callie started for their suitcases, Ben's mind already focused on what he needed to do to keep Callie safe.

"Ben!" Raul called after them, even as he approached and hoisted their suitcases onto the bed for them. "This happens sometimes but it almost always comes to nothing. The story will die down and be forgotten in a day or so and..."

"You don't understand," Ben interrupted, trying to keep his panic from making him sound angry or unkind. "Callie's in danger. We left home primarily to keep her out of harm's way. If the lunatic who's after her connects this story to me or the car, he could track us. She's already been shot once and had another unsuccessful attempt on her life. There's no way I'm taking the chance of it happening again."

A familiar tightness seized his chest as he contended with the unspeakable pain of ever losing Callie. His weakness frustrated him, and though he knew he and Callie had saved lives, he almost regretted the risk he'd taken by leaving her vulnerable, as his ability to protect her was diminished due to the consequences of the ordeal.

Elena and Raul's faces paled, and they began helping them prepare to leave, gathering their things and placing them in a pile as Callie and Ben transferred them into the suitcases.

"But Ben..." Callie grasped his arm. "How will you drive and stay awake? You need to rest and..."

Placing his hand on hers, he tried for a reassuring smile, but it didn't hide his alarm.

"I'll be alright, and if I'm not, well, you seem to be an excellent backup driver, Miss LeVray." Ben tried for the joke, hoping to relieve her distress, but the tension of the moment didn't allow for the humor to have its full effect.

"Drink plenty of water and eat regularly," Raul suggested, patting Ben on the back. "I sincerely wish we could help you, but we are headed in the opposite direction. You can always pull over when you get out of sight and rest if necessary." He shook his head, the gesture evidence of the doubt he held in Ben's ability to accomplish the long drive.

But Ben had no choice. He had to find the strength to do what was necessary to protect Callie, as this was his highest priority.

As Raul helped Ben check out and load the car and Elena and Callie gathered some leftover lunch into a bag for them to take on the road, Callie pleaded with Elena.

"Is there anything I can do for him? Please. I know Succouri don't like to share information about the bonding, but if there's anything I can do…"

Callie knew full well that Ben wasn't well enough for this. Just a few hours ago, he'd been unable even to talk with her or take care of his own needs. His conscious thought had returned, and he could move around with difficulty, but he wasn't recovered enough for a full day of driving, and she'd be unable to help by sitting apart from him in the passenger's seat. Indeed, it wouldn't even be prudent to hold his hand as drawing anything at all from him would only make things worse. Though she understood his urgency to leave, this plan seemed impossible.

Elena sighed, understanding Callie's frustration and concern. "You're right. The bond is so personal and individual, couple to couple, bond to bond. What works for one pair doesn't necessarily work for another, and, things seem to happen when they need to happen. Often you don't find out what works until you need to know it, and everyone respects the mystery of that."

She couldn't argue with Elena as they'd just experienced that very thing for themselves when the bond had enabled her to drive mere hours before she needed that ability to rescue Ben.

Elena stopped gathering up the food and placed her hand affectionately on Callie's shoulder. "The two of you are very special in more ways than just Ben's early acquisition of the gift. You're going to be a powerful force for good in this world, I can tell without a doubt, and I feel privileged to call you both friends. You'll know what to do, Callie, trust me. For being so newly bonded, you and Ben share a deep connection. It's beautiful. You'll know how to help him."

Warmed by Elena's kind affection and prediction, Callie smiled. Elena resumed packing the food, silent for a moment before continuing. "Are you and Ben planning on getting married soon?"

The question caught Callie off guard, and she took a deep breath before answering. "Nearly since the moment I met Ben, our lives have been on a virtual rollercoaster ride. With my father's stroke, the threats to my life, Ben's discoveries about his identity, and our need to flee from danger, we've been a little busy literally dodging bullets and therefore haven't had much of a chance to sit down and discuss our future in that way. But I do think getting married is our intention at some point, maybe soon." Smiling again, Callie recalled Ben's words to her when she'd cleaned his face and professed her own love for him.

"Raul and I married two weeks after we met. I wouldn't recommend that for non-Succouri couples, but the bond works crazy fast and powerful, and, if you're a couple who is more traditional in your values..." Callie smiled and nodded, and Elena paused as she interpreted her expression. "Well, you know how it is then. You will find helping Ben easier after you're married. There's something about saying the words, making the vows, and giving your whole self to the other that cements the bond. That's all I will say."

Though she appreciated Elena's words, she still wished for more actionable advice to address her immediate problem. It was hard to be patient and wait for their relationship to develop and for the bond to deepen when the moment's needs were so pressing. Despite the knowledge she'd recently gained on how to help him, she didn't share Elena's confidence that it would be enough to get him through this long day.

CHAPTER 9

THE ARRIVAL

After Ben, Callie, Elena, and Raul exchanged handshakes, warm embraces, and contact information, Ben and Callie headed out on their last day of travel. As Raul had predicted, there was a light coating of snow on the ground, but it wasn't enough to create problems for them as Ben's vehicle was well-equipped for winter weather conditions. It was after one o'clock when they left the hotel, and they had eight hours of driving to accomplish before reaching Ben's childhood home near Boston.

For an hour, Ben's anxiety over the threat caused by the newspaper article kept him alert and focused. He could sense Callie's concern for him even as she made light conversation. She kept her hands folded in her lap, and though he abhorred the distance, he respected what she was trying to offer him by avoiding draining any additional strength, which he couldn't afford to lose. Since he was already anxious about his ability to protect her in his current state, he temporarily cooperated with her in this effort. Still, he didn't intend to allow the distance to last too long. He'd spent enough of their time together suffering barriers between them, and he had no intention of returning to that torture.

When they'd put sufficient miles between themselves and the town where he'd become somewhat famous, and his alarm started to ease, exhaustion descended on him with its full force. From the back of his neck to the lower muscles in his legs, everything throbbed. Though he drank water continuously, Callie thoughtfully placing a full bottle in his cupholder whenever he drained one, he still felt constantly thirsty, and he had to expend conscious effort to keep his eyelids from involuntarily closing from heaviness. Though he tried to manage his fatigue without worrying her, Ben knew Callie was aware of his struggle.

"Ben, how are you doing?" she finally asked, staring at him even though he knew she couldn't read his face.

Ben patted her knee. "This situation makes me nostalgic for the days when vehicles had bench seating in the front. I could sure enjoy this drive a lot more if I had you much closer to me for more than one reason," he chuckled. "But, I'm managing, for now."

Callie rubbed the side of his arm, and Ben mused bitterly at how they were indeed back to touching each other through barriers, but it was better than not touching at all.

Ben let his mind wander back to how it had felt that morning when he'd awoken with Callie in his arms. It took him several minutes to register the knock on the door and for the total disorientation concerning where he was and how he'd gotten there to settle enough for him to think clearly, though he remained stunned at how Callie had accomplished it all.

He couldn't definitively remember anything after he left

the burning house, retaining only a few flashes of disjointed images, mainly of Callie lovingly caring for him while he was incoherent. His mind held a memory of Callie gently wiping his face and kissing him and her telling him that the baby was normal and he'd saved both the man and the child. He recalled the feel of his hand on her cold cheek, and then his cheek pressed against hers. His most vivid flashes of memory were of her gently washing and brushing his hair, the kind and intimate act nearly bringing him back to full consciousness.

As he'd lain there, allowing it all to display in his mind like a disorganized slideshow, he'd felt her breath on his skin and looked down at her. For several seconds, he was sure it was a dream, as the circumstance matched the content of so many of his dreams, but as he moved his hand and felt the warmth of her skin and then the power of the pull toward her gripped him, he realized it was real. He panicked when he became aware that he wasn't clothed, worrying about what they'd perhaps already done while he was not in control or even aware of his behavior, but he quickly banished the thought, confident that Callie would have protected them from that. She was clothed and wrapped in her own blanket, and she'd obviously taken care to separate them as best she could while remaining close enough to continue to help him.

As his mind cleared and the flashbacks began to organize themselves into a more cohesive sequence, Ben understood what Callie had needed to do to take care of him, and he could barely contain his gratitude for the blessing that this compassionate woman was in his life.

Regardless of the logical reasons for their current circumstance, the reality of Callie's angelic face resting peacefully on his bare chest and her body pressed up against his caused his pulse to race and a sudden flood of heat to rush through him. She was irresistibly beautiful, with her curls spilling across his skin and her serene expression. She was deeply asleep, and Ben was grateful for that as it gave pause to any actions he presently considered. He desperately wanted her, needed her at that moment.

The Succouri part of him pleasured in the strength her nearness was pouring into him as his whole body ached from the complete drain of strength the night before. The power of that need overwhelmed him with an almost primal craving for closeness, pushing him forcefully toward her. As it did, the part of him that was Ben, the man, readily assented, also wanting her, but in a different yet equally powerful way. He loved Callie with all of him, body, heart, and soul, and he desired to express that love to her and receive her expression of love for him.

So, as he lay there watching her sleep, he fought both natures as they worked together to break down his resolve because, though his body had no counterarguments, his mind did. If he intended to ask Callie to give herself to him wholly, he needed to offer himself to her first. This meant giving her everything: his binding promises, possessions, and name. What she would give him was too valuable to offer any less than everything he was and had in return. He knew, in the core of his being, that this was right, the proper way to truly love a woman. As he gazed at her lovely face, Ben felt no hesitation or sense of sacrifice at the idea of offering this extraordinary woman all of that forever.

Nevertheless, Ben knew that if she woke up now and signaled her desire, he wouldn't be able to resist so, though he desperately needed more of the strength she was giving him, he carefully pulled away, doing his best not to wake her. Though each step away from her pained him, he needed a moment of distance to regain control as he fought for them in a fierce, private battle.

Because of all that had happened in the last couple of days, Ben now faced a situation similar to the one he'd confronted on the night of their first date. When Callie had made contact with his skin for the first time, and he'd realized he wouldn't be able to contain his secret anymore, he'd made up his mind to tell her everything, to go forward instead of backward, to advance rather than retreat. Now, their bond and level of intimacy had reached the point where the associated temptations were becoming irresistible for him. Determined to do right by her in every way, it was time to make some choices that would, once again, change both of their lives forever.

Despite his struggle to focus on the road, the new and exciting possibilities that came with his decision that morning excited his heart, and Ben's plans began to take shape in his mind. He didn't have a single reservation, but he would wait for resolutions regarding the questions about his past and the threats to her life.

"Ben, would it be alright if I run a few pondering thoughts and questions by you? I mean, will that be too much to focus on?" Her inquiry returned his mind to the present.

"Sure, please. It might help keep me alert."

"Alright, then. First," Callie started, "last night Raul told me that Succouri can't help other Succouri. I asked him to help you, but he said he couldn't. But, I remembered you telling me about offering Louis a moment of strength when you shook his hand at the funeral, so..." Callie turned to look at him, awaiting his thoughts.

"That's interesting and something I didn't know," Ben considered. Though he continued to fight to keep his mind focused, the effort did seem to be helping him stay awake.

"I was curious about that myself as I didn't feel anything from Raul when we shook hands. Did you? Could you see when he shook your hand?"

"Yes..." Callie confirmed, but she said the word so tentatively that Ben glanced at her in confusion.

"It sounds like there's a 'but' coming?" he questioned, remembering that with their present prohibition on touching, Callie couldn't see his facial expressions. Ben had become so accustomed to reaching out and touching her during conversations so she could tune in to the visual cues that he was now a bit out of practice at verbally detailing what she couldn't see.

"Well, my only contact with a Succouri up to that point was with you, and we have the bond between us. So, I guess I just didn't realize that the touch of another Succouri would be so different."

"How do you mean?" Ben asked with surprise and a little concern. She had his full attention now, and it was definitely keeping him alert.

"It's a little hard to explain. I just never knew that so much of what I feel in your touch comes from our bond and isn't what would normally be offered by a Succouri. When you touch me, yes, I can see, but there's a lot more to it than that. I can tune in to your heart, connect with your character, and feel your affection for me. Without that, it's so... shallow in comparison. It's impossible to put into words, but I guess it's kind of like watching a black-and-white movie compared to watching a color one."

Ben chuckled at the metaphor. "I do hope I'm the color one."

Smiling, she nodded her head in confirmation.

"I can easily relate to what you're saying as I feel the same way about giving to you versus giving to others. But then, I had fifteen years of the black-and-white variety to compare the color version to, so I noted the distinction the first time I touched you. It is, however, nice to know that it holds true on the receiving end as well."

"That makes sense. It certainly makes the whole bonding thing that much more miraculous and special."

"It certainly does," Ben agreed as he reached over and placed his hand on her knee again, frowning at the irony of discussing how it feels to touch each other while avoiding touching each other.

After a few seconds of silence, Ben allowed a teasing smile to return, hoping Callie would hear it in his voice. "You'll be sure to let me know if anyone else's touch puts color into your movie experience, now won't you, Miss LeVray, as that would be something I'd definitely want to know about."

Laughing, she stretched across the console to quickly kiss his cheek. "You'll be the first to know, just as long as you also let me know if someone puts color into your touch."

"It's a deal." He grinned and squeezed her knee. "As for the experience with Louis, I don't know. Perhaps because he had already passed on his gift, so he was in a different phase of the whole thing…"

"That was my thought as well. Did he ever say anything to you or act surprised about the transfer of strength?"

Ben shook his head. "Not that I can recall, but I was pretty focused on you and your father's passing that day. I'm not sure I was paying much attention. We'll have to ask him about it when we get back."

Callie fell silent, and as Ben glanced over at her, he saw her head lower and her smile fade.

"I know you must miss him terribly," Ben said softly, knowing that the mention of her father's funeral prompted the sad reaction. The traumatic events of the last two days hadn't afforded her time or opportunity to deal with her grief.

"I am," she sighed, turning to look out the window. "I wish he could be here, and I wish you both had gotten the chance to know one another. He would have enthusiastically supported us in this life of purpose and service, and he would have been so proud of what you did last night. I've been extremely privileged to love two great men in my life. I just wish each had had the chance to know the other." Her voice was wistful but not despairing.

Ben's heart warmed at the compliment as Callie considered him worthy of comparison to her father. "I truly wish I had had the chance to know him better and also to thank him for helping you to become the strong, courageous woman you are. I'm in his debt, as I'd be lost without that strength. And Callie, he'd be very, very proud of what *you* did last night as well."

Callie smiled, and they enjoyed a sweet moment of reflection and appreciation as they remembered Ronald LeVray. Though Ben had only had a few moments with the man, he was thankful for the encounter as it helped him relate to Callie's memories. If it weren't for his gift, the only image of him that Ben would carry would be one of his unconscious face as he lay helplessly hooked up to machines. He would never forget Ronald's bright green eyes and his warm, accepting smile as he asked Ben to take care of his family. The trust her father placed in him when he made the request touched Ben's heart so profoundly that the memory of it brought tears to his eyes. The fact that a great man like Ronald LeVray saw something in Ben that made him comfortable enough to release and entrust the welfare of his son and daughter to his care deeply impacted Ben, changing forever the way he saw himself. Certainly, he would never forget his promise, and he continued to be motivated by the desire to be the man that her father had perceived him to be.

"Ben," Callie finally said with a soft tone of compassion. "How are you feeling about facing the memories of your mom and your past? Are you... ready for that?"

Ben blew out a long, resigned breath and reached for Callie's hand, not caring about the consequences but simply needing to connect with her. She allowed him a few moments before gently pulling away.

"I suppose it's like running into that burning house last night. I know I need to do it, so I'll just put one foot in front of the other and take what comes. If you weren't with me, I'm not sure I could face it, but I do want to move forward with my life, so this is what I have to do. And I definitely need answers about my past. That's important for both of us. It's long past time for the truth to come out and whoever caused my transformation to be revealed and held accountable for the good and the bad."

"I agree," she said with a single nod, but Ben could hear that there was more, so he waited for her to continue. "I was thinking... wondering about how different your experience as a Succouri was and is because you were so young when you received the gift. Do you think..."

As she left the sentence hanging, Ben glanced over and observed her fidgeting nervously with her sleeve. "Go on," he encouraged. "You *can* ask me anything, Callie."

"I don't know quite how to word my question." She

paused for another moment before continuing. "Do you think you're unique, different from other Succouri, perhaps in significant ways, because you didn't have a chance to fully establish your own human maturity and individuality before the Succouri part was introduced?"

Ben thought about the question carefully. "Maybe. I don't think we have enough information to answer that question with certainty. It has always been difficult to recall who I was before this came into my life. Admittedly, it sometimes feels impossible to delineate the Succouri in me from the man in me. It was something that, prior to understanding what the Succouri gift was, made me angry and still does a little, I suppose. I resent being denied the opportunity to really be a kid for very long, to develop in my own way first, and become whatever I might have been without the rest of it shaping my destiny. At times, it feels confining to be defined by something beyond yourself, which sets its own demands on you and compels you with its powerful influence."

Lowering her head, she sighed. "Yes, I know exactly what you mean."

Ben's heart twisted in his chest. Of course she knew exactly how he felt. Unlike him, she hadn't even been granted twelve years of living without her limitations defining and confining her world. Except for brief moments when he touched her, Callie's blindness had always been a part of her reality that couldn't be forgotten or ignored, impacting who she had become.

Ben blew out a slow breath, expressing amazement at the similarity in their experiences. "You certainly do," he said, shaking his head in wonder at how the bond had so wisely chosen her for him and him for her. "I remember, on our date, you pointed out that it can be hard to separate who we are in our truest selves from who we've become due to adaptations we've been forced to embrace because of the influences of circumstances beyond our control. I can completely relate to that sentiment."

"But I also emphasized that the person we are in here," Callie put her hand over Ben's heart, "is where we can anchor ourselves, find true north. Ben, I know who you are, and I'll never let you lose that solid ground."

Placing his hand on hers, he stroked it with his thumb. They fell silent for a time, retreating into their thoughts and reflections.

It didn't take long before his battle with fatigue returned, causing him to shift often as he tried to keep himself awake and alert. Just when the weariness became so oppressive that he considered stopping for a while to rest so he wouldn't put them in danger, Callie turned on the radio. She turned the knob, cycling through the stations, and Ben marveled that she knew exactly how to operate it. Then he remembered she'd told him how the effects of their bond had provided her with complete knowledge about his vehicle.

"Sing something to me, Ben," she said. "I'll flip through the stations until you hear something you know and then, sing."

Though perplexed by the request, he complied. The first song he recognized was an old rendition of "Stand by Me" and he sang softly with the music through the first verse.

When the song reached the chorus, Callie joined him, singing quietly at first. Stunned at how beautifully she sang and how perfectly her voice blended with his, Ben stopped singing for a moment to laugh in delight.

"Why, Miss LeVray! You've been holding out on me."

"Not holding out." She grinned, putting up a finger. "Just waiting for the right moment."

They sang together, one or the other picking up the harmony, and the thrill in it was so invigorating that Ben's fatigue nearly vanished. He'd only ever sung with his mother, but she couldn't sing on key. This was the first time he'd ever sung with a partner who harmonized with him and complimented his voice so beautifully.

They laughed at forgotten or mistaken lyrics, and they relayed memories associated with different songs. They sang some songs loudly and energetically and others softly and tenderly until they stopped for dinner. Though the weakness remained, Ben easily stayed focused and alert as they enjoyed this new and gratifying way of connecting. The pure fun in the experience reminded Ben of their first date, and it lightened both of their hearts after the heaviness of the last few days.

AFTER A FULL MEAL, Callie was pleased to observe that Ben's struggle with fatigue had eased as they completed the last few hours of their journey. She was thankful that the singing had worked, giving him the distraction and energy he needed to continue safely. Elena had once again been right in her prediction that Callie would know what to do exactly at the moment when the knowledge was vitally important. She wasn't sure what had prompted her to reach for the radio dial, but as her hand moved to grasp it, the idea of singing together suddenly flashed through her thoughts. And it had worked. Callie wasn't sure if she'd ever get over the wonder of this mysterious bond and its magical manifestations. Ms. Essie's description of life with

Ben being an incredible adventure was certainly proving to be wholly accurate.

Though Callie didn't bear the weight of weakness that Ben carried, she shared in the exhaustion. The idea of settling in one place for a while was appealing. As the hour approached eleven o'clock, they exited the highway, traveling on curved and narrow roads as they neared their destination.

Ben was quiet and contemplative, and Callie fought her urge to reach out for him in comfort, knowing these surroundings triggered memories and emotions that were raw and painful.

Ben hadn't told her much about his former home. She knew it was located an hour and a half from the city itself, and from some of the memories he'd shared with her, she knew it was near a river. Often, she'd wanted to inquire about it during relevant conversations, but she hesitated to bring up the topic, knowing how and why he left.

At last, Ben made a final turn, and they came to a stop. Putting the car in park, he reached for her hand. A large iron gate blocked the road in front of them.

"I'll be right back," he said, squeezing her hand and offering her a smile which, though intended to reassure her, betrayed the stress he was experiencing.

He exited the SUV, and Callie heard him speak to someone through an intercom before the iron gate squeaked open. Returning, Ben drove them through, and Callie began to understand why he was more confident in his ability to protect her here.

Since Ben needed both hands to steer as they approached the house, all Callie could see were the outdoor lights outlining a circular driveway. They slowed and then came to a stop, but Callie remained still, sensing that Ben needed a moment to wrestle with his emotions.

Shutting off the engine, he exhaled slowly. Callie unbuckled her seatbelt and reached over, gently rubbing his neck.

"Six years is a long time," he said flatly. "It doesn't look much different, though."

"But you're different," Callie said, almost in a whisper.

"True. Thanks to you, I am." Ben's voice betrayed his exhaustion, and she knew that it, as well as his physical weakness, was amplifying the emotions of the moment.

Approaching her side, Ben took her hand as she got out of the SUV. When she looked around, her breath caught in her throat.

Though dark and shadowy, the lights around the driveway were sufficient for her vision to focus on an enormous, two-story, red-brick house. The front door was recessed inside a covered brick porch, which had an elaborate arched entry.

Callie was shocked by the size and elegance of the house. This was no less than a small mansion, sprawling and beautiful in its craftsmanship and architecture. Though she hadn't had any detailed expectations regarding what his former home would look like, she wasn't expecting this.

As she stood, frozen in stunned confusion, the clues she'd missed began to line up in her mind. Ben had told her he wasn't working as a driver for the money. In fact, after picking her up that fateful morning, she wasn't sure he'd ever returned to that job. On the run for years, he'd never stayed long enough in one place to make progress at advancing in a career, yet he had a nice vehicle and stylish clothes. He never expressed the slightest concern about finances or expenses, and he had certainly provided her with the best accommodations possible on this trip.

Yet Ben had a remarkably humble and unassuming manner that would never lead anyone to conclude that he came from wealth. There wasn't an ounce of pretentiousness or entitlement in his character, so the notion had never occurred to her.

Callie thought about Ben's mother and his statement about her successful modeling career, but that alone didn't seem enough to account for this level of opulence. Her head swam as she mentally flipped through dozens of conversations and interactions with him, suddenly seeing the breadcrumbs she'd obliviously passed right by during her time with him.

Tugging her hand, Ben tried to move her toward the front door, but she resisted and turned to face him. "Um, Ben? This is your house? This is where you grew up?"

Ben stared at her, his expression confused at first but then shifting as he seemed to recognize the reason for her surprise.

"This house has been in my family for a long time. My mother loved it, and yes, I grew up here. As I'm the only Sawyer left, it now belongs to me, but..."

Before he could finish, the front door opened, and a man and woman excitedly approached them. They looked to be in their sixties, both short and round with etched wrinkles that spoke of a life of hard work and acquired wisdom. The woman's hair was mostly gray with a few lingering black strands, and it was loosely pulled back into a bun. The man was nearly bald, with a few patches of gray hair on the sides of his head. Their smiles filled their faces and made their dark eyes shine. Their enthusiasm at Ben's arrival filled Callie's heart with joy and endeared them to her instantly.

The man approached first, gripping Ben's shoulder with one hand as he reached to shake Ben's hand with the other. Ben let go of Callie so he could match the gesture. Before her vision faded, Callie saw tears in the older man's eyes.

"Ben! It's about time. It's been so many years, way too many years. Welcome home." The man's voice trembled with emotion.

Before Ben could respond, the woman approached, and grasped Ben's face with both hands, looking long into his eyes. Callie had no idea who these people were, but it was clear that they deeply loved Ben. Astonished at how freely they touched him, she wondered if they knew Ben's secret.

"Mr. Sawyer! You are a sight for these sore eyes," the woman said as she exhaled in relief. The sorrow she felt at Ben's long absence carried in her tone. "I'm not sure how it's possible, but you're even more handsome than the last time I saw you. Welcome home, dearest boy. Welcome home."

Tears of joy caused her voice to quiver as the woman kissed Ben on each cheek and embraced him, and Callie's own eyes moistened at the emotional reunion.

Ben returned their warm and enthusiastic greetings, but he quickly stepped back to grasp Callie's hand and pull her forward.

"Rosa, since when do you call me Mr. Sawyer," Ben said. "I'm still just Ben. Leo, Rosa, I want you to meet Callie LeVray." Ben turned toward Callie. "Leo and Rosa have worked with my family for a long time. They've cared for everything around here, including me, for many years."

Callie smiled, both at the pride in Ben's voice as he

introduced her and at the humble and appreciative way he referred to those who worked for him.

Rosa stepped forward, and Ben released Callie briefly so she could accept Rosa's warm embrace. As she'd done with Ben, Rosa placed her hands on Callie's cheeks and patted her affectionately.

"My my! I never thought it possible that Ben could find a girl whose beauty would outshine his own good looks, but you make him look almost plain in comparison, Miss Callie." Rosa laughed good-naturedly. "It's a real pleasure. Yes, a real pleasure." The emotion in the woman's voice told Callie that Ben had already informed them about her.

"Thank you." Callie smiled appreciatively at the warm welcome.

Leo grasped Callie's hand with both of his rough, large ones and patted it gently. "So happy you're here," he said simply, but the sentiment was deep and genuine.

"We'll get your things," Leo offered, releasing Callie back into Ben's care. "It's late, and I'm sure you're terribly tired."

"Thank you, Leo," Ben said with a sigh. Callie was glad that Ben now had help, as she knew he had to be at the very end of his strength.

Leo moved behind them toward Ben's SUV as Rosa gestured for them to head inside. She followed them through the large front door and into the house. The floors were smooth white marble tiles, and the vaulted ceilings made their voices echo as they spoke.

"I'm gonna draw Miss Callie a nice warm bath and put out some night clothes," Rosa announced. "You two get some rest, and I'll see you both tomorrow for breakfast."

Rosa paused to look again at Ben with tears on her rosy cheeks. "It's so very good to have you home again. I've worried and wondered 'bout you every day for all these many years. Seeing your precious face again does good for my soul, so very good."

Smiling, Ben quickly embraced her once more before she turned and headed out of the room.

Moving in front of Ben, Callie grasped both of his hands as she looked up into his eyes, which shone with unshed tears.

"I never said anything to them," Ben said sorrowfully, lowering his gaze. "When I ran, I didn't say goodbye. Leo and Rosa were like grandparents, always caring for me and trying to fill in some of the gaps left by my mother's inadequate parenting. I should have reached out to them and at least let them know I was safe. It was selfish and ungrateful to disappear like I did."

Callie embraced him and he leaned against her, his weakness evident.

"You were hurting and confused. I'm sure they understand. I don't think they feel that way; I think they just really missed you and were worried about you. They obviously love you deeply."

As he lingered in the embrace, he sighed in response.

"Do they know?" Callie asked.

Ben leaned his head back to look at her, but he stayed close, and Callie guessed he was grasping the moment of strength offered by their nearness as they'd both been denied the contact for most of the day.

"I can't say we ever had a conversation about it directly, but they were around for all those years, watching and hearing what went on in this house, so I expect they likely know a lot, but they were gracious and discreet about my mother's illness, and I guess they've afforded me the same courtesy."

Callie nodded in understanding, and Ben retook her hand. As they passed through the foyer, Callie looked to her left and saw a curved stairway leading to the second floor, and to her right was a large sitting room with expensive white couches and chairs, delicate glass lamps, and side tables with intricately carved legs and edges. As Ben walked her through the living room, dining room, kitchen, and a large luxurious office, Callie marveled at the spaciousness and elegance in every light fixture, piece of furniture, and accessory. It was like a home out of a fancy magazine, professionally planned and designed. And everything was white: the rugs, the furniture, the marble kitchen counter-tops, everything except for some of the rich wood tables and accents.

As she walked slowly with Ben and scanned the space around her, she couldn't believe a child had ever lived here. What would it have been like to grow up like this? Callie's home was beautiful and certainly not small and cramped, but it was comfortable, and she and Lee could run and play, even spill and make messes, without fear. But this was a white porcelain palace, everything expensive, fragile, and easily stained.

Seeming to sense her astonishment, Ben squeezed her hand and spoke in a flat, resigned tone. "My mother loved white."

"She did," Callie replied with a slight grimace. "How could you ever be free to just be a kid in this... beautiful but utterly delicate place?"

"I couldn't," he answered, with a hint of bitterness in his tone. His past statements about his lack of any real childhood began to make sense.

Letting go of his hand, she walked to one of the nearby white chairs, lowering herself into it. She leaned back and frowned. "Nope," she said, shaking her head. "Not much better than those wicker chairs on the porch back home. Definitely not up to our new and improved standards in seating choices."

Laughing, he came over to retake her hand and lift her out of the chair, and Callie was glad to lighten his mood.

As they passed through another luxurious room near the back of the house, which Callie guessed was meant to be a family room but was decorated like another formal, untouchable magazine cover page, they stepped through a doorway into a smaller room with large windows and a cozy brick fireplace. A single couch was positioned in the middle of the room with its matching ottoman, and in contrast to all of the white her eyes had taken in as they'd moved from room to room, this couch was a dark gray and looked soft and inviting. Ben gestured for her to sit and then walked to the fireplace, flipping a switch and staring as the flames came to life. He returned and wearily lowered himself beside her, pulling her close and leaning back with a contented sigh.

"This was my favorite room," he said with nostalgia. "There's no white nor anything fragile in here, and it's simple. Plus," he smiled, "the couch is comfortable. The windows look out over the river, and it's peaceful. Of all the places in this house, the crazy overkill of it all, this was the one place I most wanted to share with you. I suppose it's one of the only spaces in this house that feels like home to me."

"It's perfect." She sighed and closed her eyes, appreciating that, though Ben obviously had money and access to any luxury he might want, he preferred the simple, practical, and more homey things in life.

Callie's eyelids felt heavy, and she yawned as she leaned

against Ben's shoulder. He yawned in response and then chuckled.

"As much as I sincerely want to, I don't think I can carry you to your room tonight, sweetheart, so I'd better escort you there before you fall asleep on me."

"This is a big house," she mumbled, feeling nearly intoxicated with sleepiness. "How far do I have to walk? Are you sure we can't just sleep right here?"

Stroking her cheek, he smiled playfully. "If I can make it, you can make it."

Rising slowly, he crossed the room to turn off the fire, then returned and reached out his hand.

"Come on, sleepyhead. I heard something about a warm bath from Rosa. Don't want it getting cold."

She took his hand and, with another yawn, rose and moved slowly to walk with him. They laughed at themselves as they leaned against each other and laboriously dragged themselves up the curved staircase, each step feeling more and more toilsome.

Though she could barely keep her eyes open to look around, she noticed a tranquil library space at the top of the stairs with bookshelves and some comfortable-looking leather chairs.

Turning right, they headed down a hallway, passing several doors before coming nearly to the end and entering a large bedroom. Centered on the right wall was a king-size bed with carved bedposts and an elegant, embroidered navy-blue bedspread. There was a sitting area along the back wall and several dressers and a wardrobe scattered around the room; still, the space was so large that it felt nearly empty.

Ben circled the room with her, even stopping in the doorway of the enormous en suite bathroom to let her take everything in while she still had his touch to focus her vision. As they returned to the center of the room, Ben stopped leaning on her and took her hand, leading her to a door and opening it with a sly smile.

Inside was a huge closet, about half the size of Callie's bedroom back home, well stocked with clothing.

"Whose clothes are these?" she asked curiously, assuming someone had been staying here or renting the place while Ben was away.

Ben chuckled and began searching through the racks. He pulled out an item from the selection of what looked to be brand-new clothes.

"These are yours, Miss LeVray," he said with amusement.

Staring at him with wide eyes, she was sure she hadn't heard him correctly.

Ben pulled the selected item out of its plastic protective bag and held it up proudly. It was a long black dress with a plunging neckline and a slit up one side. It was almost identical to the dress she'd worn on their first date. Stunned, she stood with her mouth open, confused about what was happening.

"And somewhere in here," Ben said, glancing around the closet, "are those shoes, which I promised to replace for you as well."

"I... Ben... I," she stammered, unable to make her tired, stunned brain work with her mouth.

"I think Rosa organized these by more casual to less casual or some such thing. I'll have her fill you in on the system in the morning." He paused, and his smile faded as she continued to stand there speechless. "I had Rosa coordinate with Grace on your size and between her input and what I already knew of your tastes and preferences, we tried to get things you'd like, but if you don't..."

"Ben!" Callie finally managed. "You didn't need to. I mean, this is so incredibly generous and extravagant and..."

Callie watched as Ben's smile lit up his face again as he took in her appreciation and surprise.

"Thank you. I... I can't believe you went to all this trouble and expense for me."

"This wasn't trouble," he said, hanging the dress back up and moving to stand in front of her. "This was fun, and watching your face made it all the more so."

Callie wrapped her arms around his waist. He kissed her softly several times, but he didn't linger and she was confused by his hesitation. She knew he needed her, needed to stay near her to replenish the strength he still obviously lacked, but his rushed affections indicated that staying wasn't in his plan.

"Ben," she whispered. "Are you... are you staying with me tonight? I mean, don't you still need my help?"

Before speaking, he pressed his cheek against hers for several seconds, and the force of their bond intensified.

At last, he whispered into her ear, speaking slowly, each word carrying such intense longing that it made Callie's heart pound fiercely in her chest. "Yes. I need you, Callie. Need you, want you, with everything I am, all of me. But, if I stay here with you, I won't be satisfied to simply lie next to you. I love you, deeply and genuinely love you, so I have to walk out of this room for now, to protect us both, though that is the very last thing I want to do."

The fire moving between them was so powerful that Callie didn't care about boundaries anymore. Though she wanted to protest, to tell him to stay, she couldn't breathe, much less speak. She was dizzy and overtaken by feelings that drowned her in deep waters of desire. She needed him too, wanted him recklessly.

For another moment, Ben lingered, his uneven breathing confirming the passion of his words. He pressed his lips to hers, only for a second, and then pulled away.

"Good night, Miss LeVray," he panted, still speaking in a whisper. "I'll be nearby, and I'll see you in the morning."

And then he was gone.

CHAPTER 10
THE MEMORIES

Callie wrestled with conflicting thoughts as she rolled over in bed and stared into the hazy light streaming through the bedroom's large windows. Despite her exhaustion, she hadn't slept well as emotions related to Ben's swift departure the night before tormented her.

On the one hand, she appreciated his discipline as he fought to maintain control of his own passions toward her, desiring to do right by her in every way. Precious few men would fight so hard to maintain their convictions, especially with the valid reasons he had to disregard them. Truly, in her rational mind, she agreed with him, possessing the same goals and intentions.

But then there was the rest of it to consider. Their relationship was far from normal. It wasn't just simple attraction and passion that pushed them to abandon their course, but it was also sheer necessity. Callie was Ben's Succouri partner, his only aid in times of severe need. Though he could eventually recover without her, it took far longer, leaving him diminished unnecessarily. Though the closeness required to assist him triggered temptations that were increasingly difficult to resist, it was intolerable to Callie to deny Ben the help he needed because of this concern.

She recalled Elena telling her how it would be much easier to help Ben once they were married and the boundaries of their consciences no longer restrained them, but then, Elena and Raul had married quickly and had not faced the obstacles and challenges confronting her and Ben. In many ways, those challenges amplified the difficulty as the intimacy and closeness resulting from confronting each hardship together accelerated the natural bonding between them. As they grew closer through these experiences, it was only natural for them to want their physical intimacy to keep pace with the merging of their hearts.

Sighing in frustration, Callie sat up in bed and contended with these conflicting realities. One thing she was sure of: she hated withholding from Ben what was in her power to offer. She'd rather help him, even if it meant taking the risk of them going too far than play It safe and leave him suffering unnecessarily. Since she was the only one who could give him what he needed, it felt immoral and cruel to withhold assistance, no matter what the reason.

Grunting, she flopped back onto her stomach, momentarily burying her face in her pillow in exasperation. When she heard a soft knock on her door, she flipped back over quickly, pulling the sheets over her.

"Come in," she said tentatively, assuming it was Ben, but after what had transpired last night, surprised that he'd come to her room now.

The door opened, and the sound of a kind, familiar voice caused her to relax. "Miss Callie, it's Rosa."

Callie threw back the covers and rose, pulling on the soft robe that had been left on her bed the night before and tying it closed as she moved to greet the older woman.

"Rosa. Oh, please," Callie beckoned, "Come on in."

Rosa approached cautiously and affectionately touched Callie's cheek. "Good morning, Miss Callie. I hope you slept well. I know it can be hard to rest in an unfamiliar place, but I want you to feel right at home here."

Callie smiled at the sincere kindness in the words.

"Ben asked me to bring you this." Rosa carefully passed Callie an insulated cup with a secured lid. Before she took a sip, she could smell the chai tea.

"Thank you. That's very kind."

From Rosa's careful and intentional approach, it was evident that Ben had considerately instructed Rosa on how to work with her low eyesight. "Won't you sit with me for a few minutes?" Callie invited, turning toward the sitting area, which provided two chairs with a small circular table between them. After Callie had observed the affection between Ben, Leo, and Rosa the day before, she wanted to get to know the couple better and learn more about Ben's childhood and past from them.

"Surely," Rosa replied enthusiastically, though she seemed surprised by the invitation.

Rosa stayed protectively close by Callie's side as they moved to the chairs. Since Ben had given her a chance to survey the room visually, Callie was quite comfortable navigating here, even with her limited eyesight.

As she settled in the chair and set her cup on the small table, Callie heard Rosa let out a slight groan, revealing physical discomfort. Feeling concerned, she wondered if Ben had felt a draw from Rosa or Leo when they'd touched him, and she made a mental note to ask him about it later.

"Miss Callie," Rosa said, "I can't tell ya how delighted Leo and I are to have Ben home again. We love that boy like he was our own, and we've been worried sick, knowin' how and why he left and the terrible burden of sorrow he carried away with him."

Callie lowered her head, feeling empathy for this kind couple's pain for so many years as they wondered what had become of Ben. She didn't have the heart, nor was it her place, to tell them how terribly Ben had suffered in loneliness and confusion.

"Ben and I only met a short while ago," Callie explained. "He was… he was and still is working on healing so many deep wounds, but Rosa, he *is* healing, and he's an incredible man." Callie smiled with pride as she spoke the truth about him.

Rosa leaned toward her, and Callie wondered if Rosa hoped she could read her expressions, though unfortunately, the effort was in vain as the distance was still too great for her to pick up much of anything from Rosa's eyes or face.

"I can see that," Rosa said with a breathy sigh. "When you two arrived, I looked into his eyes and I saw it! He's finally whole. Praise be! I can't tell you, can't express how my heart rejoices." Relief and joy resounded in her voice, and Callie's eyes began to fill with tears.

"What do you mean?"

"We've known Ben since he was young, six or seven, hard to recall after all these years. That tender heart, I'm sure you know well, has always been in him. A kinder, gentler soul you'll never meet, not in your life!" she emphasized.

Smiling in agreement, Callie leaned in, wanting to hear more about Ben's childhood. Sensing her enthusiastic interest, Rosa continued. "Even as a child, Ben was as humble and selfless as his dear mother was…" She paused, struggling to appropriately phrase her next statement. "Well, self-focused and distant. How nature coulda put in Ben a soul so completely opposite of the one in his genetic predecessor, I'll never understand. Forgive me; I don't mean to be unkind. Adalynn Sawyer fought her own demons, and I suppose none of us can rightly judge how another bears their load. She never wanted to be a mother, and though I suppose she did at least keep Ben safe and provide for his basic needs, she never embraced the role. Though naturally even-tempered and compliant, Ben interpreted his mother's shortcomings, dissatisfactions, depression, and distance as evidence of his own deficiencies as a son and later, as a man. We tried very hard to convince him otherwise, but I'm afraid we were unsuccessful." A despairing sigh passed through her lips before she continued. "Ben was born with the heart of a knight, needin' to save a princess. As year after year went by, he tried to be better and do more but still she couldn't be rescued and refused to be saved; it emptied him, robbed him of his confidence, and tore at his heart. Though Adalynn may have ultimately been incapable of expressing motherly love, Ben loved her unconditionally and loyally, which made her disconnection all the more destructive."

Profound helplessness colored Rosa's voice as she told the story, and Callie's heart throbbed in pain as she related to the attributes in Ben that Rosa described. Knowing Ben as she did, it was easy for her to understand how his heart would have been broken by his mother's behavior and reactions to him. A tear escaped her eye and traced down her cheek.

"When… when it all ended so tragically – when

Adalynn's demons won out – I..." Rosa fell silent, the emotions too powerful for her to continue. She took several deep breaths before trying again. "Miss Callie, I thought Ben would suffer the same fate as his mother, and I couldn't bear the thought. Right before he left, and I suppose even years before that, I'd look into those tender eyes and see sorrow, an emptiness, not like hers, but still heartbreaking. The hole went deeper after his illness. It worried us and broke our hearts. That precious boy was an angel straight from heaven, a beautiful, compassionate soul who deserved much more than he was given as a child. Oh, he had money, but that wasn't important to him; it certainly wasn't what he needed. If his mother had only been capable of seeing it, looking beyond herself, and giving to him, or at least letting him give to her, perhaps things would have ended very differently."

Now tears flowed freely as Callie understood, for the first time, the significant voids left in Ben's heart by his childhood experiences. Rosa had been lost in her own sorrow as she spoke, but now, noticing Callie's tears, she reached over to again pat Callie's cheek.

"But," Rosa said, her voice shifting to express joy, "at long last, he has what he needs. I don't know how you did it, how you healed and filled his heart, but I see it in his eyes, and Leo and I can finally be at peace knowing Ben's alright and has at last found the life he surely deserves. You are a special soul too, Miss Callie. I understand why Ben loves you so deeply. He found another heart like his, someone who understands and connects with his... unique burdens. Our hearts can breathe now, knowing he's not alone and broken anymore. We are most grateful to you, most grateful indeed!"

"Rosa!" Callie spoke in a gasp between the soft sobs

that shook her. "There is a kind, wise woman back home who helped Ben and me find each other and work through our early difficulties. You remind me so much of her. One night, as I worried about Ben's broken heart and wondered if I'd ever be able to break down his walls, she told me that there was still hope for him because he hadn't yet forgotten what love was. She was convinced that because he remembered love, he'd eventually be able to open his heart and let me in. After hearing your story, I'm certain you and Leo planted the seeds of love in Ben's life. Ben never forgot what love was because the two of you showed him love and affection. Because I didn't know the whole story, I'd thought it was his mother, but now I understand. Your care for him and your constant reminders of his worth and value kept love alive in him, eventually bringing him to me and my family and holding him in one place long enough to begin to heal."

Now Callie heard Rosa softly crying as well.

"You made the difference first," Callie said with conviction. "It's likely because of the two of you that he stayed sane, didn't follow in his mother's footsteps, and didn't give in to total despair." Callie smiled at Rosa despite her tears. "Thank you, Rosa. Thank you for loving my beloved Ben before I even knew him and keeping his heart alive."

They warmly embraced, each crying softly as their love for the same soul connected their hearts.

ROSA INSTRUCTED Callie on how the clothes Ben had provided for her were organized in the closet. In addition, she discovered that several drawers had been filled with sleepwear and casual sweats and T-shirts. There were so many choices, overwhelming her as she tried to decide what to wear. Her own closet at home didn't have this kind of selection. Finally, she laid out a pair of gray slacks and a lavender sweater, and Rosa left her alone to shower and get ready for the day, promising to return to help her down for breakfast.

"Ben's friend, Donovan, is in the kitchen and wants to talk with you when you're ready," Rosa informed her before leaving.

Callie smiled, looking forward to getting better acquainted with him as well.

"Where's Ben?" she asked, concern rising as she hoped, despite her lack of assistance, he was feeling stronger today.

"He left early. Said he had an errand to run. He made sure Donovan was here before he left, not trusting your safety to anyone else. He should be back soon," Rosa said with a reassuring smile.

Callie was surprised, not at his trust in Donovan, but that he'd felt strong enough to get up early. She got the feeling Rosa knew more than she was saying, but she didn't press her for details, though she was curious about the mysterious errand.

As she dressed and fixed her hair and makeup, she pondered Rosa's description of Ben's mother. Until that morning, everything she'd known about Adalynn Sawyer had come from Ben. His perspective was rooted in the love and loyalty of a kind and forgiving son. Ben believed his mother loved him, though he freely admitted she'd had very few parenting skills.

It was enlightening to hear about the woman from the perspective of someone who didn't have that kind of familial tie, though Rosa did feel that way about Ben. Though she and Leo had no doubt witnessed a lot as they cared for this house and its grounds, they wouldn't have been present for all the moments Ben shared with his mother. He possessed some cherished memories, like singing with her, and his mother did know his secret, and Ben felt that she empathized with his difficult plight. Still, having a broader perspective on Adalynn's character provided Callie with a much clearer understanding of Ben's pain and helped her to better discern how to aid him in his healing.

In addition, Callie found Rosa's statement that Ben was born "with the heart of a knight needing to save a princess" particularly insightful. She knew the Succouri part of him endowed him with this trait. Ms. Essie had told them that the gift came with a lack, a strong need to help others. As Callie tried to distinguish the qualities in Ben that came from his humanity from the qualities that were Succouri in origin, she'd wondered about the genesis of this particular characteristic, assuming it to be from the latter rather than the former. After speaking to Rosa, she was convinced his heroic heart had always been a part of Ben's nature, the gift only enhancing the pre-existing trait. Apparently, in so many ways, Ben's natural personality coincided with his adopted one. No wonder *he* struggled to separate the two sides in his own mind.

The conversation with Rosa had also helped Callie with her dilemma from that morning. She better understood why Ben was driven to protect her, even at the cost of his own wellness. It was more apparent to her now why, when they'd first met, he'd been so intent on guarding her against the pain he associated with his secret and why he'd believed he was poison for others, especially those whom he wanted so desperately to help. Between his largely fruitless efforts to help his mother and the fact that the healing offered by his Succouri touch didn't last, Ben's earnest need to rescue had largely gone unsatisfied for years. Though none of that was his fault, he'd taken it to heart as a personal failure. Only recently, beginning with his successful rescue of her, had his attempts to save others yielded far more positive results, and she could see how that was changing him, giving him confidence and filling up empty places inside.

In the same way, he wanted, needed to do right by her. It was another way he protected and cared for her, and he needed to win this fight. Though she still didn't like the restrictions it placed on her ability to help him, she determined not to hinder this crucial struggle. However, she sincerely hoped Ben wouldn't need to give so much of himself away again before circumstances changed, and she could be freer to provide him with all he needed without hesitation.

When Callie had dressed and was ready for the day, Rosa returned and offered her arm, guiding her down the curved staircase and into the kitchen. Ben still hadn't returned, but Donovan rose to greet her warmly. "Good morning, ma'am. It's nice to see you again. I'm glad you and Ben had a safe and pleasant trip."

Callie smiled, knowing that because Donovan didn't know Ben's secret, there were a lot of details about their journey Ben hadn't been at liberty to share.

"Donovan, please just call me Callie," she said, laughing. "After all, I'm several years younger than you are. It's good to see you as well."

"I'll try," Donovan said, sounding doubtful about the prospect. "It's not about age. It's about respect, and I have much of that for you, ma'am... Callie."

Callie laughed good-naturedly at his failed attempt to

comply with her wishes. Rosa released her and Donovan took over, guiding her to a chair at the large white marble kitchen island. Again, Callie took note of Ben's thoughtfulness in taking the time to make sure that the people who would be helping her knew exactly what to do.

When she had settled herself in the high, padded chair, Rosa brought her a plate of breakfast, which smelled heavenly. Pancakes, fruit, and sausage, all cooked to perfection, made her mouth water as she suddenly realized her hunger. She thanked Rosa as she eagerly took a few satisfying bites. Rosa affectionately patted her shoulder before exiting the kitchen, apparently wanting to leave the two of them to talk privately.

"Did you sleep well?" Donovan asked politely as he sat across from her. He wasn't eating, and Callie guessed he'd probably already finished his breakfast, as she knew he'd been there since early that morning.

Callie smiled, wanting to be honest but appreciative at the same time. "It was a little hard getting settled, but the accommodations were very comfortable."

"This is quite a place," he said a bit sarcastically, and she guessed the eccentric nature of the décor was likely the reason for the tone.

"Yes, it is," she agreed. "I had no idea that Ben grew up like this." Callie gestured at the space around them.

"I bet it was quite a surprise. If I'd met Ben apart from knowing about his family and their wealth, I'd have never guessed that he came from this kind of environment either. Ben is so different from all of them."

"What do you mean, 'all of them'?" Callie inquired, lowering her fork and focusing her gaze Donovan's way.

"Our families have run in the same circles for generations. My parents knew his mother, and my grandparents knew his grandparents; I think my grandparents even stayed at some of the other Sawyer properties sometimes on vacations. They were all... well, let's just say that generations of handed down wealth had not brought out the best in them."

Callie again felt stunned. How many properties did Ben own? She was already overwhelmed at the revelation that this colossal house was his, but it seemed this was only one of many. Though she wanted to ask Donovan for more details, she didn't want to put him on the spot as he obviously assumed she knew more than she did. The information was really Ben's to share anyway whenever he felt he wanted to do so, and no sooner.

Callie sighed, remembering the story Ben had told her about Donovan's parents and their rejection of him. "That certainly isn't true of Ben or you, Donovan. I am grateful for your service to our country and now to Ben and me. I want you to know how much Ben admires you and how highly he regards you, and I the same."

Donovan was quiet for a moment, and Callie wished she could read his face.

"I sincerely appreciate that," he said humbly, "but I have to tell you that I believe you to be a great hero in your own right as well, ma'am. When I met up with Ben a few years ago, he was afflicted. I tried my best to help him, but I couldn't get through to him or break down his defenses. From the start of our friendship, he's always been a downtrodden, though incredibly generous soul, but after the last time we were together, I thought he was lost beyond the point of return. I've seen people suffering in a bad way, soldiers with PTSD. Ben was not far off from that. It troubled me as I've always thought he possessed a uniquely courageous heart."

Nodding, Callie expressed understanding of Donovan's assessment.

"I tried to get him to move in with me, to remain in one place for a while, and he genuinely seemed to want to, but..." Confusion colored his tone as he finished. "He couldn't accept the help, even from me, even though he had helped me in much the same way early in our friendship. I know what happened with his mother crushed him, but I'm not sure why he felt he had to carry all that alone."

"I know," Callie said, almost in a whisper. "When I first met Ben, it was very, very hard to break through his walls."

"I don't mean to pry, and certainly don't feel obligated to share anything you don't feel comfortable sharing, but can you tell me what Ben was running from? I mean, I get the sadness, and I, of all people, understand wanting to escape from the way we grew up, but there was just more to it, something I couldn't put my finger on or figure out. It was like he was running from himself."

Callie's heart ached for Donovan's confusion, as it was rooted in deep affection for Ben, but this wasn't her secret to tell.

"I can only say that I understand your confusion. I've felt it, struggled with it. There are reasons, and Ben turning down your help and running had nothing to do with you. He thinks of you as a brother; he told me that. He admires you for your choices in life and your courage to serve despite opposition. The reasons why Ben ran are complex. He did want to accept your help; even now, he wishes he had."

"Well," Donovan sighed, "regardless of the past, I'm so glad he's anchored now. He's a totally new man. It's like he's the person he was supposed to be without all the weight and sorrow. It's fantastic, ma'am, and such a relief.

You are a truly extraordinary person to have accomplished that, and I hope to learn more someday about how you did it. But, for now, if we can get this monster who's after you behind bars, you can both move forward with your lives."

"Do you know where Ben is this morning?" Callie asked, increasingly concerned as the time passed and Ben didn't return.

The several seconds of silence that lapsed before he answered told Callie he did. When Donovan spoke, Callie's heart relaxed as the tone was light and playful.

"There may be one or two of Ben's secrets I do know about but am not at liberty to share. I'll just say, to quote the lovely lady sitting across from me, 'There are reasons'."

Callie smiled warmly, though she couldn't help but feel sad at being left out of whatever important thing Ben was doing. They'd barely been apart in weeks, and they'd shared so many personal experiences. Since the day he told her his secret, Ben had been open with her, and it wasn't like him to exclude her from his life in any way. Even as she had these thoughts, she scolded herself, recognizing that, though they shared a Succouri bond, Ben had no actual obligation to include her in everything he did, and it was unreasonable to expect that.

She and Donovan enjoyed more light conversation while she finished her breakfast. Callie found him to be just as Ben described: kind and easy to be with. He casually worked in several questions about Grace, asking how they met and how long they'd been friends. Though she couldn't tell if they'd exchanged phone calls or texts, she was now sure of Donovan's interest in her friend.

After Callie had finished eating, Donovan presented her with a new phone. He assisted her in setting it up with the accessibility features she needed to operate it efficiently with her visual limitations. He'd already programmed it with the contact information from her previous phone, and he'd also updated it with Lee's new number.

Sensing her eagerness to get in touch with her brother, Donovan kindly excused himself so that she could have a private conversation with Lee, saying he needed to do a security sweep. Callie smiled in appreciation as she excitedly dialed his number.

CHAPTER II
THE TRUST

Late in the morning, Ben returned, excited about what he'd accomplished but tired and eager to reunite with Callie. He'd felt torn about leaving that morning, but what he had to do had to be done without her, and he thought the timing would be right as she'd likely sleep in because of their late arrival the night before.

In the previous weeks, he'd spent little time apart from her, and even though he'd been eager to accomplish his errand, he was shocked at how lonely he felt without her by his side. Callie had become a part of him, maybe the best part of who he was, and the void he felt at her absence only confirmed the purpose and necessity of his outing.

As he parked his vehicle and walked toward the front door, feeling stronger than the previous day but still far from normal, Ben recalled the emptiness of waking up that morning without her next to him. Though he'd only been blessed with two mornings of that blissful reality, it was enough to make him greedily never again want otherwise. He'd done the right thing when he walked out of her room, though he tossed and turned for a long time, battling his desire to return. Even with his plans firmly in place, he wasn't sure how long he could hold his resolve. She'd invited him to stay, wanted him with her, and though he wasn't clear whether the invitation offered more than just helping him recover his strength, the intense desire he'd seen in her eyes thrilled him beyond words and caused his own desire to surge. Staying with her was not only what he fervently longed for, but it also eased his worry over leaving her alone while the threat to her life lingered.

While he was reasonably assured in the steps he and Donovan had taken to secure the house and surrounding property, certainly more confident than he'd been at the hotels they'd stayed in, after she'd been attacked in her bed, Ben couldn't relax while leaving her alone in that vulnerable state.

His conflict between the two ways he wanted to protect her collided. Keeping her safe from harm was his top priority and overshadowed every other consideration, but he also needed to guard her from his own passion. It was beginning to feel impossible to accomplish both tasks satisfactorily, especially if she was no longer in the fight with him. If Callie had decided she was comfortable now allowing all restrictions to fall away, he wasn't confident he could resist her for long; in fact, he was significantly more confident he could not.

As Ben entered the house, Rosa met him at the door, and Ben smiled triumphantly at her as he passed her a small box, committing it to her for safekeeping. Her returned smile filled her whole face, and Ben got the feeling she and Callie had connected that morning in such a way that now enabled her to release unrestrained joy and support regarding Ben's decision.

As he moved past the foyer, Donovan approached, his face also displaying an enthusiastic smile.

"Ben," Donovan said as he came up and patted him on the back in greeting. "That lady of yours is... much more than you deserve," he teased, but Ben could see and hear his genuine admiration for Callie.

Ben nodded his head and smiled. "There's no doubt about that. She most definitely is," he agreed wholeheartedly, marveling at how Callie had won over the entire household in the few hours he'd been away.

"She's curious about your errand though, just to warn you. I hope you have a good explanation prepared."

"Where is she?"

"Talking to her brother. I set her up with her new phone, and I could tell how much she wanted to speak with him, so I left her in privacy in the kitchen, but I've been hanging close and keeping an eye out."

"Thank you for your help today so I could step out for a bit."

"Mission accomplished?" Donovan asked in a formal tone, betraying his military background.

"Yes." Ben smiled. "Everything's set."

"You're a lucky man. I'll head out for a bit, but I'll check everything and be monitoring. Be back later."

Ben patted Donovan's back in appreciation, then turned to find Callie. As he entered the kitchen, he heard her saying her goodbyes to Lee, so he waited in the doorway until she was finished. The sound of her voice made his heart both relax in relief and pound with excitement. As always, Callie looked breathtakingly beautiful. He was pleased that the clothes he arranged to have available for her fit nicely and complimented her perfect feminine figure.

"Well," Ben said when she had finished her call. "After

telling Lee about our trip, am I going to be known by any new nicknames when we get home?"

Callie spun around, a look of relief filling her face. "Ben!" she exclaimed, offering him one of her heart-stopping smiles. Her ecstatic joy at seeing him thrilled his heart. They moved swiftly toward one another, and Callie almost knocked him over with her embrace.

"Wow!" he laughed, gripping the back of a nearby chair for balance. "I should go away more often," he teased.

"Don't you dare!"

"Remember, I didn't have you with me last night, sweetheart, so I'm still not as strong as you are. Go easy on me." Grinning, he ran his fingers through her curls.

Easing back, she looked into his eyes. "How are you? Are you better today?"

Ben sighed but held his grin. "A little, but I'm hoping for some quality time with my favorite girl on my favorite couch today."

"You got it!" she said, happiness reflecting in her green eyes.

"It's a perfect day for that anyway," he noted.

Seeing the confusion in her expression, he took her hand and led her to the nearest window. She gasped, obviously unaware of the weather. It had snowed overnight, continuing through the morning. A blanket of soft white covered everything, and icicles hung from gutters and tree limbs. It was like a crystalized fantasy world, and Ben could see the awe in Callie's face as she took it all in. It filled him with joy as he was sure this was the first time she had seen snow like this, with full vision.

"Welcome to winter in Massachusetts," he chuckled.

"It's so beautiful!" Her voice was an enchanted whisper.

"But… You were out driving in this?" she asked, suddenly panicked.

"Hey, I'm here, back safely. It's too late to worry now," he said in defense, holding up a hand to halt her concern.

"Why? I mean, what was so urgent that you needed to risk life and limb in this weather?"

Ben could hear her hesitancy in asking the question, even with her concern for his safety. Though he felt regret that she had any reservations about asking him whatever she wanted, in this one case, he had to be evasive.

"Why, Miss LeVray!" he said, trying to convey fun and playfulness. "I'd happily risk life and limb to put a smile on your face any and every day, but do remember that it isn't as much of a risk for me as it might be for you."

"Hm," she said, turning away from the window to face him and placing her free hand on her hip. "Not talking, huh?"

"Nope," he said with a broad grin and a shake of his head.

"Not even offering a deal this time?"

"Nope," he repeated, holding his grin.

Callie sighed in resignation. "Wow, you're tough. Alright, well, as long as you don't make it a habit, I'll forgive you this time."

Ben laughed and put his hand on her cheek. "I have no further plans to leave your side, Miss LeVray."

Callie leaned in and kissed him. "Good," she said with a flirty smile, which melted Ben's heart.

THEY SPENT the rest of the morning contentedly curled up under a thick blanket on Ben's favorite gray couch, watching through the large windows as the snow fell onto the picturesque landscape. From this room, they could see the river winding through the deep valley below, though presently, because of the snow, the details of the scene blended with only soft edges of distinction in the white wonderland.

Callie's head was comfortably tucked into Ben's shoulder, with her forehead against his neck and his arm wrapped around her, holding her against him. Callie had been concerned that, after his abrupt exit the night before, he might be distant, unwilling even to let her help him in a circumstance that didn't place them in a potentially compromising position. But when he'd eagerly pulled her into his arms, she realized she hadn't needed to worry. Ben wasn't retreating from her but rather genuinely striving to do the right thing, and she breathed easier at this realization.

Even with the current contact level, the fire between them raged, reassuring her that Ben was receiving the help he needed. After the fire rescue and their subsequent intimate moments, the magnetism between them had increased, making it even more challenging to focus on anything but her feelings for him when they were this close. Nevertheless, after her talk with Rosa that morning, Callie was determined to partner with Ben in their choice to hold some boundaries for a while longer.

"Your mother must have loved it when it snowed," Callie said with a smile as she thought about Adalynn's affinity for all things white.

Ben chuckled, following her line of thought. "Surprisingly, she didn't. When the weather would get bad like this here, she'd take off to Florida and stay there for a few weeks, sometimes months."

Hearing the strain in his voice as he spoke of his

mother, she guessed that when Adalynn did this, she left him behind with Rosa and Leo, demonstrating little regard for his feelings. Since their arrival, Ben's attitude toward his mother had shifted somewhat, perhaps because being there, where so many difficult memories lingered, re-balanced his previously more positively biased perspective.

"Ben?" Callie started to ask a question but then changed her mind, wishing she could take back her inquiry.

He waited for a moment, but when she didn't continue, he pulled away to look at her.

"Callie, truly, you can ask me anything. Well, almost anything. The one exception being where I went this morning," he smiled mischievously.

Though she appreciated his reassurance, her stomach churned as she worried about him potentially misinterpreting the motivation behind her question.

"Well," she said, lowering her gaze from his spellbinding eyes. "I was quite caught off guard by all of this." Callie gestured at the space around her as she continued. "Maybe I should have realized, seen the clues, but I genuinely had no idea you grew up like this."

Ben sighed. "It wasn't exactly a secret. It's just not who I am, not really something I'm proud of or even necessarily very comfortable with. I didn't earn this. I'm simply the last man standing, so..."

"I understand, and, truly, you could be the poorest or the richest man on earth, and it wouldn't change anything for me; you know that. But I'm trying to understand your world, relate to it and, I guess, figure out how I fit in."

"I don't intend to live in this world. I left it at the time primarily because of what happened to my mother, but I would have left eventually anyhow. I don't want to fit in or be like many who love and embrace this life. I never fit in before, and I don't desire to fit in now or in the future. If what I have can help us serve others, live a life where we can give easily and often, and enable me to protect you from harm, then I suppose it serves some noble purpose, but that's the extent to which I plan on giving it a foothold in our lives."

Callie nodded, admiring and agreeing with his perspective. Given his experiences, she understood his disdain for this world. Her curiosity over Donovan's revelation remained, but she wouldn't push for more information until Ben wanted to share.

"Well, regardless," she said, leaning back against his shoulder. "I appreciate what you're doing to provide extravagantly for me and protect me."

Ben was quiet, pondering something.

"Callie, I don't... I don't know how to talk about this very well since it's something I'm not that comfortable with myself, and it only became mine anyway when my mother died, so in a lot of ways, it's all new to me. But whatever you want to know about it, I'm happy to tell you, show you the extent of it, whatever. What's mine is yours, and I'll want your input and help anyway, deciding what in the world to do with it all when we go back home."

Callie took a deep breath. "It's not my place or my business, Ben. I'm sure, absolutely certain, you will do the right thing."

Abruptly, Ben pulled away, sitting up and turning his whole body to face her. Alarmed, she moved to match his posture so that they sat directly facing one another.

"It *is* your business." His voice sounded wounded, like she'd hurt him. "Don't you intend to continue sharing this life with me, being my partner in everything? Isn't that what you told me in the park the other night when you very persuasively convinced me that this,"—Ben gestured between them—"was a forever thing? Did you mean that, or did I misunderstand?"

The hurt in his voice broke her heart and certainly hadn't been her intent. "No! Ben, no! I mean, yes, I meant it, absolutely every word," she stammered, tears forming in her eyes.

Seeing her distress, he put his hand on hers. "I'm confused then," he said, shaking his head but softening his tone.

"I just want to respect your privacy. I mean, I'm not your... we're not married, and though this bond makes us feel like our lives are one life rather than two, and our hearts are deeply connected, we're not legally there yet, so I don't want to presume anything and..." Callie covered her face with her hands as the confusion over how to classify their relationship and determine proper boundary lines made her feel suddenly insecure.

Sighing in understanding and compassion, he pulled her close and kissed her hair as he tried to calm her nerves. He held her quietly against him for a moment before leaning back to look at her again.

"I'm sorry for the confusion. There's no doubt you and I are traveling through uncharted waters here. I appreciate your thoughtfulness and the intentions of your heart, but your concern for my privacy and autonomy is unnecessary. In our relationship, there's only one area where I'm trying to keep some boundaries in place, and that's just tempo-rary. After all, thanks to our little fire incident the other night, in part, those lines have already been breached, though admittedly unequally to your advantage." Ben smiled and winked at her playfully. "But, Callie, the rest of it... You can know it all, have it all if you want it. Don't you see? I'd freely sign it all over to you right now if you asked me to; that's how much I trust you and feel assured about our future together. I want you in my business, invite you into my life without reservations or limits, gladly, completely. And I know you invite me into yours as well. If I asked you how much money you had or anything else, would you hesitate to tell me?"

"Not for a second," she answered quickly.

"Then why would you worry about asking me?"

"I don't want you to get the wrong idea," she said, finally directly speaking her fears. "I don't want you to think my motives for asking are, well, anything other than just wanting to understand you and be a part of your world."

Ben cocked his head to the side, and an amused look filled his face. "Hm... Let's see. You accepted that I'm Succouri, a crazy, unbelievable, and foreign thing no person could easily accept. You embraced this unpredictable life with me, which puts you under stress and often leaves you on your own, protecting both of us. You accepted that I will likely die young and you'll have to take care of me for years as I weaken. And, to top off all that heartbreak and hardship, you've now accepted that staying with me resigns you to a life without the ability to have children of your own. Honestly, sweetheart, I would have thought the 'three strikes and you're out' rule would have applied long ago. I have no idea why, but you, Miss Callie LeVray, have loved me through it all, accepted me, and by some miracle I can't fathom, you still want me. And that all came true while you believed I had little more than a few dollars to my name." Ben paused to shake his head in wonder.

"But now, you're worried that if you ask me about my financial situation, I might think you're after me for my riches?" Ben smiled and shook his head again. "I'm positive there's not enough money in all the world to even out that scale."

Callie lowered her head, unsure how to respond but overcome by his extraordinary kindness and humility. What about all he'd given her? What about the fact that he'd saved her life twice, given her the ability to see every day at the cost of his strength, and accepted her without hesitation when she couldn't? What about the love and care he lavished on her continually without expecting payback? He spoke as if none of that were real or significant.

"Ben," she said softly. "I don't see it that way at all. You don't understand what you've given me; continue to give me daily. I wish... I hope someday I can make you see who you are. You're one in a million, Ben, the kind of man I didn't know even existed anymore, much less hoped to claim as my own. Everyone sees your rare and beautiful heart: Lee, Rosa, Leo, Donovan, everyone. The fact that you offered your heart to me, chose me to partner with you... that's reward enough for a lifetime."

Now, Ben lowered his head, profoundly touched by her words. "Well, then, Miss LeVray," he said, his voice thick with emotion, "can we agree that we're in the same place? I'm free to ask you anything, and you'll happily share, and you're free to ask me anything, and I'm privileged to oblige, with the one exception of this morning's little outing." He offered her another playful smile.

She looked straight into his eyes, which shone with sincerity. "Agreed," she confirmed, smiling and squeezing his hand.

"Alright then," he said, rising to his feet and pulling her with him.

He led her to the large office and pulled two white chairs up to the desk, gesturing for her to sit in one of them. Hesitantly, she complied, noting with pleasure how Ben was already moving around and walking more easily. Sitting beside her, he pulled a piece of paper and a pen from the desk drawer and set them in front of him.

"The Sawyer family has a lot of real estate, which has been passed down from generation to generation, adding to it as it moved down the line. Most of it is rented out, with a handful of properties like this one remaining unoccupied and available for use. Honestly, I don't know why I've left any of it like that since I haven't used it in six years and really have no intention to do so. When we're done here, I'll probably turn it over to the same real estate company that manages the rest of the confounded mess unless you have other thoughts on the matter. I don't really do anything except oversee the statements and make sure everything is managed on the up and up. It's too easy, really. Like I said, I've done nothing to earn it except be born,"—Ben paused to chuckle bitterly—"accidentally so, into the family name."

Pausing, he looked at her, but she had no questions, so he continued.

"All of the properties are owned and paid off by now, so when the rent payments come in each month, after I pay the company that manages it, the rest gets deposited into several accounts in my name, some short-term and some long-term investments. This..."—he stopped talking to write down a number—"is approximately how much I have put away for... well, later, I suppose, in long-term investments."

Ben held her hand and pushed the paper toward her.

Though Callie was still uncomfortable knowing all of

Ben's private affairs, she'd started this conversation and this was a genuine gesture of trust, so she looked down and focused on the number he'd written. Despite her intention not to react, Callie gasped and put her hand over her mouth in disbelief.

Ben retracted the paper and jotted down another number. "And this is approximately how much is in my accounts for immediate access."

But Callie didn't want to look at it. "It's okay, Ben. I get the picture," she said through the tightness in her throat.

"Callie, it's just a thing, but it's a thing I need your help with, your partnership in, and your input about. Please, I know it's a little crazy. Imagine growing up with it."

Callie blew out a breath and focused again on a number she could barely comprehend. "I don't know quite what to say," she shrugged. "I... I feel totally intimidated by that," she gestured toward the numbers on the page.

Ben smiled in understanding. "Yep, I relate to that sentiment."

Ben grabbed the paper and bent below the desk, running it through a noisy paper shredder.

Staring at the disappearing page, he continued. "And that's about how significant it is in the grand scheme of things. It makes very little difference unless you let it. And I'm never going to let it, and since I know your heart well, I can confidently say you're never going to let it either."

He took her hand, and they headed into the kitchen for lunch. Though Callie's head still spun with shock, she did her best to put the whole matter out of her mind. Nevertheless, Ben's kind words and profound display of trust continued to touch her heart deeply.

· · ·

AFTER LUNCH, as Rosa and Callie chatted casually, Ben stepped away to contact Elena's father. When he completed the call, and Rosa left the room, Ben returned to the kitchen, sitting next to Callie.

"Doctor Navarro was very kind," Ben explained, and Callie's concerned expression relaxed. "Since I'd permitted Elena to tell him about me, he only had a few initial questions, preferring to discuss it in greater detail when we meet in person the day after tomorrow. It will take us a couple of hours to drive there, so I wanted to wait until the snow cleared."

"Was he..." Callie paused, looking for the right word. "Was he as surprised as everyone else has been about your story?"

Ben nodded. "Yes, maybe more so, though I think the fact that Elena had prepared him by giving him some information, so he had time for it to sink in, tempered his reaction. But he still seemed hesitant to believe all of it, though not in a rude or unkind way. He expressed a definite interest in learning more and helping us discover any answers and facts he possibly could, though he warned me that this whole thing, even in normal conditions, is still a wonderous mystery."

"Do you need to prepare in any way? Like"—Callie smiled, looking awkward at asking the question—"like fasting for a blood draw or anything like that?"

Ben chuckled, sharing her amusement at the idea of doing something normal in relation to something completely abnormal. "No, he didn't indicate anything like that, but he did ask me if I was, how did he put it...'at full power'." They both laughed at the euphemism. "I told him I would be by then, presumably, if no one needs me between now and then. I alerted him to our unique situation and the small draw that results from it. He advised minimizing contact for an hour or so before we see him, but honestly, he didn't seem too concerned about it."

Callie leaned forward, resting her chin on her hand. "Hm, I may need to buy you a new pair of gloves," Callie teased.

"No way!" Ben said emphatically, shaking his head and reaching for her hand. "Whatever it is when we get there, it is. I'm sure it will be just fine."

"So," Callie considered, drumming her fingers on the countertop. "If we're going there the day after tomorrow and we're stuck here by the snowstorm for another full day…"

"Yes," Ben interrupted, anticipating Callie's question. "Tomorrow, if you're up for it, we'll start going through some of my mother's things and see what we can find."

Ben's heart constricted at the idea, but this was, in large part, what they'd come to do, and though it was painful, he wanted to resolve the questions so he could move ahead with his plans with Callie.

Callie placed her hand on his cheek. "I'm sorry for the pain of facing the past, but there's light and new life on the other side."

"Yes, there certainly is," he agreed as he gazed deeply into the future he could see in the green eyes staring back at him.

They took advantage of the remainder of the afternoon to rest, mostly back in the comfort of the gray couch, both of them contentedly napping for a time. They had several days of early mornings and late nights to make up for, and Ben was still recovering from the fire rescue.

By the time dinner came around, Ben felt significantly stronger, largely thanks to Callie's help throughout the day.

Though their safe level of contact didn't provide him with a rapid influx of strength, the amount of time they'd spent in relatively close contact was ample enough to help him regain solid ground. After enjoying a hearty dinner with Rosa, Leo, Callie, and Donovan, Ben felt very nearly normal.

When they had eaten and they all moved to clear the table, Ben caught a look from Donovan that alarmed him. He stared at him for confirmation, and Donovan nodded his head. Ben retrieved Callie from the kitchen, apologizing to Rosa for leaving her alone with the cleanup, which caused Rosa to laugh and remind him that he was paying her for the work.

When the three of them were seated around the dining room table, Ben holding Callie's hand so she could see but also to provide comfort as he perceived Donovan's news might be difficult, Donovan cleared his throat and looked apologetically at them.

"Through a series of phone calls today, beginning with Officer Evans and ending with a man named Wes Taylor at the FBI, I'm afraid I've been informed of some unpleasant news. It seems that the authorities are now fairly certain they've learned the identity of Callie's shooter." Donovan reached down into a bag and retrieved a file. Setting it on the table, he opened it, and pulled something out. After taking a deep breath, he slid it across the table to Ben. Ben reached to slide it closer and then stared, recognizing the face at once. This was the man whose profile he'd seen through the window of the Dodge outside of the courthouse days before Callie was shot.

Ben let out a long exhale as he slid the photo toward Callie. "That's him," Ben said flatly. "But if they know who he is now, that sounds like good news, not bad."

"It would be, except... except for a couple of things.

Charro Ruiz is a cousin of the man Callie's father convicted for life. He's just as evil and dangerous and he's got a motive that frankly, he's not likely to let go of. The FBI wants this guy too, as he's either certainly connected to or suspected of being connected to several open investigations. That's why they're now involved. I've worked with the FBI before, but this, Taylor, is new to me. Evidently, he's done a ton of undercover work with drug gangs, and he's familiar with this particular ring of thugs. The problem is, they've lost track of him. He was confirmed to have been out you all's way for a while, but not long after you two left, he disappeared."

Ben's heart began to pound and Callie's hand tensed at the news.

"Does that mean... Donovan, do you think he knows where we are?"

"Unlikely," Donovan replied, shaking his head. "It doesn't sound like you two left any tracks behind, and I've been sure to erase any evidence of hotel reservations, credit card use, or anything like that, so I can't think of any way for him to have tracked your direction."

Ben looked at Callie just as she looked at him. There was evidence, a way to track them, though he had no idea how revealing it might be. Telling Donovan about it now seemed the only safe choice. Protecting Callie was his priority, but filling Donovan in on the details of their trip meant much more than simply directing him to a small-town newspaper article.

"Donovan," Ben said. "Could you please give Callie and me a moment, and then we'll get right back to you?"

Though Donovan looked confused, he nodded and rose quickly, moving out of earshot.

"Ben!" Callie's voice shook as she clung tightly to his hand and tried to avoid looking at the picture on the table.

Ben slid it away so it wouldn't be right in front of her and he reached for her other hand to turn her body toward him. "I think we have to tell him, Callie," Ben whispered. "He needs to know about the fire and the newspaper article. I wish we could just give him a general statement about it, not reveal everything, but he's too good for that. He'll find the article and read it along with anything else that's come out about us from that incident. If we don't tell him, we leave out important information that he needs to keep you safe."

Sitting back, she blinked at him for several minutes, trying to hold back tears. She was scared, and Ben's heart ached, wanting her to feel safe and at ease.

After a moment of silence, she refocused on his face and nodded her head in agreement. "He'll understand. He already suspects something. He asked me earlier what you'd been running from. I put off the question, but I didn't alleviate his suspicions or confusion."

Ben sighed resolutely. "Alright, since we're in agreement."

Callie nodded again, and Ben took a deep breath before calling Donovan back into the room.

For the next twenty minutes, Ben did his best to explain who he was to Donovan, how he had saved the family from the fire, and the subsequent newspaper article. Donovan sat speechless, and Ben could tell by the look in his eyes that he didn't believe any of it. Callie, evidently seeing it too, tried to help, offering her own story of learning about Ben, how he'd saved her when she'd been shot, and how she could see when he touched her, but Donovan still said nothing, looking confused and unconvinced.

"Donovan," Ben pleaded, "I understand your doubt, and I know this sounds completely crazy, but..."

"Not crazy, impossible!" Donovan said at last, trying to be kind but unable to contain his skepticism.

There was a long silence before Ben took a deep breath and spoke in his most compassionate tone, drawing on every special Succouri gift of empathy he could muster. "Donovan, I know you're not well. I know you're ill or injured somehow, and it's pretty serious."

Donovan's face paled and Ben rose and went to sit in the chair beside him. He gazed intently into Donovan's brown eyes.

"I...I haven't told anyone about that except for my doctors," Donovan whispered. "How do you know?"

"Because what we're telling you is true. Incredible, unbelievable, I understand, but true, nonetheless. When I shook your hand, I felt strength go out of me into you, temporarily curing whatever it is that's wrong. I can't tell exactly what it is, but the draw of strength is strong enough that I know it's serious. Are you in pain?" Ben asked as his own heart hurt for his friend.

"Always." Donovan huffed in evident frustration at having his privacy violated and appearing weak, but also expressing honest anger at his condition.

"May I?" Ben asked, holding out his hand but not yet touching Donovan.

He stared at Ben, momentarily unsure, but finally nodded in consent.

Ben placed his hand on Donovan's arm and the room fell silent. As Ben experienced the same substantial draw of strength he had before, he watched Donovan's face and eyes as his emotions shifted from doubt with a touch of anger, to confusion, and then finally, to wonder and acceptance.

He stared at Ben for a long moment, unable to speak. When Ben was confident that Donovan now fully believed, Ben removed his hand and leaned away, sighing.

"I wish, for both you and Callie, that my gift was permanent healing, but unfortunately, it isn't. You don't have to tell us what's wrong, but I hope you'll let us help you in any way we can. If you need further evidence, you can look up that newspaper article, and I think the information you'll read there will substantiate what Callie and I are telling you."

Ben watched Donovan's eyes as he wrestled with conflicting thoughts and emotions. Giving him the time and space to work it out in his head, Ben sat patiently.

"I went through a lot overseas," Donovan started, speaking slowly, the anger gone from his tone. "I was shot twice in an attack that, frankly, I was lucky to have escaped with my life. On top of that, I took a hit from an IED, and I've got shrapnel embedded in my body that will still be there when I die. All of that has caused some pretty serious internal damage, which results in a myriad of different issues. I'm managing it, but I don't know how long treatments will work. The long-term prognosis isn't encouraging."

Ben lowered his head, and as he glanced quickly at Callie, he noticed tears on her cheeks. "I'm so sorry," he whispered. "You offered to help me once, and I should have taken you up on it. I know I didn't but I should have. Maybe you understand now why I ran, why I couldn't stay in one place, and why I was terrified of anyone knowing me well enough to find out about all of this. But please, let me offer you the same. Whatever we can do to help, please, we won't push you, invade your privacy, but..."

Donovan rose and patted Ben on the shoulder. "I appreciate that, Ben. Give me a little time. I need to process all of this. I'm going to find that article, see what the damage is, and think through what the consequences might be. I still believe our security measures here are adequate, but"—he paused and gestured toward Callie—"stay close to her. Don't let her out of your sight. In terms of a bodyguard," Donovan said, chuckling, "you're definitely the right man for the job. I'll get back to you two tomorrow."

Ben and Callie smiled in understanding but didn't follow him, giving him the space they knew he needed. When he'd left, Ben sat back next to Callie, and they pondered the night's events quietly for a few minutes.

"He'll be all right," Callie finally said softly. "Once it all sinks in, he'll be all right. In the end, he'll be able to help us much more proficiently now that he knows everything, and he'll be an even closer friend for you too, Ben."

Ben agreed with her, but presently, he was preoccupied with his worry about Callie. Knowing her shooter was on their trail, maybe even had a good idea of the direction they'd been going, filled him with anger and fear. The thought of a soulless killer hunting this remarkable woman, the light of his world and heart, was unfathomable and awakened every protective instinct he possessed.

"I'm sorry I put you in danger by helping that family," Ben said. "I didn't even consider, just reacted."

"No. Don't be, please. If I'd known then what we know now, I'd still fully support you in saving that man and baby. It's what we have to do, you and me. In some ways, it will always be a risk, and I suppose we'll get better at protecting ourselves, but we have to accept the risk too."

Ben shook his head and exhaled. "I can accept the risk of my secret being discovered, Callie, but not of you being killed. That's not an acceptable risk, ever." Ben's voice shook with the passion behind his words.

Callie turned to stare at the picture Donovan had left. She trembled as she stared into the vacant, dark eyes of the man who hunted her. His anger burned hotter from a deep place inside him. He flipped it over, breaking its insidious hold on her.

"I'll protect you with my life, Callie. I swear I will."

A tear traced down her cheek, and Ben pulled her to him.

"That's what I'm afraid of," she whispered through trembling lips.

CHAPTER 12

THE STAND

L ater that night, after thoroughly checking the security measures around the house, Ben walked Callie to her room. They'd done their best to enjoy the evening, trying not to dwell on the unknown dangers and unanswered questions. Now, as they walked down the hall toward her bedroom, every dangerous possibility, every potential hole in the security around the house, and every horrifying regret he would have if he left her and something happened played like a 3D movie in Ben's mind.

As he stood outside her door holding her hands, he felt paralyzed, unable to tolerate the idea of leaving her alone, causing her to be far enough away from him that he wouldn't be immediately aware of a threat, and therefore, potentially unable to respond in time if the worst should happen.

"Ben?" Callie questioned, looking into his eyes. "I'll be alright."

He knew she said the words for his benefit. She didn't look alright at all. She looked scared and shaken as she had for most of the night since seeing her attacker's face. But after his statements the night before, Callie knew staying with her would mean a battle for him, so she kindly offered him an out.

Taking a deep breath, he pulled her close. He breathed in the scent of her, memorized the feel of her against him, and leaned into the strength offered by the familiar, comforting fire of their bond. He tried not to imagine the nightmare of life without all these things, which were now as critical to his survival as oxygen to his lungs.

As he held her, unwilling to let go and unable to pull away, she spoke softly, her own need for him evident in her voice. "What if we make another of our famous deals?"

Ben leaned back just enough to look into her exotic eyes, his heart aching as he again observed the fear in them. "I'm listening."

"What if you stay here with me, but we wear sweats, sleep in our own blankets, and keep our distance? I won't even kiss you goodnight." She tried for a smile, but it was weak and forced.

"Hm," he considered, working hard to take on a teasing tone. "I'll take the first part, but no deal on the last part of that offer."

"The goodnight kiss?"

Letting go of her and stepping back, he crossed his arms. "I'll take my kiss now, out here where it's safer, please." He smiled and drummed his fingers, feigning impatience. "Or no deal."

Her smile grew as she began to relax. "You drive a hard bargain, Mr. Sawyer, but alright, if I must."

Standing on her tiptoes, she pressed her lips to his. Ben returned her kiss, softly at first, kissing the corners of her mouth and brushing his lips across hers.

But soon, his desire grew, and Ben encircled her waist

with his arm, lifting her off the floor, and drawing her to him. She laughed in pure delight, and Ben turned them around, bracing her against the wall as he deepened and intensified the kiss. As she clung to his neck, they both got swept away by the flood of passion and fire that enveloped them.

Slowly, he lowered Callie's feet to the floor as he continued kissing her passionately, and he ran his hands down her sides, letting them come to rest around her narrow waist. Her fingers traced down his back and then, she surprised him by lifting his shirt and sensually sliding them up the bare skin of his back, sending intense waves of thrilling heat through his whole body. Her touch on his skin was ecstasy, and he wanted more, much more.

And he wanted to reciprocate, to touch her soft, smooth skin. As his heart pounded, longing filled every thought and began seizing control of him.

In the second before he surrendered to it, Ben pulled back just enough to speak, his voice thick and breathless. "Are you sure, Callie? Are you absolutely sure that this is what you want?"

They were about to cross a line of no return. His disciplined mind had only so much power to resist the cravings of the human man and the Succouri in him, both of which eagerly wanted the same thing at this moment. There was a faint nagging thought at the very farthest corner of his mind that whispered to him that they were both currently emotionally vulnerable and shouldn't be making choices as crucial as this one in such a state. From the other corner came a voice that countered, arguing that they deserved the comfort the closeness offered them.

Gradually, Callie withdrew her hands and put them back around his shoulders. They froze as Ben waited for her answer, and Callie, indecisive, fought her own invisible battle.

"I... I love you," she finally said shakily. "I need you. I know we're trying to do this right, but I've already slept in your arms, and I was certainly conscious enough to remember how heavenly it feels."

Reluctantly, Ben stepped back, ashamed of placing her in this situation. Though telling her seemed the wrong thing to do at this moment, he fought the same battle, also having awoken with her in his arms and lingering for several blissful moments in that perfect reality.

But it was his fault they'd ended up in that situation. As a consequence of who he was, the rescue debilitated him and left her to care for him in the most intimate way. Though he had no doubt Callie did her best to respect his privacy, she couldn't avoid seeing him, touching him, and lying next to him. If the situation were reversed, Ben could imagine how difficult it would be to return to stricter boundary lines after that encounter.

"I'm so sorry I've caused you all this confusion," he said, taking another step back.

"No, Ben! That's not what I meant." She stepped forward, filling the space between them. "You didn't do anything wrong. I'm the one who crossed the line just now. But the truth is," she smiled at him. "I can't think clearly when I'm in your arms anymore. I don't even want to think clearly; I just want you, and I'm not ashamed of it."

Ben returned her smile, thrilling at her desire for him and relating to her dilemma. He touched her cheek, stroking it lightly, then tucked a few curls behind her ear.

"Callie, you are beautiful, exquisitely and captivatingly beautiful. Your internal beauty has already disintegrated every fortified wall I thought I'd solidly built around my heart, and now your external beauty is doing the same to my control. I want you too." Ben sighed and shook his head. "You have absolutely no idea how desperately. Since our first kiss, we've fought very hard to follow a healthy path despite the enormous and unusual temptations we face. Truthfully, given all we've been through, I'm quite proud of our resolve. But I'm weary of fighting it as well. I want nothing more than to love you with abandon, no limitations; me all yours and you all mine." He pulled her back into his arms.

"So, what do we do?" she asked as she rested her head on his chest.

"I don't want to look back someday and regret anything. I want to do right by you, Callie, in every way. So, I guess we do our best to hang in there a little longer, only a little longer."

They breathed slowly as they leaned against one another for a while, letting the passion ease, but at last, Ben reluctantly let go of her and stepped back, holding her hands again and looking into her eyes.

"So," he said, teasing her, yet also speaking the truth, "goodnight kiss solidly checked off the list at this point."

She smiled at him. "I guess it's time for the sweats and distance."

Ten minutes later, they lay together on opposite sides of the large bed, keeping enough space that the pull of their bond was manageable. As Ben lay on his back with his hands behind his head, staring at the ceiling, he listened for anything amiss and tuned in to his instincts, which he now knew would warn him with that familiar feeling of dread should there be a problem.

"Ben?" Callie spoke into the darkness, a laugh in her voice.

"Yes?"

"Do you realize this is the first time we've done this where one of us wasn't unconscious?"

Ben chuckled and turned his head her way. "That's true."

"I'm glad you're here," she sighed. "I couldn't have slept without you nearby."

Ben reached over and squeezed her hand. "And I couldn't have slept for the worry of you being here alone."

There was silence for a few moments before she spoke again. "Was the draw from Donovan tonight the same? Still strong?"

"Yes, maybe more so, or perhaps it just felt that way because the contact was prolonged."

"And he noticed the effects this time." Though she said it as a statement, not a question, Ben remembered that he hadn't held her hand when he touched Donovan's arm, so she couldn't have seen how his emotions had shifted.

"Yes. There's no doubt he believes us now."

"I'm worried about him. He's such a hero and a kind man too. He doesn't deserve to suffer like that."

Ben's heart was touched by the genuine concern in Callie's voice, proof of her deep affection for his friend. "I completely agree. I really hope he lets us help him."

"So do I." She paused to sigh. "Are you feeling alright? Did the encounter set you back at all for meeting with Doctor Navarro?"

Ben chuckled again. "Our goodnight kiss in the hallway more than took care of that. I feel about ninety percent recovered at this point."

"Good," she said, exhaling in relief. "This morning, I noticed that Rosa expressed discomfort when moving around. Did you feel anything from her?"

Ben smiled into the darkness. "Callie, there are very few people over sixty who don't draw something from me when I touch them. Arthritis, back pain, or something is usually causing discomfort at that age. But I didn't feel anything unusually strong, so don't worry."

"I guess I never thought about that, but it makes sense."

"The one exception is Ms. Essie," Ben said curiously. "She must be at least seventy, but nothing seems to be at all wrong with her."

"And she looks so young too," Callie added.

"Yes, she does."

"Do you think it's the bond somehow?"

Ben pondered the question. "Could be. It makes sense that years of contact with a Succouri might have some long-term effects."

Ben thought about Callie and wondered what the effects might be for her after years of sleeping next to him, holding his hand, and experiencing the closest kind of intimacy. As she was quiet as well, Ben guessed she was wondering the same.

"When you lived here, which room was yours?" she asked, changing the subject.

"This one."

Callie raised up and turned toward him. "Ben! You didn't need to give me your room."

He chuckled softly. "Well, we seem to be somewhat sharing it at this point, but..."

Ben trailed off as he wasn't sure how to express his mixed feelings regarding the memories brought to the surface by this room and house.

"Callie," he finally continued, knowing she was patiently waiting for him to finish his thought. "When we're done here and ready to go home, I'd like to give this place to Rosa and Leo. They've taken care of it for years and I owe them an unpayable debt of gratitude for all they did for me when I was young, as well as for how I treated them in leaving as I did. They can live here or sell and move elsewhere; I don't care. I don't ever want to come back here. I might want to take you to some of the other properties to visit at some point, but not this one." Ben's voice was somber and tight.

"Is being here that painful?" she asked in a concerned whisper.

"When you lose someone and time passes, it's easy to remember the good things, hold on to them, and begin to make them the prominent narrative in your mind. But being here has flipped that upside-down. Besides Rosa and Leo, my life here was not happy, though there were a handful of happy moments. Every room, every white piece of furniture resurrects haunting ghosts, most of which aren't particularly friendly."

"We could redecorate?" she offered.

Ben shook his head. "They'd still walk the halls. I need to walk out, lock the doors, and let the past go. My life with you is so different, in the best way. With you, I feel like I'm who I really am, like I've found myself, if that makes sense. The chains of the past threaten to imprison me here, so once we've learned all we can from the remnants of the past, I need to make a clean break."

Ben paused, turning onto his side to face her. "But, as we discussed earlier, as my full partner in everything, I want your candid opinion about the idea, and I won't do anything we don't agree on."

Callie reached for his hand in the darkness, and Ben helped her find it. "It's a wonderful, generous, and perfect idea, and if you're sure it's what you want and need, I wholeheartedly agree," she said enthusiastically with a luminous smile that brightened up the dark room.

Ben breathed out a relieved and very contented sigh. Though he'd had no reservations or concerns about sharing the extent of his fortune with Callie, her easy approval of his proposal confirmed every bit of trust he'd placed in her heart.

"Thank you, sweetheart."

She held her smile, and her eyes sparkled with tears of admiration and love. "You know what, Ben Sawyer? Your heart is exquisitely beautiful."

WHEN CALLIE OPENED her eyes in the morning, it only took her a few seconds to realize she was, once again, firmly secured in Ben's arms, the top half of her body draped across his chest. Since they'd both worn sweats and T-shirts, the contact wasn't as intimate as the last time this happened, but she was still startled to find herself there as they took great care to keep their distance, and she had no recollection whatsoever of their shift toward one another.

She raised her head to look up at his sleeping face, musing at how this was the first time she'd awoken before him and, therefore, had the chance to let her gaze linger on his handsome features.

Struggling to free one of her arms from his surprisingly firm grasp, she stroked his face, pushing aside a few strands of dark brown hair from his forehead. She worried, knowing that the day would likely be painful for him as they planned to go through his mother's belongings, looking for clues about his father's identity or anything else that might provide Ben with answers about his past.

After he'd told her of his plans to give the house to Leo and Rosa, her heart had ached at the level of pain she hadn't realized he suffered by being here. His extravagantly generous heart didn't surprise her, but his desire to permanently cut ties with the past and physical reminders of his mother did.

Apart from his mother's suicide, she had not been aware of the extent to which memories from his past haunted him until her conversation with Rosa and her observations of his reactions to the house. Though she hated seeing him hurting and wanted to shut off sources of any continued flow of pain, the agenda for the day would not accommodate that desire.

Callie kissed him gently, first on the chin, then both cheeks, and finally, softly on the lips, as she determined to do her utmost to remind him that the past was powerless, holding no influence over his future.

As she continued to enjoy tracing the perfect features of his face with her finger, Ben stirred and slowly blinked his eyes.

"Good morning," she said, smiling playfully.

"Callie?" His smile was dreamy and delighted at first, but his look quickly shifted to surprise with a little light scolding.

She laughed at the expression. "Hey, don't look at me like that. I'm stuck here."

She tried to move but couldn't, the action revealing how securely he was holding her.

Releasing her quickly, he sat up, his face shifting to an apologetic expression. "I'm sorry. I have no recollection of doing that."

Alarm and confusion filled his face, and Callie placed her hand reassuringly on his arm. "Ben, it's fine." She giggled at the unintentional predicament. "You've got clothes on this time, so no harm done here."

Ben still looked concerned and bewildered. "Do you remember us... well, me, doing that?"

Callie shook her head, still smiling. "Not at all," she said, speaking with a light tone as Ben was far more frantic about the situation than necessary.

He shook his head several times, concentrating hard on trying to solve the mystery.

"I think it's the Succouri part of you," she offered as she put the pieces together in her mind. "You did the same thing the night of the fire when I lay beside you. Even though you were nearly unconscious and very weak, you pulled me pretty tightly against you."

"I'm sorry, I..."

"Ben!" She grabbed his other arm and turned him toward her. "I promise, it's really alright. It makes sense. If being near me fills you with strength, gives you something you need, it makes sense for you to lean into it, or"—she stopped to laugh again—"pull it to you. You might be able to counter that instinct in your conscious state, but when you're asleep or unconscious, it's likely not under your control. Nothing happened here, Ben. You just pulled me into an embrace. We do that a lot. I know it's a bit more intimate in, well, in bed like this, but I didn't even know about it until like sixty seconds ago so, please, don't worry."

"But I'd never want to force you into anything you didn't want or... Callie! Was I hurting you?" Horror at that possibility darkened his expression as her words, intended to comfort him, seemed to be having the opposite effect.

"Oh no, Ben! Not at all!" she nearly shouted, heartbroken at his alarm. She softened her voice as she continued, and she smiled flirtatiously. "I rather enjoy it...

Actually, really enjoy it. Trust me; I didn't put that much effort into trying to escape. Remember, the way this works is I get something, and you get something; that's the beauty in the whole thing. I truly love being held by you; nowhere else I'd rather be."

His face relaxed, but his eyes still held concern. "But it makes it harder for you and me; that's what we were trying to avoid."

Grinning, she shrugged her shoulders. "I'm afraid that ship has sailed. I told you I couldn't lie by telling you I would forget what I saw and experienced the other night. You could stop holding me in your arms from here on out, and I'd still remember and be tempted by my attraction to you." She paused to smile suggestively. "Thankfully, it seems the Succouri in you won't let that happen."

Ben smiled and sighed in surrender, tracing his thumb down her cheek. "The man in me would never allow that to happen either, Miss LeVray."

"Good, then, we're okay here." She kissed him quickly on the lips.

Eyes shining with gratitude and love, Ben shook his head in amazement. "No matter what crazy new thing you learn about me or what it means to be with me, you just keep accepting it all with kindness and grace."

She stared into his eyes, reflecting the same look of love. "Loving you, Ben Sawyer, is the easiest thing I've ever done or will ever do in my entire life."

AT BREAKFAST, Ben told Rosa and Leo about their plans for the day.

"I put your mother's things; pictures, files, anything I could find, in her room," Rosa said.

"I noticed there wasn't much around the house. Thank you for collecting it all and being thoughtful."

Though Callie couldn't read Rosa's face as she and Ben were sitting too far apart at the table for him to hold her hand, she could easily hear the concern for Ben in Rosa's voice. Callie marveled at how Rosa's protective motherly instincts appeared to be stronger than those of his own biological mother.

After a few moments of silence, Ben spoke up again, his voice gentle and cautious. "Do either of you know anything about my father? Who he was, whether my mother knew who he was, anything?"

Leo and Rosa didn't answer immediately, and Callie was certain that the hesitation came from their desire to protect Ben.

"When you were sick, a man came here, only once, and Rosa and I have always believed that it was your father, though we don't have any proof, and your mother was sure to dismiss us before we could overhear or verify anything," Leo said, his voice tentative and somber.

Ben shifted in his seat. "What made you think it was my father?" he asked, surprised at the revelation.

"He looked like you, a lot like you; same hair, same eyes, though not quite the same soul. But more than that, he had the look of a worried parent, not just an aloof well-wisher," Rosa explained.

"Why didn't you ever tell me?" Ben's tone held a hint of betrayal.

"We planned to if we were ever certain or if he ever came back, but neither ever happened." Rosa spoke softly and lowered her head. "You were so young and troubled at the time. We didn't want to add to the confusion by giving you information we weren't sure was even accurate."

Ben sighed, processing this new information, which reshaped some of his previous perceptions.

"So, you believe my mother knew who he was and how to contact him?"

"Yes," Leo replied, his voice reluctant and strained. "But, Ben, that's the only time we ever saw him. What kind of father only comes to check on his boy when he's ill and never shows up again? I don't want you hurt by what you'll likely find if you dig in that hole."

"I understand, and I appreciate your concern for me, but this is more than a search for a lost parent. There are other questions about my past I'm trying to answer and, though I have no idea if my biological father is connected, I may need to turn over every available rock and look underneath in my quest for answers."

Their silent response spoke of their respect for Ben's decision while it also revealed deep concern. In addition, Callie wondered if the lack of any follow-up questions might indicate knowledge of Ben's secret and their continued discretion on the matter. During her conversation with Rosa, Callie had noted her reference to Ben's "unique burden" which was perhaps further proof of their knowledge of the issue.

Mid-morning, before they'd had a chance to start their search through Adalynn Sawyer's belongings, Donovan returned, and the three of them did their best to settle comfortably in the front room, though the furniture was stiff and awkward despite its elegance.

As Donovan settled in his chair, he chuckled, allowing Callie's nervousness regarding his acceptance of Ben's secret to ease.

"Ben, I think we might be more comfortable sitting on the floor," Donovan teased.

Ben grimaced in response. "Comfort wasn't one of my mother's priorities."

Donovan nodded sympathetically. "It was a weird world we grew up in, a very weird world. And, speaking of weird worlds..." He smiled and opened the file he'd been holding. "I read the article, and there was a follow-up the next day, as well as a short blurb about it on one local evening news station. Big picture, it gave away your vehicle and your first name, Ben, and a very basic description of you, but I saw no mention of Callie's name anywhere, though they did report that there was a woman with you."

"Nathan's wife was probably too distraught to remember our names," Callie said.

"Probably," Ben agreed, "and I only told Nathan mine, not Callie's."

"The story was... remarkable, unbelievable really. Anyone who read it or heard it likely wouldn't believe most of it." Donovan chuckled again. "Well, as I also didn't." Donovan paused, and Callie and Ben waited.

Closing the file, he looked into Ben's eyes, admiration clear in his expression. "It was a shock to find out that my long-lost friend is a superhero, but"—he smiled—"I'm very honored and a little intimidated to have been trusted with this sensitive and sacred secret, and I consider it a privilege to come alongside you both, primarily as a friend but also as someone in the fight with you as we continue to keep Callie safe."

Donovan leaned forward and offered Ben his outstretched hand. Grasping it firmly, Ben smiled in gratitude at his generous statement of full support. "I appreciate the kind words but, truly, I'm the one who's been honored, for a long time now, to enjoy the friendship of a real-life hero."

As both men exchanged affectionate smiles, Callie's eyes filled with tears at witnessing the two incredible men before her display mutual pride and respect for the courage of the other.

"Anyone who would run into a fire like that to save people he didn't even know… well, you're a fellow soldier in my book," Donovan added, leaning back awkwardly in his uncomfortable chair. "Now, all of that aside, and I'll briefly add that saving lives is always worth the risk, this does complicate things a bit."

Nodding, Ben leaned back as well.

"From what you've told me about the night of Callie's shooting, Ruiz likely saw you there, saw your vehicle, and connected you to Callie. The first thing he probably did when he discovered Callie was gone, was look into you, find out your name, etc. Though you've moved around a lot, and that might make it harder to pinpoint where you might go, the Sawyer name is somewhat well-known because of your mother and your fortune. This article and subsequent news story might just be enough to confirm or at least narrow down a general vicinity of where you were headed, maybe even more specific than that if he's any good at tracking."

"Do we need to go somewhere else?" Ben asked, anger rising in his voice.

Donovan crossed his arms. "I guess that depends." He looked back and forth between Callie and Ben as he continued. "He'll find you again, so if you run, you're just buying time. If we don't take this guy out, get him off your back, the two of you will spend your life running away. That's an option, but not one I'd personally want to embrace." He paused as he studied their faces.

The thought of constantly running and hiding made

Callie's stomach ache. That wasn't the kind of life she wanted. She wanted family, friends, and a full life with Ben.

"If you stay here," Donovan continued, "take a stand, we'll have the FBI's help. Agent Taylor is very committed to catching this guy. He has numerous resources and is willing to put them all behind helping us. And he knows what he's doing as he's got over twenty years of experience. You've got a secure place here, and if we're fairly sure he's coming, which I am at this point, that gives us some advantage rather than being caught off guard."

As he finished his analysis, he continued to look back and forth between Callie and Ben.

"Ben," Callie said softly as she turned to look into his eyes. She could feel the rage in him building. "We have to take a stand here. We can't spend our lives running. How will we help people, build a life together, and fulfill our mutual purpose if we're always looking over our shoulders, afraid to stand out or leave a trail? I want to live, but I also want a life."

A tortured look settled on Ben's face and Donovan rose and put a hand on his shoulder. "I understand why you love her," he said, nodding toward Callie. "She's got the strength and courage of a warrior. I'll give you two a minute alone to talk about this. Let me know what you decide, and I'll do everything I can to help you either way."

When he'd left, Ben turned his eyes to Callie. Though she appreciated Donovan's words, she didn't feel courageous or strong. Her body shook and her heart pounded, and she knew Ben was fully aware of her fear.

"Let me just make one thing very, very clear." He started, speaking with uncharacteristic firmness. "While being Succouri and all that that entails matters to me, it doesn't come close to the importance of keeping you safe.

You're my life, period. I'd run with you until the end of my days if that was what was needed to keep you with me, and I'd do it gladly."

Lowering her head, she tried to calm her trembling. "I know you would. I know you'd run with me, and I know you'd give up your life for me." She lifted her eyes to meet his. "But I don't want either of those options. I want a real, full life with you, and for that to happen, I need you to be alive. I know you're tough and can heal fast and all of that but, Ben, you're not invincible. If we stay here, we'll have help and backup, so there will be less chance you'll have to protect me by yourself. Please, you're doing everything you can to protect me, but I want to protect you too, because I'm also very willing to give up my life for you."

Leaning forward, Ben rested his forehead on hers as they wrestled with the terrible choice before them. Through the aid of their bond, Callie could feel Ben's struggle, his anger at her shooter, and his desperate need to protect her, and she guessed he could read her emotions as well.

As they sat together, not moving or speaking but tuning in with their total concentration to each other's hearts, there came a new and incomprehensible experience, a kind of mutual vision playing out in the intangible shared space of their bond. The experience manifested in Callie's mind as if their thoughts and feelings, Ben's and hers, were lined up like you might arrange missing puzzle pieces adjacent to their intended yet vacant spots. Then, in rapid succession, each thought dropped, one by one, into its proper place, and the answer came clear and sure, like a discernible image coming into focus as the last puzzle piece fell into place.

When the answer, produced by the merging of their shared thoughts, dawned in their minds, they both raised their heads, looking at one another, the wonder of the strange experience showing in their bewildered expressions.

Ben smiled at her. "I guess we know what we're going to do then."

Callie stopped trembling as the confidence born from the inaudible, yet fully engaging collaboration brought a sense of peace. "Yes, I guess we do."

CHAPTER 13
THE LETTERS

Ben informed Donovan of their decision to stay and take a stand, and Donovan wholeheartedly supported the choice. The three of them spent time strategizing new security measures with the increased threat level, including Donovan moving into the house full time to provide additional protection as well as constant surveillance as he coordinated with his contacts at the FBI. Ben and Donovan filled Rosa and Leo in on the updates, as these changes and threats affected them as well. They were gracious, responding with offers to help in any way possible. Callie regretted putting their lives in danger by her presence there, but they kindly extended to her the same loyalty and affectionate commitment they offered Ben.

Ben told Donovan about their plans to go to Cape Cod the next day, letting him know it had something to do with his life as a Succouri but that he couldn't be more specific than that without first getting permission from everyone involved. Donovan didn't push for more information but worked with them on precautionary measures to make the trip as safe as possible. Ben considered canceling the appointment, but Callie protested, and Donovan encouraged them to go, reassuring them that since the location was somewhere Ben had never been before and out of town, they were likely in less danger there than staying at the house.

It wasn't until after lunch that they could finally refocus on their original plan for the day. As Callie and Ben reached the top of the stairs and turned left, heading toward a closed door at the end of the hallway, Callie could feel the tension in Ben's hand and posture. The day had already been an emotional one, and this task would only add to that stress.

Just before they entered the room, Callie stopped, and Ben turned to look at her questioningly. "I just want to tell you that I love you. I know this is hard but this is the past, a time in your life that no longer has any power over you. You know who you are now, and nothing can take that away."

Offering her an appreciative smile, Ben brushed her cheek with his fingers. They gazed at each other silently, communicating love, support, and understanding. Then Ben turned and opened the door.

As Callie had expected, the room was massive, and everything was white. In reality, it was more like two rooms as there was a spacious offset seating area, complete with a couch, shelves of movies and books, and a wall-mounted TV. The bed was ornate and covered with what looked to be an expensive embroidered white lace spread. Thick white rugs were scattered around the room, and the dressers and side tables were made of the same rich dark wood found in the rest of the house.

The pictures on the walls caught Callie's attention immediately. The rest of the house had tasteful, predictable artwork, mostly of landscape scenes, but this room had paintings and portraits of people, their faces captured in a moment of emotional expression, primarily variations of sadness or at least somberness.

As she looked around the room, her gaze lingered on a large portrait hanging over the bed. The woman pictured there wore a flowing white evening gown, and her face was stunningly beautiful. Her golden hair was loosely gathered into a complicated updo. Her porcelain white skin and piercing ice-blue eyes captured Callie's focus. Though her facial features were almost ethereal, her solemn expression dulled their impact. As she stared at the woman's straight, closed lips and tight jaw, she imagined how much more radiant she would look with a smile, and she wondered why anyone would choose this expression for a portrait.

As Ben stood watching her, noticing her interest in the portrait, he shook his head and let out a resigned sigh. "My mother didn't believe in smiling for pictures. She thought it made people look silly and fake."

"That's your mother?" Callie gasped, turning to look at him.

He nodded, and Callie looked back at the portrait. Ben hadn't been exaggerating when he said his mother had movie-star good looks, but though Ben also possessed extraordinarily handsome features, Callie was surprised at how dissimilar they looked. Adalynn's hair color was different, and her skin much paler. The eyes were blue, but Ben's were a much deeper and more brilliant hue. There were some slight resemblances in the nose, and Adalynn seemed to have the same thick, abundant hair, but there wasn't much else that betrayed the genetic connection.

"She's enchanting, but she doesn't look much like you," Callie observed.

"No," Ben agreed with a humorless chuckle and a shake

of his head. "I always thought I must favor my dad, and I guess Rosa and Leo sort of confirmed that for us today."

Leading Callie to the side of the large bed where a sizable collection of boxes and framed pictures had been gathered, Ben sat on the floor with her. He had to let go of her hand to begin sorting through the boxes. As this left Callie without much sight, she felt a little powerless to help him in his search, but at the same time, the task was something he needed to do mostly on his own anyway, so she contented herself with simply offering her presence, hoping it provided him with some comfort.

For the next half an hour, Ben meticulously sorted through folders and old pictures, stopping a few times to touch Callie's hand so she could enjoy looking at photos of him when he was a boy. There weren't many, which saddened her, and most of them were formal; Ben clad in the uniform of the private school he attended, looking straight-faced and very posed, which Callie now understood as likely a mandate from his mother. Even so, his gentle, warm nature was evident. There were a dozen or so more candid shots, a few with him smiling, and Callie couldn't help but laugh in delight at the boyish charm in his grin as it was something he'd never fully outgrown. Rosa was right when she said Ben was "an angel straight from heaven." Even as a boy, his features were striking, his vivid blue eyes conveying humility and compassion. There were no pictures of Ben with his mother, which Callie found puzzling, and she wondered if most of the more candid ones were taken by Rosa and Leo. There were very few of Ben after his illness, and they were all of the more posed variety. Still, it was rewarding for Callie to watch the progress of the man she loved as he changed and matured from boyhood to manhood. It made her feel more connected to his past and the life he'd lived before she'd known him.

Watching her delighted expression as she took in the images, Ben commented on how he looked forward to seeing pictures of Callie as a girl. She laughed and told him her dad had taken so many that it might take days instead of hours to get through them all.

Callie placed the photos of Ben in a separate pile, receiving his permission to take them along when they returned home. The framed photos were of Adalynn, taken in professional modeling sessions before Ben was even born. As Callie took in the various expressions on her face presented in the significant collection, she matched some of them with similar looks she'd seen Ben express, causing her to slightly revise her previous conclusion that Ben bore almost no resemblance to his mother. In a few photos, Adalynn offered a forced-looking smile, but Callie observed that this expression was particularly dissimilar to Ben's as there was nothing at all contrived in his smile.

When they'd made it through the large pile of items and had found nothing of significance in their quest for answers, Ben took her hand and rose, leading her to the closet. The space inside was enormous, and she was shocked that it still overflowed with clothing, including an extensive collection of fancy gowns and shimmering jewelry. Though it had been six years since Adalynn's death, it appeared that none of her possessions had been stored, discarded, or donated, and though she knew Ben had immediately run and left all of this behind, she was surprised that all of Adalynn's belongings had been so well preserved.

"Where did she possibly wear all of these fancy

gowns?" Callie asked as she ran her hand along the elegant silks and satins of dozens of dresses.

"Unlike me, she jumped at any opportunity to attend a fancy party or charity event, like the one I met you at for our first date." Ben smiled briefly, and Callie guessed the happy expression was related to the memory of their date rather than the formal events his mother forced him to attend.

"Don't like parties, Mr. Sawyer?" she asked.

"Not ones where I have to wear a tie and make small talk for hours with people I know care nothing about me and vice versa."

"Hm." Callie crossed her arms. "Well, I can certainly understand that. I'm not sure I've ever been to such a party unless I'm the entertainment." Smiling, she thought about how often she'd performed at events like that with Grace and Lobster but had never really been part of the crowd.

"Now," Ben said playfully, crossing his arms to match her posture, "I might be persuaded to change my mind if I could see you wearing a gown, like the one from our date, with more frequency."

Broadening her grin, she tilted her head to the side. "I'm happy to oblige you in that way anytime, and you don't have to suffer the party torture. Just cook me a nice dinner, and I'll happily dress up for you."

Ben pondered, stroking his chin. "Now that's an idea, Miss LeVray, a very wonderful idea."

Ben began searching through shelves and looking on the floor beneath the tightly packed racks of clothing, and Callie could sense his frustration as the effort yielded nothing of consequence. She was about to suggest they take a break when Ben emerged from beneath a rack of thick, flowing gowns with a small box. He blew a cloud of dust off the lid and opened it. She heard the shifting of papers and then Ben returned the lid, placed the box under his arm, and reached for her hand.

"Ben?" she inquired as they walked out of the closet toward the adjacent sitting room.

"This looks like a box of miscellaneous letters, but there's quite a few here, so I thought we'd have a seat while I sort through them."

Though she wasn't sure why, Callie felt nervous for him as she sat down beside him on the couch, and he began investigating the contents of the box. He pulled half a dozen items out, looked at them briefly, and then set them aside before lingering on first an envelope and then the letter he extracted from it. Before inquiring, she gave him the time to read and consider it. "Something interesting?"

"Maybe." He stared at it for another moment before continuing. "The return address just has the initials T.T. but no address and the letter is signed the same."

"What does it say?" Callie asked, perplexed by the unusual correspondence.

Ben read it to her in a puzzled tone.

> Addy, I sincerely appreciate the contact and information. While I wish for so much more, his well-being is most important to me, as is yours. I wish I could further explain, but doing so would not be prudent. Trust me when I say this is the wiser course of action. Someday, things might be different, but I understand it might be too late by then. Nevertheless, I'm grateful for your willingness to allow me this small favor. Sincerely, T.T.

Callie considered the cryptic message for a moment before speaking. "Is there a postal date?"

Picking up the envelope, he quickly scanned it. "It looks like it's about nineteen years old," he said, his voice revealing a bit of tightness now.

"Any others in that box with the same information in the return address?"

Ben flipped through the remaining content, setting aside one other letter before reaching the bottom of the box. He returned the rejected content to the box before refocusing on the selected envelope and scanning it for a postal date.

"It looks like this one was later, about…" Ben paused and sucked in a breath. "Fifteen years ago."

Callie placed her hand on Ben's knee as he slowly pulled the small letter from the envelope. This time, he read it out loud to her immediately rather than reviewing it on his own first.

> Addy, I'm so very sorry I've been out of
> contact for a while, and I'm overtaken
> with sadness at your news. My life has
> recently changed in profound ways, but
> none of that is important now. You have
> my firm guarantee and promise that I
> will do whatever it takes to turn this
> situation around. I won't let him die.

Stunned, Ben fell silent, and they stared at each other. Callie could feel Ben's heart pounding, and he breathed irregularly for a moment before finishing the letter.

> I can't tell you more than that, and I may not

be able to contact you for a while after this, but all that matters is that he pulls through. If possible, I will visit you in the next few days before I take action on this situation. Sincerely, T.T.

"Ben!" Callie gasped. "This has to be your father! Do you think he was Succouri? Do you think he's the one who donated marrow?"

Covering his face with his hands, Ben tried to focus through the disorientation and confusion caused by this unexpected turn of events.

Lowering his hands, he shook his head. "He couldn't be. If he were about the same age as my mother, he'd only have been about thirty-three when I had the transplant. Even if he'd become Succouri, he wouldn't have reached the ripening stage by then for sure."

"Maybe he knew one that was, I mean, a Succouri that was ready to donate," she said, squinting as she tried to solve the mystery.

"But," Ben shook his head again, "Everyone's told us no Succouri would ever do this, ever donate to a child like that. The ones we've met didn't even believe it to be possible. And, even if he convinced one to do it, why would they do it anonymously and leave me in the dark like that?"

"And then," Callie added, softening her voice as she tried to ease Ben's turmoil, "how would he work out the whole problem with the hospital finding out that the donor wasn't, well, normal, and how would the marrow match and..." Callie trailed off as the idea of his father being a Succouri or knowing the donor suddenly seemed out of the question.

"So, if we assume that T.T. is your father" – she tried

again after a moment of silence – "what was he talking about here, and why was he so confident in his ability to help you?"

"I don't know."

Retrieving the envelope, he once again stared at the postal date. "Callie, this is almost exactly when my transplant was. I can't remember the exact date, but I'm sure this is very nearly it, maybe a few days off, if that."

Callie sighed and rubbed her forehead, trying to still the dizzying thoughts. "Okay, maybe we just need to put together the things we can conclude with some certainty from these letters."

"I think," Ben started, the words halting and strained. "I think T.T. must be my father. The timing of these is right and the tone too."

"I agree." Callie nodded.

"So, my mother knew who he was; that's settled for certain. It also seems they had some consistent contact with one another, at least about me, though"—Ben paused—"my father didn't seem to want or feel he was able to be in my life."

"What did he say in the first letter? Something about wanting more, but it not being 'prudent'?"

Ben retrieved the first letter and scanned it. "Yes, that's the exact word. Who knows what that means? It could just be an excuse or justification for his lack of involvement," Ben said a little bitterly.

"Maybe, but it doesn't sound like that. This letter was sent when you were"—she paused for a moment to do the math,—"about eight. It almost sounds like this is the first contact with your mother."

"That would be close to the age when I started asking her about my father."

Callie drummed her fingers on her knee as she thought. "Then I wonder if this is when your mom told him of your existence. I don't know; it's just a strange letter to write if he'd previously known about you."

Ben nodded in agreement as he continued to stare at the letter.

"So, assuming he wanted contact, which is what it sounds like from the letter, what would have prevented him from it? I mean, why wouldn't it be prudent?"

"And why the hiding?" Ben added. "Why not give your name and a return address? It sounds like my mother knew where to find him or had given him some information about me, so why the secrecy since she likely knew the information anyway?"

They fell silent as neither had answers to these pressing questions.

"In the last letter, he refers to a visit," Callie noted. "That must be the one where Rosa and Leo saw him. They said he never came again after that. He indicated that helping you would cut him off from communication with your mother somehow. That's strange too."

Rising, Ben paced frustratedly. "There's just too many holes here. I wish my mother had left me a letter. I've always thought it odd that she didn't. If she knew she was going to... not going to be around anymore, why not tell me about all of this; at least leave me something?" Anger mingled with hurt at his mother's lack of provision for him, even in death.

As there were no good answers to Ben's questions, Callie changed the subject, trying to move Ben past the difficult moment. "I think our next step might be to contact the hospital and see what records we can find of your transplant. Likely, we won't get a donor's name, but maybe we could see if the doctor might speak with us about the circumstances surrounding the donation."

Returning to the couch, he flopped down defeatedly beside her. "I don't know that we've made much progress here. We still don't really know anything."

Callie turned and softly encircled his hand with both of hers. "Specifics, no; we don't have many of those. But, Ben, we know your father knew about you and was interested in your well-being. When he found out you were sick, though we don't know what exactly he did or how, he desperately wanted to help you, he was determined to do so. Somehow, he felt that being in your life wasn't a good thing for you, so he kept his distance, but he cared, Ben, he cared deeply about you; that's hope worth hanging onto."

Turning toward her, he put his arm around her shoulders.

After a moment, he abruptly straightened, stood, and returned to the gathered items next to the bed. She waited, hearing the shifting of papers and files. Then he returned to the couch, carrying something in his hand.

"I was thinking," he started as he sat beside her. "I was wondering why there were only two letters. If my mother was communicating with T.T., providing him with updates about me, shouldn't more have come from his side than just these two?"

Callie tilted her head. "It seems so, but..." The incomplete statement hung in the air as a question.

"When I was looking through the files, I found this but didn't think anything of it until just a moment ago." Ben touched her hand, and Callie saw he held a small brown envelope. The number 23 was written on the outside.

Opening the flap, he turned the envelope upside-down, dropping something into his hand. Staring at the item, he was still for a moment before passing it to her. It was a small key, and Callie turned it around several times as she tried to discern the connection Ben was making between their discoveries about his father and this item.

"Post office box or... safety deposit box?" she finally exclaimed.

"When my mother died, I got all her records, inherited all her accounts, and was informed of the extent of her possessions. The lawyers were meticulous and detailed. But, Callie, I don't remember anything about a box."

"How do we know where this is? I mean, which post office or bank?"

"I can make some calls. If it was in her name, I should be allowed access since I'm the designated heir."

"It's worth a try."

For the next hour, Ben and Callie separated, each making their phone calls. Callie called Lee again, updating him on the latest news and the progress of their search, and Ben made a series of calls, first to the hospital where he'd had his transplant and then to several nearby post offices and banks.

Shortly before dinner, Ben led Callie to their favorite gray couch, and they reclined comfortably while filling each other in on their phone conversations.

"Lee's worried about both of us. I didn't give him all the details, but he knows me too well, so he read my voice. We're his only family now, and he feels helpless being so far away. I can tell he's itching to join us here, but there's no way I'd let him."

"Agreed. No need to put another LeVray in harm's way. Have there been any problems, threats, anything like that?"

"Thankfully, no, and since we know my shooter's not there anymore, they're easing security around him, though Ms. Essie will, I'm sure, be keeping a solid eye out."

Ben nodded.

"Any luck on your end?" Callie asked, trying to bridle her intense curiosity.

"Yes and no," Ben answered, wobbling his head between a nod and a shake. "I found the bank where the safety deposit box is located, and evidently, someone is still paying for it, though I'm confident it isn't coming from me or the estate, so..."

"Your father?" Callie gasped.

"Perhaps. They wouldn't give me the names on the account over the phone. The location is on our route for tomorrow, so on the way home, we can go by and check it out. They acknowledged my right as heir but, interestingly, my name was already listed on the account as someone who could gain access, even without that provision."

Surprise registered on her face, mimicking his own initial reaction to the news. "Wow! That's... that's progress for sure and may confirm your instincts about how your parents communicated."

"Maybe," Ben said, sounding skeptical. "I just don't understand why my father would keep paying for it after my mother died. I mean, there wouldn't be any more letters or messages from her end, so why keep it? And if my name was on the account, why didn't anyone ever tell me about it? None of this makes sense. I feel like I'm missing a big, important piece of the puzzle here."

Ben rubbed his forehead, and though it wasn't possible for him to have a headache, all the questions were overwhelming his mind and causing him to feel dizzy.

Callie leaned against him, and her warmth eased the stress brought on by all the unknowns.

"Maybe there will be something in the box that can answer our questions," she offered. "There must be a reason that your father kept it going and, maybe this is a way you could reach out to him; put your own letter in the box if you're interested in doing that?"

The possibility she presented caught him off guard. He hadn't thought about that. If he did discover that his father held the other key and paid for the continued reservation, would he want to reach out to him? He knew so little at this point, and despite his unexplained excuses, it was hard for Ben to get past the fact that his father knew about him but never reached out or involved himself in his life. Though he sadly now knew this was not a possibility, Ben was unwaveringly sure that if he'd ever become a father himself, he would have moved heaven and earth to be fully involved in his child's life.

Kindly offering him some space on this subject, Callie switched gears. "And the hospital? Any luck there?"

"Some. I confirmed the exact date of my transplant, and it was four days after that letter was postmarked. I also got the name of the doctor who performed the procedure, Doctor Roy Clemens." Ben couldn't help the disdain that crept into his tone when he spoke the man's name. "He's retired now and the hospital offered to reach out to him for me, but I'm pretty much at the mercy of whether he chooses to call me back. Given what I remember about him, I'm not holding my breath."

"Can you get a copy of your records?" Callie asked as she stroked the back of his hand.

"Yes, but they let me know that neither the identity nor any detailed information about the donor would be included, and it will take thirty to sixty days to make them available, so no quick answers there."

They were silent for a moment, though Callie continued to gently stroke his hand.

"I know it feels like we haven't made progress because we now have a lot more questions than we did this morning but, Ben, we've actually made tremendous strides today. We likely know the initials of your father's name, that he knew about you, that somehow he was involved in your transplant or at least knew of your illness, and that there's a safety deposit box where you might be able to communicate with him. That's a lot, a whole lot more than we knew a few hours ago."

Though he knew Callie was right, it was hard to feel any satisfaction in their discoveries when everything they'd learned was inconclusive and only led to more questions.

When he let out a defeated exhale, Callie turned to kiss him on the cheek. "Are you alright?" she asked as she looked into his eyes.

"I'm confused, but I think I'm alright," he reassured her. "I couldn't do this without you. Thank you for your strength and help as we sort through this tangled mess."

Kissing him again, she smiled lovingly, anchoring his heart to something solid and real.

As they moved into the dining room to join Leo, Rosa, and Donovan for dinner, Callie whispered softly in his ear. "Whatever I've got is yours, Ben Sawyer. My strength, my heart, all yours."

As he smiled and squeezed her hand in response, he thought about the little black box he'd entrusted to Rosa's care. He hoped, very soon, Callie might be willing to make that promise official and permanent.

CHAPTER 14

THE DOCTOR

That night, as they lay together in Ben's old room, keeping some distance but not being quite as cautious as the night before, knowing that Ben's Succouri nature would eventually draw them together anyway, Callie spoke up, her voice breaking the silence of the night. "I was thinking, wondering…"

Ben chuckled. "That has been the general state we've been in all day."

"Well, I think this is something you will be able to answer for me," she said with a smile.

"Good. It would be nice to offer a firm answer about something."

"I know your mother knew about your gift, though neither of you understood exactly what it was, but how did she explain it? I mean, she had to have been frantic trying to figure out what happened to you."

Ben didn't speak immediately as he thought about how to answer her question.

"Callie," he finally said, offering a resigned sigh before continuing, "you have to understand that the relationship I had with my mother was nothing like the one you had with your father or the one you have with Lee. We weren't close in that way. At the time, I guess I thought we were, but now that I have other families and other relationships to compare it to, I realize what I had with my mother wasn't normal; definitely not what a son-mother relationship should've been. She largely lived her own life and was away much of the time. When I fit into her schedule, she spent time with me, but that wasn't often. A nanny raised her, so I'm not sure she knew what mothering was supposed to be like. It was truly only because of her depression that we connected at all, as her sadness often kept her sleeping all day or holed up in her room. I'd watch movies with her, sing to her, and hold her hand, and she cheered up, but it didn't last."

"But what did she say when you told her about some of your experiences, like the story about the baseball incident and other difficult moments like that?"

Again, Ben was quiet for a time, staring blankly at the ceiling. "You are the first and only person I've ever told that story to."

Abruptly, Callie sat up, crossing her legs as she turned to face him. "You went through all of that alone?" she asked, horrified at the idea.

Ben turned his head toward her. "My mother wasn't even here at the house when that happened and again, that just wasn't the kind of relationship we had. I helped her or tried to anyway. She loved my presence when she was sad, lonely, but..."

"Oh, Ben!" Callie put her hands over her face as her heart ached. She'd been under the impression this whole time that Ben had shared the burden of his confusion and pain regarding his secret with his mother, and she'd offered him some measure of comfort. Callie hadn't imagined he'd carried it all alone for the entire fifteen years. She knew he'd been isolated in his confusion for six years after his mother died, but she'd not understood that, until he met her, he'd never had any real help in his struggle, even as a vulnerable child. Her heart couldn't fathom how lonely and desperate that reality must have been.

"I... I didn't know," she stammered, unable to accept the truth. "I thought... I thought she knew all of it and helped you. I'm so sorry."

Ben reached across the bed and rubbed her knee. "I did have Rosa and Leo, well at least their love and kindness. As I said, we never talked about my secret."

"Then how can you be confident your mother even knew about it?"

"Because she felt better when I touched her. Of course, I thought I was relieving her depression, not just her physical symptoms, but regardless of that error, she noticeably responded when I held her hand, and I told her I could help people when I touched them. She never questioned that statement as her personal experience backed it up."

"But..." Callie shook her head, trying to understand the odd relationship between Ben and his mother. "Didn't she ask questions or want to take you to the doctor or something? I mean, if my child came to me and said he could cure people with his touch, I'd sit up and take notice and certainly want some answers."

At the question, Ben sat up, mirroring her posture as he faced her. He exhaled, and as he spoke, sorrow and regret dominated his tone. "That's because you would be a loving, caring, and fully engaged mother, Callie."

A sad silence lingered as they lowered their heads, each contending with heartbreak and shared loss.

At last, Callie raised her eyes, trying to focus on his face in the darkness. "And you... you would be a wonderful father, Ben, and I'm not giving up on that possibility someday, just so you know."

Gently taking her hand, he intertwined his fingers with hers. Her vision focused on his expression, sad yet contented as he gazed into her eyes.

"So, if you and your mother never really talked in depth about your gift, then she probably never told your father about it, assuming she even had contact with him at all after the transplant."

"Probably not," Ben acknowledged.

"So then, even if your father knew about the Succouri somehow, he may not know you're one."

"Not unless he was involved directly in acquiring the Succouri marrow."

After a moment passed, Callie kept ahold of Ben's hand but slowly lay back down as she continued to wrestle with her emotions. Ben lowered himself back onto his pillow as well.

"Just when I think I can't possibly be more inspired by you or fall deeper in love with you..." she whispered.

Ben turned to look at her with an appreciative but confused expression. "What do you mean?"

"I honestly don't know how someone who has gone through what you have, carried what you've carried, and spent years alone without support and guidance could turn out so... so wonderful, kind, compassionate, and warm. It's extraordinary!"

"Callie, you..."

"No. I mean, I hope I've helped you begin to heal, but I saw your heart the first day I met you. You've had this heart all along; Rosa confirmed that for me. You were born with a good soul. I'm just privileged to watch it fully emerge into the light. You may not have chosen the Succouri gift, but it couldn't have encountered a more suited match."

Ben turned onto his side, positioning himself closer to her. He took a deep, shaky breath, revealing the depth of his emotions at her words. "That's truly the kindest thing anyone has ever said to me, but please, please understand that if I hadn't met you when I did, if you hadn't loved me, accepted my secret, and joined me in this life, I'd be irredeemably lost right now; of that, I have no doubt. It is your soul, your heart, that saved me from utter despair, and it's your love for me that makes any of this – looking for my father and searching for answers about my past – worthwhile."

Turning onto her side to face him, she smiled and placed her hand tenderly on the side of his face, focusing on the moonlight reflecting in his eyes. "I love you, Ben Sawyer," she whispered.

Closing the gap between them, he came alongside her, raising onto his elbow as she rolled onto her back. He leaned over her to kiss her lips gently, stroking her hair as he gazed intensely into her eyes. "And I love you, Callie LeVray."

As they lingered in the intimate moment, the fire began to move and build between them, and they enjoyed its familiar presence for a few seconds before Ben smiled at her, brushed her lips once more with his, and then retreated to his side of the bed.

After a moment, Callie laughed out loud, and Ben turned his head.

"You know, when you don't need to protect me anymore, I'm really going to miss our late-night chats."

Ben chuckled, and she heard him reply so softly that she

wondered whether he'd intended for her to hear him. "Not for long."

BEN AND CALLIE had an early breakfast the following day before heading out for their appointment with Doctor Navarro. Rather than his Range Rover, Ben drove a Mercedes left in the oversized, detached garage on the property, faithfully maintained over the years by Leo. Since a description of Ben's vehicle had been one of the details revealed in the news story about the fire, switching it out for this one was a precautionary measure they'd decided on as they increased security.

Once again, Donovan followed them for a while, making sure they weren't being pursued before leaving them on their own. The weather had turned warmer, with temperatures above freezing, so the roads were slushy with the melting snow and water dripped from trees and rooftops, but traveling was smooth and easy.

A few minutes before ten o'clock, they pulled into the driveway of a tasteful countryside home thirty miles outside Cape Cod, and Ben turned off the engine. The house was remote, away from the main thoroughfare, with no other houses in sight.

"I'm not sure what I expected," Ben said, staring at the spacious but not overly extravagant home. "I guess I didn't realize we were meeting him at his house."

Callie smiled reassuringly at him. When he opened her door, she took his arm cautiously, determined to follow the doctor's request to avoid drawing anything from him for at least an hour before their visit. Ben wasn't as concerned about the issue, but he appreciated her thoughtfulness, so he cooperated with her effort.

As they walked together toward the front door, Ben was surprised to feel a little nervous about the appointment. He didn't know what to expect, and, realistically, he wasn't sure he'd learn much definitively, as no one they'd met thus far had ever heard of a Succouri like him. Still, a twinge of anxiety pushed some adrenaline through his veins.

A few seconds after ringing the doorbell, the front door opened, and an older couple greeted them with friendly smiles.

"Welcome, welcome. I'm Ed, and this is my wife, Silvia," the doctor offered enthusiastically.

Doctor Navarro was a short man with thick gray hair and suntan-brown skin. He wore stylish glasses that enhanced the intellectual impression that came with his title. His wife's hair was also gray, cut into a neat, short bob. She was several inches taller than her husband, and her skin was a lighter shade of brown.

Ben introduced himself and Callie as he accepted the offered handshakes. Knowing Callie couldn't see well, the doctor and his wife thoughtfully reached out for Callie's hand rather than expecting her to see theirs, and Ben smiled at the kind consideration.

After the initial greetings, they were led into a room near the front of the house where a sage green curved couch and two matching chairs were arranged in a near circle, positioned to maximize ease of conversation.

"I call this my office." The doctor chuckled as he gestured for Ben and Callie to sit on the curved couch while he and his wife took the chairs. "Sure beats meeting with people in a sterile examination room."

Ben smiled and nodded as the warmth of the people and atmosphere began to ease his anxiety.

"Your daughter, Elena, is so kind," Callie said once she'd

settled beside Ben. "She and Raul helped Ben and me in a tough situation."

"And they spoke very highly of the two of you as well," Silvia replied. "Though your story surprised them, they were inspired by it and the love you two have for one another, and I can see why."

Ben and Callie smiled appreciatively at the compliment.

"They filled us in on the basic details, but, Ben, it is hard to believe," the doctor said, shaking his head. "What I understand is that you had leukemia at age twelve and received a marrow transplant at a regular hospital. Then you recovered quickly and, shortly thereafter, began manifesting the Succouri gifts. Do I have all of that correct?"

"Yes," Ben said hesitantly. "But I had no idea what they were, and I only connected them recently to the marrow transplant. For fifteen years, until I met Callie and we learned about the Succouri together, I had no understanding whatsoever of what it was or how I'd come to possess it."

"Remarkable!" Doctor Navarro exclaimed, leaning back in his chair. "No one ever approached you, warned you, taught you?"

"No, no one."

"And you had no bonding until you met Callie?"

Ben nodded. "Right. Actually, I knew nothing about the bonding, so when I met Callie and it all started happening, we were baffled and overwhelmed by the experience." Ben looked over at Callie and saw her smile in recollection, as he also did.

"I can imagine," the doctor chuckled. "And it was Ms. Essie and Louis who filled you in on who you were?"

Ben stared, surprise showing on his face as he hadn't

mentioned Ms. Essie or Louis to Doctor Navarro or Raul and Elena.

"I received a phone call from them just before you called me. We're old friends," the doctor explained. "It's a very small and tight-knit community, Ben. They didn't know about you meeting my daughter, of course, but they told me a little about you and that you wanted to connect with the Succouri network in hopes of finding some answers. It's a great coincidence that fate had already made that connection for us."

"Yes, it is," Ben agreed, still bewildered.

Ben filled the doctor and his wife in on everything he knew: the hospital where he'd had the procedure, a little about his family background, and even the recent incomplete but possibly connected discoveries about his father.

"You don't know his name?" Silvia asked.

"No, only what we think might be his initials. We hope to learn more later today when we follow up on a potential lead. Would you happen to know anything about a Succouri donating marrow around that time?"

"I have only been aware of the Succouri for ten years, involved in working with them directly for eight, so this would have been before my time, but I will inquire through some contacts I have and see what I can learn," the doctor offered.

"Thank you, and if we uncover anything relevant to me becoming Succouri after following up on the lead regarding my father, I'll let you know about that as well," Ben said.

The doctor sat silently, processing the information Ben had given him for a few moments before speaking.

"Well, Mr. Sawyer, your situation bewilders me on several fronts. First, it has been the understanding of all who have researched this phenomenon that full human maturity was an absolute requirement for compatibility with the Succouri additive. The best we can understand it, the Succouri DNA, if you'll allow for that not entirely accurate terminology, comes alongside the human DNA, working as a partner. Even in the blood, we can observe the additive, but it *is* only an additive. The composition of the person's blood isn't changed. I can't say that I've ever known anyone who has tried to give the gift to a child, as the ethical ramifications of that are dubious at best. Still, the nature of the merging of human and Succouri biology in the simplest terms, doesn't seem compatible with one who hasn't fully matured yet. Then there is the issue of the secrecy. A Succouri in the ripening stage is compelled, by his nature, to give away what he has, but that's not just physical. I've been privileged to be a part of several transfers, including Raul's reception, and it is wonderful to watch the parental-like bond that forms between the giver and the receiver. A unique connection develops, and I don't understand how any Succouri would or could tolerate the absence of that experience when they're in that stage. Lastly, and this may be the most puzzling of all the quandaries, I don't understand how you survived, seemingly healthy and mentally sound, as you sit here before me, for fifteen years without the bonding. Bonding isn't an option for Succouri; it's an absolute necessity, both for his physical and mental well-being. The fact that you were so young and much of what is involved in the bonding wasn't really appropriate or possible for you as a child, complicates matters, but it doesn't explain how you managed to survive without it."

The doctor paused as he stroked his chin thoughtfully. "You may be turning a lot of what we thought we knew upside-down, Mr. Sawyer."

Blowing out a breath, Ben leaned forward, looking the doctor in the eye. "Well, then is it possible that I'm something different in some way? Like... a variety of Succouri no one has known about or even something else entirely?"

The doctor shook his head. "Not from what Ms. Essie told me. Why don't you tell me about your experiences using your gift, how it feels, what you can do, and maybe a little about your and Callie's bonding process, though I don't want to invade that sacred space any more than necessary."

Ben shared, as best he could, his experiences: the sensation of the draw, the kickback, the weakness he experienced, and the effects he'd observed. Callie offered her perspective as one who had received and benefitted continually from Ben's gift, both in the extreme, when she'd been shot, and every day, as he gave her sight. Ben talked about the fire and helping the child and Nathan simultaneously, and they shared the story of Ben's revival of Callie's father.

"Most of this sounds advanced for sure, but fairly standard in terms of normal Succouri abilities. Since you've had the gift for fifteen years, I would have anticipated this higher level of skill, though the stories never fail to leave me awestruck. Now, I won't ask you to share any details you don't feel comfortable divulging, but could you tell me a bit about your bond? How has it manifested, how long has it been in place, and what was its progression? Whatever you are comfortable with, remembering that all information shared here is confidential and will never leave this room," he reassured.

Trading off, Ben and Callie shared a sketch of the progression of their bond, starting with the simple sensation of heat in their hands, the rapid healing that they believed the bond provided for Callie after her surgery, the ability it had given her to drive, how the magnetism had helped them find each other after the fire, and their recent experience with the inaudible collaboration they'd undergone when trying to make an important decision. They kept private the passion and fire that the bond intensified between them, though they guessed that the doctor was likely already aware of this effect as it seemed like a typical result of the bonding. The doctor and his wife listened with great interest, and Ben observed as their expressions revealed more and more surprise with each newly relayed experience.

When they'd shared all they felt comfortable revealing, Doctor Navarro leaned forward and tapped his finger on the coffee table in front of him as he spoke. "Now, this is interesting," he said excitedly. "For as short a time as you two have been bonded, your experiences are quite advanced. It's almost as if..." He ceased tapping his finger and looked straight at Ben. "As if the bonding process is trying to catch up with the advanced stage of your Succouri maturity. To help you, give you what you need to function fully at your level, I can see how that would be necessary. An immature bond wouldn't be beneficial to a mature Succouri. Typically, a new Succouri finds a partner quickly, sometimes already having a spouse who instantly takes on that additional role, and the bond grows at a parallel rate with the growth of the gift. But Callie came along fifteen years after your reception so, in a manner of speaking, you two had fifteen years of catching up to do." Doctor Navarro chuckled delightedly at the idea.

"But I didn't use it much before I knew Callie," Ben explained. "Since I had no idea what it was, and I hated it due to that confusion, I avoided using it, so I'm not sure how advanced I really am."

"Even so," the doctor insisted, "having the ability for that long puts you in a different place than someone who's just recently received it. Not using it might have slowed you down a little, but not significantly. In a way, it's like a child growing into an adult. It happens whether they want it and cooperate with it or not."

"So," Callie interjected. "I want to make sure I understand. Are you saying what Ben and I have experienced with our bond is unusual?"

"Unquestionably, yes! For the length of time you've been bonded, very unusual," the doctor confirmed emphatically. "For example, while some magnetism is part of every Succouri bond, what the two of you described is extraordinary. It seems that your bond is not only providing Ben with what he needs but also filling in the gaps for Callie's visual limitations, making sure she has everything she needs to be a full partner in this journey. I've never heard of a bond's magnetism helping partners physically find one another as yours did after that fire. This manifestation is unique, and the need for this compensation is likely another significant contributor to the mature state that your bond is currently in. If Ben hadn't had the gift for such a long time when he met you, Callie, the level of his Succouri maturity wouldn't have been adequate to provide that compensation, though I openly admit that even with that explanation, it is still confounding. To offer a further example, the skill of transferring knowledge, as when the bond allowed Callie to drive, as well as when it enabled you to mentally collaborate, is a manifestation that requires a very high level of Succouri maturity and bond development, typically taking years to reach. We might conclude that, as Callie is clearly the perfect match for you, Ben, the fifteen years without a bond was the preparation time necessary to perfect your current partnership. It's astounding, but that's a word which certainly characterizes this phenomenon."

Doctor Navarro shook his head and grinned in amazement as Callie and Ben also smiled at one another despite their stunned expressions. If all those years of turmoil were part of the broken road leading him to Callie, to quote the song he'd sung to her only days before, then that was suffering well worth enduring.

"I don't mean to get too personal here," the doctor continued, "and again, forgive me for trespassing on sacred ground but, with the maturity of your bond, well... I know you two aren't married, and I don't know your moral convictions, but..."

Ben put up a hand. "It has been quite challenging for us, and that's probably as far as we want to go on that subject."

Though their efforts of late to maintain some boundary lines in regards to their physical intimacy had been a bit precarious, the doctor's stunned expression, which communicated his surprise that they'd accomplished the feat at all, gave Ben a renewed sense of pride in their accomplished restraint.

"Remarkable!" the doctor repeated, articulating each syllable as he leaned back again in his chair. "You two are indeed unique and unquestionably remarkable."

"We've faced many complicating circumstances, which haven't afforded us the privilege of focusing exclusively on developing our relationship or understanding our Succouri bond," Ben explained. "I won't get into all of that, but in very real terms, we've been surviving day to day."

"Yes," the doctor acknowledged, nodding. "Ms. Essie filled me in on the basics." The doctor's expression shifted, becoming suddenly serious as he focused on Ben. "Mr.

Sawyer, I have no doubt you're doing all you can, but let me just emphasize how essential it is to keep Callie safe, for her sake, of course, but also for you, for your survival as a man and as Succouri. I've had the misfortune of knowing one Succouri who tragically lost his partner." The doctor and Silvia's faces dropped in sorrow. "The consequences are terrible, indescribably terrible."

Ben put his arm around Callie's shoulders affectionately and protectively. "I assure you, anyone who wants to do her harm will have to take me out first," Ben asserted with no hint of compromise, and Callie trembled at the statement.

"Well," the doctor redirected, lightening his tone. "I'd say you're unquestionably Succouri, but a very unique one. Learning how this came to be will undoubtedly be the key to unraveling this mystery, but I'd like to take some blood samples and study them if you're willing. It might be that, by comparing your blood to that of a Succouri who came by the gift in the common way, we can learn something, maybe answer more questions."

"Yes, that's fine," Ben agreed.

The doctor rose, and Ben looked at Callie.

"It perhaps would be best if she stays here with Silvia while we draw the blood," the doctor suggested. "It's a little complicated with a Succouri and might not be much fun to witness."

Seeing the other question in Ben's eyes, the doctor added, "I can assure you, we have the highest level of security here. As you can imagine, that's a necessity. She'll be safe."

Ben turned to Callie to see what she wanted to do.

"I'll be okay, Ben," she said softly, but he could hear her alarm at the doctor's cryptic description of the procedure.

He squeezed her shoulder and turned to follow the doctor out of the room and down the hall, passing the kitchen and living room before coming to a locked door. Ben assumed it was to the garage, but when the doctor unlocked the door and opened it, Ben stepped into a room that bore no resemblance to a garage at all. It was as if he'd walked straight into a medical research facility, complete with white floors, hospital beds, expensive medical equipment, computers, microscopes, and even the wheeled stools you'd expect to see in a doctor's examination room. Ben whistled in amazement, and Doctor Navarro chuckled next to him as he gestured for Ben to sit on one of the beds.

"This is something, Doc.," Ben complimented. "Just a few weeks ago, I believed I was the only person in the world with this ability. It's still sinking in that there's more like me out there, much less that there's places like this that support the whole thing."

Patting Ben on the shoulder, the doctor smiled in understanding. "Well, in your case, you may not have been too far off with your original assessment. You've had quite a journey, and, in many ways, it's just begun."

Moving to a supply cabinet, the doctor began collecting items.

"Can I ask you a couple of questions while we're alone?"

The doctor turned and gave Ben his full attention. "You're wondering about the lifespan issue," he speculated.

"Yes, and the childless issue as well. Do you think there's any possibility either of those might not be the same for me, given my situation?" Ben tried to keep his tone even, but the emotions broke through, nonetheless.

Doctor Navarro took a deep breath and crossed his arms. "I'd be surprised if the childless issue was different for you. Unfortunately, that just seems inevitable with the acquisition of the gift, but of course, I can't say with absolute certainty. Since that's a part of this whole thing we can't pin down and scientifically explain, I'm not confident any amount of testing will provide us with a definitive answer on that issue. As far as the length of the Succouri lifespan, I'm very curious about that myself. We might be able to learn more about that through some of these tests, as there is a noticeable change in the amount and behavior of the Succouri additive as one matures. If, and this may be a big if with you, but if your blood is similar to what would be" he paused to chuckle at the next word, "normal for Succouri, then that might give us some educated guesses on the matter. You're unique, though, Ben, and I wouldn't take any previous forgone conclusions as necessarily applicable to you, at least not until we know a lot more."

Ben nodded in understanding, and the doctor turned, resuming his preparations as he asked Ben to remove his shirt for the blood draw.

A moment later, Doctor Navarro approached holding a strange-looking needle, and Ben raised his eyebrows as he stared at it.

"Okay," the doctor said with a sigh. "This is the not-so-fun part. Because Succouri heal rapidly, taking blood the usual way is impossible, at least if you want any significant amount. I, and some other doctors with me, have developed this special device with the needle inside of this tube-like barrier." He pointed to the relevant parts of the device as he continued. "This helps to hold the wound open so it doesn't heal before I can extract any blood. But it's not fun. Because of your quick healing, no anesthetic, even local, works, so this is just a grin-and-bear-it type of thing. Succouri aren't impervious to pain, as you likely know. It's just that rapid healing takes care of a wound so quickly that there's not much time for pain. I know you probably haven't experienced much pain for a while, so this might shock your system, but I'll make it as quick as I can."

"Go ahead, Doc. Do what you gotta do," Ben said with little more than curiosity.

Though he thought he'd been prepared, Ben soon realized that the doctor hadn't been exaggerating when he said the procedure would be painful. Ben found himself gritting his teeth and bracing himself with his free arm as the device pierced him, feeling like someone was driving dull-tipped nails into his arm. He thought of how Callie must have felt when she'd been shot, developing a new and profound respect for the pain she'd endured.

When it was over, Doctor Navarro patted Ben on the back. "I'm impressed with your grit," he praised with a smile. "We've got a good sample here. I'll study it and get back to you in a few days. Maybe you'll learn more on your end about your acquisition in the meantime, and we can put together a more cohesive and helpful analysis for you and Callie."

Pausing, he looked at Ben with curiosity. "Before we go back, I hope you don't mind, but I have to ask you, why haven't you married that lovely girl?"

Ben smiled as he glanced at the deep wound left by the blood draw, which was already beginning to heal.

"I do have plans regarding that firmly in place, but I was hoping to know more about my past and my unique situation before asking her, wanting her to have a fuller picture of what she was getting herself into before giving her answer."

Doctor Navarro laughed. "Ben, even if there are some significant findings from this blood draw, we won't be able to answer all of your questions. I guarantee you that beautiful girl doesn't care about your past, at least not in a way that would affect her answer. She loves you deeply; I see it clear as day in her eyes. Succouri bond aside, if you're waiting until your questions are all answered, and the unknowns are resolved, you'll never get there, and the two of you are torturing yourselves unnecessarily. I've been involved with the Succouri phenomenon for a long time so, doctor to patient here, as I guess I'm the closest thing you've got to a family doctor at this point, I prescribe allowing the bond to progress freely, or you're going to drive yourselves crazy as you try to fulfill your purpose with one hand tied behind your back."

Ben raised his eyebrows, not entirely understanding what the doctor meant. "But I want her to be safe first, out of danger, and more free to…"

"Ben," he put up a hand, "you'll never be able to guarantee that, even when they've caught this idiot. And anyway, wouldn't it be easier to protect her, or at least just as easy, if you were married?"

"But we've only known each other for a relatively short time and…"

Doctor Navarro shook his head, causing Ben to stop mid-sentence. "I understand that because you haven't known what you were for fifteen years, it's hard to think like a Succouri. Your human training has dominated your thoughts, actions, and judgments, and you've not had the necessary education on this whole other part of who you are. But, Ben, when it comes to your bond with Callie, you will have to begin to let the Succouri part of you control your decisions or at least have a much more substantial influence. My daughter married Raul two weeks after the bond was initiated, and they weren't anywhere near as advanced in the bonding process as you and Callie are. It's simply a different experience when you're Succouri, resulting in a completely different developmental timeline."

"But she's not Succouri," Ben protested. "I don't want her to feel pressured, like she has to move at my pace because..."

"Ben!" The doctor looked at him with bewilderment, raising a hand and shaking his head vigorously. "Callie absolutely *is* Succouri! Succouri is not one, it's two; the word itself is not singular but plural. You're not understanding how the bond works. The bond changed her, in much the same way as the transplant changed you. I've studied the blood chemistry of bonded partners and, though I can't explain the science of it all, the chemistry of the bonded partner's blood changes too. I know, somehow you've survived alone, so you don't understand the full truth in my words regarding the necessity of the bond, but trust me when I say, Succouri need both partners to function. Plainly, it's impossible for you to be fully Succouri without Callie. Though your roles are somewhat different, she is now just as necessary in the calling, the fulfilling of the purpose in the gift, as you are. She is in this with you one hundred percent. There's barely a degree of separation between the two of you, except what you're creating by stalling the process, hindering her ability to be a full partner with you."

"But she didn't volunteer for this," he argued, feeling freed and relieved at finally having someone to hash out all of these questions and doubts with. "I didn't even know what I was when I fell in love with her. It isn't fair to force her into a lifelong commitment this soon just because she fell in love with me too."

The doctor continued to look confounded and

dismayed by Ben's lack of proper training, but he exhibited sincere compassion as well, and he softened his voice as he continued. "It doesn't work that way. No bonded partner can be forced into a bond. The bond won't take if that's the case. Even though the two of you didn't know what was happening, she had to be willing and cooperative in order for the process to initiate. There had to be attraction, admiration, respect, and at least the seeds of love before the bond had any fertile soil in which to grow. And, for any bond to have grown at the rate the one between you two has, even with the way you've held it back, the level of genuine love and all the rest must be very very high. I promise you, Callie doesn't feel pushed, pulled, held down, or confined by her love and bond with you. She treasures it and benefits from it as much as you do. If she didn't, it wouldn't be growing and thriving like it is."

Ben took a deep breath, considering the doctor's words carefully. Though he still didn't fully comprehend all he was saying, he understood enough to give him plenty of food for thought.

"Thank you, Doc. I obviously have a lot to learn, but you've given me quite a bit to think about."

Smiling sympathetically, the doctor moved to store Ben's blood and remove his gloves.

CHAPTER 15
THE BOX

As soon as Ben and Callie pulled away from the Navarro home, Callie reached for Ben's arm. "Did it hurt?" she asked, her voice panicky.

Ben smiled, happy to be free to touch each other again and attempting to reassure her. "Not as much as getting shot, I'm sure, but it wasn't any picnic."

"Can I see?" she asked, already pulling up his shirt sleeve.

As she pushed it up past his elbow, revealing the spot where the blood had been drawn, she inhaled in surprise, and he glanced down at the wound. He had only felt pain for a few seconds after the needle device had been retracted. Still, as the injury was significant and deep, it was taking longer than usual to heal. Presently, it looked nowhere near as bad as it had immediately after the procedure, but Callie wasn't used to seeing any wounds or marks on his skin at all, so he understood her reaction.

"Why is it so deep?" she questioned, her eyes round with surprise.

"He used a special type of needle to take the blood

because of the whole rapid healing issue. It had to hold the wound open long enough to extract an adequate sample."

"And no painkillers?"

"Evidently, they don't work on Succouri."

After staring at the wound for a few more seconds, Callie gently ran her fingers back and forth over it, the action making his skin tingle pleasantly. When he glanced down at his arm, he was stunned to observe that the wound had nearly disappeared.

"Wow, Miss LeVray! I thought I was the one with the healing touch," he teased, but he was genuinely baffled.

Callie continued to stare at his arm for a moment before responding. "Maybe you're rubbing off on me." She laughed as she pulled down his sleeve and placed her hand on his.

Ben thought about Doctor Navarro's words as they traveled in silence for a time, each pondering what they'd learned from the visit. The doctor's statement that Callie was Succouri too, that the bond had changed her like the transplant had changed him, repeated in his head. He knew she was his invaluable partner, and he knew he needed her in so many other ways unrelated to his Succouri purpose and mission, but he'd never thought about her as actually sharing in his identity. As he considered his past and how long he'd walked alone with this ability, he recognized that old habits die hard. Even though his mother knew his secret, she didn't shoulder any of the burden or participate in his reality. Then, when she died, he isolated himself in his unique, unrelatable world. Though he hated being alone, always had, it was what he knew, had known all his life. It was hard to change the expectation that, no matter how close he got to someone, this part of him would always distinguish and separate him from others, even Callie.

But the doctor had, in the strongest terms, refuted that

notion, asserting that even the definition of the word countered solitude. Though unintentional, their love had changed them both, redirecting their lives onto an entirely new path. Though Callie had convinced him that she truly loved him and was willing to walk this road, he had still felt that he'd, at least somewhat, thrust her into this life, as loving him came with inescapable consequences. Perhaps the fact that this identity had been forced on him influenced his perspective. But, if what the doctor said was true, if she also saw herself as Succouri, maybe Callie didn't feel that way about it at all. The idea that she might perceive herself that way brought a sense of peace, as it eased the isolation inherent in carrying the identity alone. But, accepting that being Succouri wasn't a solitary experience was difficult as it required him to reprogram fifteen years of alternate thinking.

As he pondered, he heard Callie softly laugh next to him. "Am I missing something?" he asked, enjoying the sound of her laughter even if he didn't know the cause.

"I just... I guess I just find it funny that we seem to impress people with our... self-control, though I hardly feel like I have much at all." She laughed again. "How many times did the good doctor call us 'remarkable'?"

Ben laughed with her. "That did seem to be his favorite descriptor of us. I get the feeling that a month of dating in Succouri time is like five years of dating in human time so, given our... our patience, I suppose we should give ourselves more credit."

"I suppose so." She smiled flirtatiously at him. "I knew we were unique and that our journey forward would be as well, but it was a little surprising to hear how very different our short time together has already been in comparison to other Succouri couples."

"Yes," Ben chuckled. "I guess no one could ever accuse you or me of being predictable or normal."

"True," she agreed with another smile. "Do you remember, the first day we met, you told me that being normal was overrated?"

"I do." He grinned at the memory.

"I have this feeling no matter what we learn about the Succouri, we're going to be different, make our own path, and live extraordinary lives. Your statement may have been more prophetic than you realized."

"Well then, I suppose I should ask, are you still up for the life of adventure I promised you?"

"As long as you promise to keep holding my hand." She smiled, but there was a plea in her tone.

Ben looked at her, sincerity in his eyes. "Always." He pulled her hand to his lips, sealing the promise with a kiss.

THEY STOPPED to enjoy a late lunch, continuing to talk about their visit with the doctor, what they'd learned, and what they hoped they might find out from the doctor's study of Ben's blood. Ben didn't bring up the private conversation he'd had with the doctor, wanting to wait for his blood analysis before giving her any information that might end up being inaccurate. In addition, he got the feeling that Callie and Silvia had also discussed some subjects that Callie wasn't ready to speak openly about yet, so he didn't press her to share, though he was curious.

When they'd resumed their drive, nearing the bank where the safety deposit box was located, Callie finally broached the subject.

"Have you decided?"

"Decided?"

"If you find a letter from your father there, will you respond?"

Ben took a deep breath. "I'm doubtful I'll find anything like that, but if I do, I think it depends on what the letter says. If my father didn't know of my existence until I was eight, I can excuse his lack of involvement or interest until then, of course. But, once he knew, well... It's hard for me to conceive of a legitimate reason for continuing to stay away. If he's the type of man who doesn't take responsibility for his actions and refuses to own up to his mistakes, I don't think I want someone like that in my or your life, Callie."

"I understand, but..."

Ben looked over at her, waiting for her to finish her thought.

"I'd just encourage you to keep an open mind. We don't know anything about him yet, his life, his circumstances. And, well, I just get the feeling he really did care about you. In that letter, when he found out you were ill, he sounded heartbroken and desperate to help. It might be hard to understand given his distance, but until you know the whole story, please, just consider keeping the door open, at least a small crack."

"I'll try," he promised, appreciating her generous, open heart.

As he exited the car and walked with Callie into the bank, Ben felt nervous. Much closer to his former home here, the thought of Callie's shooter potentially being nearby put his senses on high alert. Continuously scanning around them in every direction as they entered the building, he kept Callie close by his side.

Inside, when he presented the clerk with his driver's license and the key to the box, he asked for the names listed on the account.

"It looks like there are three people listed here; well, two and then just the initials of another," the clerk answered, puzzled as he stared at his computer screen.

Ben sighed. "Let me guess; me, Adalynn Sawyer, and T.T.," he said defeatedly, as he'd been hopeful for a full name rather than the same nondescript initials.

"That's right." The clerk looked up in surprise. "I've never seen that before. Didn't know people could do that on an account."

The clerk led them to a small private room and retrieved the identified box, setting it on the table then quickly retreating, leaving them alone.

For a long moment, Ben stared at it, not sure what he hoped to find inside. Callie didn't press him, allowing him whatever time he needed to face its contents.

Finally, he took a deep breath and opened the lid.

To his profound surprise, a single item lay at the bottom: an envelope with "Ben Sawyer" written on the front. Since he knew his mother's handwriting and this didn't match, only one possible author remained.

Though Callie had anticipated this, Ben had not believed that there was any real chance of finding something from his father, so the reality of the letter caused his head to spin and his heart to constrict with a mix of emotions.

"You were right," he whispered shakily to Callie as he lifted the letter from the box.

She put her hand over her heart and Ben saw tears already shining in her eyes. Her voice was barely audible as she spoke in wonder mixed with sadness. "That's why he kept paying for it all these years. He wanted you to find this."

The consideration from a father he'd never known lit a weak flame in a distant, deserted place in his heart.

Slowly, Ben broke the seal on the envelope and extracted the single sheet of paper as they held their breath. It took his eyes several seconds to focus on his name at the top of the page, still unable to comprehend the truth that, for the first time in his twenty-seven years, his father was addressing him.

Clearing his throat, Ben tried to control his emotions so he could speak clearly enough for Callie to hear and understand him.

> Ben, if you are reading this letter, then one
> of my very greatest hopes is coming true.
> I'm trying to put myself in your shoes, to
> understand how you must feel about
> suddenly hearing from me after twenty-
> one years of silence and only after
> tragedy has shaken your world.

Ben looked up, and Callie inhaled, both recognizing that this letter was six years old.

> I'm so sorry about your mother. The pain of
> her loss also hits me hard, though I don't
> presume to compare my loss to yours.
> Though I've kept my distance from you
> out of sheer necessity and protection, I
> can no longer justify that position, no
> matter how noble the cause, as I can't
> abide the thought of you facing this
> tragedy or the future years alone.

Ben stopped to take an unsteady breath, and he turned to look at Callie, noticing fresh tears just escaping the corners of her eyes. Despite his father's wishes, Ben had indeed spent six years alone and lost in sorrow.

> I know you likely feel betrayed, abandoned, and forgotten because of my silence, but I want to assure you, in the strongest terms, that I stayed away solely for your good. I can't say more than that without risk, but I want you to know I've watched you, cared for you, and stayed as connected as I possibly could through this admittedly cold and crude means of communication. As you probably know, your mother wasn't very detailed or consistent in her correspondence. Still, she's provided me with some information about you and a few pictures over the years, and I've treasured each offering.

Now, Callie cried in earnest, and Ben's eyes grew moist as his heart pounded in confusion and throbbed with a strange new feeling of loss.

> I'm afraid there's still reason to fear, and I'm not willing to put you at risk, no matter how desperately I want direct contact. Still, if you're willing, if you're so inclined, I'd treasure the opportunity to continue this small yet infinitely signifi-cant connection with you. I know you're

a man now, no longer a child in need of
any parental guidance or interference in
that way, but I still love you, Son.

Ben lowered the letter, his heart feeling as if it was being filled, and then emptied repeatedly as the doubts mingled with the hopes. Callie reached for him, and he gladly pulled her close, unashamedly releasing a stream of tears into her hair as he clung to her for solid ground.

"I don't understand," he forced out through the tightness in his throat. "If he loved me, why didn't he ever see me? What was it that kept him away? This doesn't make any sense."

"I don't know, Ben, I don't know." She breathed unevenly through her sobs. "But he cared, he wanted to know you, and he always loved you."

The words burrowed deep into his soul, bringing something inside of him to the surface, something that had never seen daylight before. They remained in each other's arms for a while before Ben finally regained enough composure to finish reading the letter.

Someday, I will walk up to you and embrace
        you, and I can only hope that the small
        offering, which I was privileged and
        honored to give, will permit you to
        release enough forgiveness in your soul
        to allow me entrance into a small corner
        of your heart.
Presently, if your answer is 'no' and you
        have no desire to connect with me, I
        want you to know I truly understand,
        and I will leave this option open always

should you ever change your mind. Be
well and happy, my son. T.T.

"Ben!" Callie gasped. "He's been waiting for six years!"
Agony for the loss on both sides, resounded in her cry.

"Why would he assume that I knew about this box?"
Ben questioned, heaviness pressing in around his heart,
reminding him of how it felt during the fire rescue when his
lungs couldn't get enough oxygen.

"Maybe he thought you'd go through your mother's
things soon after her death and find the key?" Callie said as
she wiped her nose and breathed deeply, trying to regain
control of her shaky voice.

Exhaling slowly, Ben suddenly felt ashamed of his
behavior in running away. "Of course. I mean, we found the
letters and the key after only one day of searching. If I
hadn't run away, I'd have found them years ago."

"But, Ben, he didn't know! I'm almost certain now that
he didn't know you were Succouri. He didn't reference it in
the letter, only a cryptic mention of him helping you when
you were sick. I don't understand how he didn't know, yet
somehow was involved in your cure, but I'm convinced he
was totally ignorant of the pain and hardship you were
dealing with after your mother died and even long before."

"Even if he did know, because I ran, he wouldn't have
had any way of finding me as I didn't stay in one place long
enough to be found." A wave of regret hit him, nearly
pulling him under with its force. He put his head in his
hands, unable to think as he wrestled with the weight of so
much wasted time.

Callie rubbed his back. "It's not your fault, Ben. You
didn't know about any of this, and you were hurting and
confused."

Leaning back, he felt as empty as when he'd given all his strength away.

"It's not too late," she said, her voice gentle and compassionate. "It's definitely not too late. He's still paying for this box, still waiting."

"I don't know what I'd say," he sighed defeatedly. "I mean, I still don't even know his name."

"You don't need to say much. Just let him know you're out there and interested in connecting with him. It's just a first step; that's all it is."

Remaining still and quiet for a moment, Ben sorted through a tangled web of emotions: regret, fear, curiosity, hurt, joy, loss, and finally hope. Callie waited silently, offering her reassuring presence as he struggled to decide what to do.

At last, Ben rose and retrieved a piece of paper and a pen from a side table. After considering carefully, he settled on a simple reply, unsure of how long it might be until his father would read it but compelled to reach out, none-theless.

> T.T., Regrettably, six long years have passed
> while I was entirely ignorant of your
> message and this box. Truly, I only
> learned about you and your association
> with my mother in the last twenty-four
> hours. I regret the time that has lapsed,
> as it has undoubtedly caused us both
> undue additional pain. Since this is all so
> new to me, forgive my general confusion
> on the matter, as many complications in
> my current circumstance make
> processing this situation difficult. Still, I

am open to hearing more from you. I don't comprehend the distance for all these years, but then, running and hiding are not realities that I'm unacquainted with. I'm not planning on being in town for long, but I will recheck this box before I leave. Ben Sawyer

After reading his response to Callie, she smiled approvingly.

"That's perfect," she praised, unashamedly ecstatic at his choice to return the correspondence.

As they completed the short drive to Ben's childhood home, he tried to bring order to the conflicting information he now knew about his father. No matter how many ways he turned and twisted the new facts around in his head, he couldn't make them fit into the holes carved by previously established truths.

His father knew about his illness and pledged to save him, but it couldn't have been him who donated marrow as he was too young. And if his father had found a Succouri donor willing to give Ben his gift, his father would undoubtedly know that Ben had become a Succouri. Even if he had found a donor willing to do such a forbidden thing as donate to a child, how did he pull off having the procedure done in a regular hospital, and how did he convince the donor not to be involved with Ben after the donation? And then there was the most crucial question of all: Why would his father want to deprive him of knowledge regarding his identity, leaving him suffering in confusion and fear? The circle of questions went round and round with no resolutions or satisfactory answers.

Callie held his hand and he sensed her concern, but he

had no reassurance to offer her right now as the emotions were simply too fresh and overpowering.

When he pulled into the driveway and Donovan rushed up to meet him before he moved to open Callie's door, the look of alarm on Donovan's face abruptly refocused Ben's attention.

"Is everything alright?" Ben asked, staring into his friend's troubled eyes.

Donovan nodded, but his eyes told a different story. "Rosa's got dinner waiting, but let's talk afterward," Donovan said in a voice that sounded like he was delivering an apology.

"Are you sure?" Ben questioned, feeling like the matter must be urgent for him to look so uneasy.

"Yes. I know you two have had a long day and need to eat and relax. Right now, everything is under control."

As Ben stared at Donovan, trying to decipher the expression on his face, he noticed that, for the first time since reconnecting with his friend, he looked ill. His face was pale, and his movements stiff and sluggish.

Though he'd admitted to him and Callie that he was constantly in pain, Donovan never showed it. He walked like a man on a mission, always straight and strong, never betraying any sign of weakness. But tonight, his frailty was showing, subtly, but enough for someone who cared about him to notice.

As the three of them walked into the house, Donovan offered a forced smile. "Productive day?" he inquired.

Ben and Callie nodded, and Ben exhaled tiredly. "You could say that," he answered sarcastically. "You could definitely say that."

. . .

CALLIE FIDGETED with her fork at dinner, her consuming worry about Ben churning her stomach and making her lose her appetite. Rosa had worked hard to prepare a delicious meal for them, and she didn't want to hurt her feelings, but she couldn't force herself to eat more than a few bites.

Though there were five of them around the table, the meal was quiet, and Callie got the distinct impression that each of them struggled with their own thoughts and feelings, though she suspected the focal point was primarily Ben.

Rosa and Leo knew Ben well enough to interpret his facial expressions and body language, but they were also polite and discreet. Though they loved Ben as family, because he was their employer, they maintained respect for him as such, making them shy about inquiring about his personal matters without his open invitation. Callie wasn't sure what troubled Donovan, but his unusual silence told her things weren't right with him either.

As she continued to push food around on her plate and tune into her bond with Ben, keeping her heart open to what she might say or do to help him, her thoughts drifted back to her private conversation with Silvia that afternoon. When Ben left to get his blood drawn, Silvia asked Callie if she had any questions she wanted to discuss while Ben was away, and Callie eagerly took advantage of the opportunity. Though Silvia and Doctor Navarro weren't Succouri, their experience with them was vast, so the chance to learn from them was too good to pass up.

"I know you've only known Ben for a few minutes, but do you, can you see a difference between him and other Succouri you've known?" she had asked, trying to confirm or reject her own impressions, admittedly based on a small sampling of others.

"How do you mean?"

"Well..." Callie struggled to put her observations into words. "I haven't known many Succouri, but in the ones I've known, I can distinguish the human part of them from the Succouri part of them. But with Ben, I can't. I've recently discovered that even from a young age, before he got the gift, he had a natural personality that mimicked many of the Succouri qualities, so admittedly that makes it harder. Still, I just wonder if his early acquisition may have led to a merging of characteristics rather than more of a cooperation of the human and Succouri natures."

"Interesting," Silvia replied. "I'd need to know him better before offering an educated opinion, but I can follow your question. Ben is certainly unique and special. I can see in him the best of the Succouri characteristics: kindness, honesty, gentleness, and courage."

"Then if I'm right about the personalities merging, would it follow this might be true for him physically as well?"

"Hm," Silvia considered. "I'm not sure how that would manifest, but logically, if much of his physical maturity happened after his reception, yes, that would make sense."

Callie sighed. "I guess I worry about what that will mean for him someday when the gift expires. I know gradual weakening is normal, but if Ben's body and personality are intertwined rather than adjacent with his Succouri identity, how will he survive at all when that part of him is gone?"

"I see." Silvia let out an empathetic sigh as she comprehended Callie's concern. "I'll talk with Ed about this. Since Ben is most likely one of a kind, the only Succouri with this potential merging quality, it might not be possible to answer that question, but we can certainly ask it and see if anything we learn gives a hint of an answer."

"Thank you," Callie said, relieved to have spoken the worry out loud.

"You love him deeply, I can see that," Silvia observed, patting Callie on the knee.

Callie smiled. "Ben is extraordinary; there's no one like him. He's experienced so much heartbreak and confusion, but he's so genuinely good and noble. He's much more than I ever dreamed of finding in a man, but..." Callie lowered her head, covering her face with her hands.

"What is it?"

"Silvia, I'm terrified he's going to get himself killed trying to protect me. If someone came for me, tried to harm me, I have no doubt he'd jump in front of the danger: a bullet, a knife, a car, anything. He's already done so."

Tears of fear and dread formed in Callie's eyes. "I know I can't stop him, and I know he can survive a lot with his Succouri healing, but he's not indestructible, and I couldn't live without him." Callie's voice trembled at the idea of watching Ben die because he was protecting her.

Moving to sit beside Callie, Silvia placed a hand gently on hers. "I understand. I'm not going to lie to you. I believe he would; he has to, Callie. That's who he is; that's part of why you love him and also part of what we were talking about concerning the merging of Ben the man and Ben the Succouri. Succouri protect, save, preserve; it's their nature, and that instinct is never stronger than it is with their bonded partner."

A tear trickled down Callie's face as she wrestled with the truth. "I understand, but I'm afraid. I know part of this life is watching him suffer, helping him after he's given his strength away. I suppose I'm still learning how to accept even that part of it. I do wish there was more I could do to help him when he's weak or helping others. I know Doctor Navarro says we're advanced in our bond, but I think, in that way, we're not where we should be. It takes a long time to get him back to normal when he's empty, and I hate watching him struggle."

Silvia contemplated Callie's words before responding. "I know it's difficult to be patient, but I am fully confident you will grow in that area as the bond deepens."

Callie looked at her questioningly.

"You have the power to help restore him; that's your Succouri gift."

"*My* Succouri gift?" Puzzled at the statement, Callie squinted her eyes.

"Yes, of course. Now that you've bonded with Ben, you are as much Succouri as he is, though your role is slightly different."

"I..." Callie stammered. "I'm Succouri?"

Silvia laughed. "Yes, you are! Forgive me. I forgot that you and Ben weren't taught about how this all works. Yes, Callie. The Succouri identity is comprised of two roles. In simplest terms, Ben's role is to sustain life with his touch, giving away himself to others. But your role is similar. You do that for him. You two might not have fully developed that aspect yet, and sometimes, it's simply hard to measure what you're offering him, but you will see it at some point and understand how you can best use your own gift. Watch his reactions and do what feels right in the moment. Your own ability and gift will surprise you."

· · ·

As they sat in silence around the table, Callie smiled at Silvia's timely words. Despite the challenges of the day, her heart filled with excitement as she recalled observing the power of her touch as it increased the healing rate in Ben's wound from his blood draw. Though Ben had been focused on driving and his own thoughts, unable to fully appreciate the miraculous experience, she'd sat awestruck, noting how, with each stroke of her finger, the wound had dramatically progressed in its healing. A lightbulb switched on as this visible demonstration of her own ability offered her clear and tangible evidence of what she offered Ben.

As Silvia had said, in many ways, it was similar to what he gave others, but different too. Ben's touch temporarily healed, but when he let go, the bodies of others couldn't hold on to the healing. But her touch reflected his own gift back to him, and his body was capable of permanently absorbing the cure.

Like wrapping oneself in a blanket to keep warm, the beneficial heat doesn't come from the blanket itself but from the person's own body. The blanket simply holds the heat in, allowing a person to take full advantage of what his body is already providing.

Callie was like the blanket for Ben. Her close physical connection with him enabled his body to reap the benefits of the healing power it already produced. The healing originated with him, but her role as the only one who enabled him to receive back what he gave out was unmistakably essential. He could eventually recover without her help, but much more slowly, and the connection provided by the assistance she offered was deep and meaningful.

Suddenly, she understood Elena's statement when she said Ben helped others, but Callie helped him. She was

Ben's Succouri, but even better as her touch cured him; the healing remaining viable even after she let go.

Joy overflowed at the purpose and wonder this new, clear understanding brought to her heart. Not only did she share a love with him, but she also shared in his identity. From his reaction in the car, Callie knew he was puzzled by the experience and didn't comprehend what had occurred. With everything he faced today, the timing wasn't right to share her enthusiasm, but privately, she was elated by the change this knowledge made in her perception of her role in their future together.

CHAPTER 16

THE DARKNESS

Ben's mind was a jumble of questions and quandaries as they finished eating and moved to help Rosa with the cleanup. He noticed that Callie, like himself, hadn't eaten much, the events of the day robbing them of their appetites. In addition, Ben's concern for Donovan was growing.

Even in the short time they'd spent at the dinner table, Donovan's condition had visibly worsened. He was pale, and every movement appeared laborious. On top of that he nervously and continually watched the feed on his phone from the cameras and various security measures around the house.

As soon as the cleanup was complete and Rosa and Leo had departed for their private residence, leaving the three of them sipping tea or coffee around the kitchen island, Ben addressed the issue.

"Alright, my friend, what's going on?" Ben asked as he settled himself across from Donovan and next to Callie.

Avoiding eye contact with him, Donovan stared unfocused at nothing in particular until finally letting out a resigned breath and looking Ben in the eye. "Regrettably, I need to step away for a bit, but I've got someone coming tomorrow to take over security here. He's very competent, Ben, and he'll ensure your and Callie's safety."

"That's fine, Donovan, but that's not what I meant. What's going on with you? You don't look well."

Callie's expression shifted to a look of concern as his words seemed to pinpoint the source of a problem she'd been trying to identify.

"I'm not," Donovan confirmed, and Ben could hear the disdain for his weakness. "I need to check back into the hospital for more treatments. I don't want to leave you vulnerable here in any way, so..."

"I'm sorry," Ben whispered, lowering his gaze. "You don't know how much I wish my gift could permanently heal."

Placing her hand on Ben's arm, Callie lent her support to him as she spoke to Donovan. "Is there anything we can do? Anything at all?"

Donovan offered a weak smile. "Well, ma'am, I could use a new kidney and a few other spare parts if you've got them lying around."

Though Ben knew he was joking, the comment sparked an idea. Perhaps there was a way to help his friend, but that particular solution would change Donovan's life forever.

"Ben, I'm kidding," he said, noticing Ben's contemplative expression. "I doubt they'd give me a kidney as there are too many other things going awry to justify accepting a donation."

Glancing over at Callie, Ben noticed her face held the same expression as his. This wasn't something they could talk to Donovan about until they knew if the idea was even a possibility, but the thought ignited some hope in him, and he could see it did in Callie as well.

Ben turned back to Donovan. "We will do everything we can to help you; you know that. You name it, we'll make it happen."

Though he smiled appreciatively, Donovan dismissed Ben's concern with a wave of his hand. "Right now, let's focus on keeping you two safe. There has been some news on that front. There is some indication Ruiz might be in the area, so we need to tighten things down and remain within the boundaries of our security here until they apprehend him. In some ways, this is a good thing as the chances are better of catching him since we know he's close and we know what he's after." He offered an apologetic grimace before continuing. "Agent Taylor's passionate about this case. He's tracking the situation twenty-four seven. We're lucky to have him on board as he's an outstanding agent with a ton of beneficial experience."

"Alright," Ben sighed. "We'll stick around the house for the time being."

"My replacement will be here at eight a.m. tomorrow, and I'll get him up to speed before I leave and..." As Donovan spoke, he rose from his chair, and Ben watched his face turn ghostly white.

Ben jumped up and rushed to him, just in time to catch Donovan before his head hit the tile floor. His body convulsed several times, and Ben struggled to hold onto him so he wouldn't injure himself further.

Gasping, Callie came and knelt beside Ben. He lowered Donovan's head to the floor so he could push up his sleeve and grasp his arm with both hands.

"Ben!" Callie cried out. "I'll call 911."

As Ben waited for Donovan's body to relax and the draw to hit him, his mind ran through the complications in this situation. For the ambulance to get here, Ben would need to drop the security grid and open the gate, and while they were engaged in helping Donovan, no one would be monitoring the cameras or the sensors' feedback. With the news that Ruiz might be nearby, disarming was the last thing they should do, but there wasn't a choice right now. His friend's life had to take precedence.

When the draw hit him, it was powerful, and Ben immediately refocused on the task at hand. He helped Callie as she directed the emergency dispatcher on where to go, and he watched for Donovan to respond to his touch.

It took a full minute of steady draw from him before Donovan's body relaxed and his eyes opened.

"How long?" Ben asked Callie, knowing he couldn't sustain this level of draw for more than a few minutes.

"They're saying ten minutes," she answered, fear and worry for both of them causing her voice to shake.

"Have them tell you when they're about two minutes out. I'll need to drop the security and open the gate."

"No!" Donovan forcefully interjected, and Ben looked down at his anguished brown eyes. "Ben, don't! No one's watching the cameras. Dropping our defenses is not an option."

Ben smiled reassuringly at his friend, overwhelmed by the strong draw but relieved at the color returning to his face. "Aren't you the one who said that saving lives is always worth the risk?"

"At least let me make a call and get some backup here," Donovan pleaded.

Nodding, Ben held tightly to his friend as he placed several calls. Because of Ben's temporary cure, Donovan's voice was steady and clear, which appeared to be making it harder for him to convey the urgency of the situation. Ben guessed that was the reason for Donovan's irritated grunt when he hung up the phone.

"You need to relax," Ben implored, his voice weary as his hands began to tremble from the strain. "I know it doesn't feel like it, but your body's undergoing trauma, and you need to stay still and calm."

Besides the way he helped Callie daily and his experiences with his mother, Ben couldn't remember a time when he had helped someone who already knew about his secret. Typically, he had to contend with the shock of the person he was assisting as they reacted to his unbelievable ability, in addition to the strain of the draw itself. In this case, however, Donovan's lack of surprise, as well as his grave concern over leaving them defenseless, made him careless, forgetting that he was seriously ill.

"Are you alright?" Callie whispered next to him, evidently feeling the drain taking a toll on him as the trembling in his hands intensified. She still held the phone to her ear, waiting for the two-minute warning.

"For a few more minutes," he whispered back, smiling weakly as he attempted to reassure her, though he knew he couldn't hide anything from her.

"They're sending someone when they can," Donovan fumed. "It might be a while. You can't drop the security, please, I'll be fine and..."

"You won't be fine," Ben said emphatically. "You don't understand; that's not how this works. It's not a cure, remember? When I let go, it will all return to how it was.

We have to get you help, and they have to be able to get in here."

Donovan gritted his teeth, angry at the situation and the unavoidable actions they were being forced to take.

Ben's hands shook violently, and he felt the weakness of the draw setting in. When he took a deep, shaky breath, Callie set her hand on his shoulder, being very careful not to contact his skin. At her touch, Ben felt a slight retreat of the advancing weakness.

"Callie," he turned to whisper to her, trying not to worry Donovan. "That's helping, thank you."

Surprised, she leaned closer and put her hand flat on his back. The change was slight but significant as he held his ground to keep Donovan well a bit longer. They'd never done this side by side together before, except for when he'd revived her dad. At the time, Ms. Essie had told Callie not to touch him, but she'd only meant to avoid skin contact, and their bond was also not as well developed then. Ben wondered if, with the new depths their bond had reached in the last few days, there might be a change in Callie's ability to assist him.

"Just for a moment, try touching my hand," Ben requested, his voice thin and weak.

"Are you sure?" she asked hesitantly.

"Yes. Just for three or four seconds."

Scooting as close to him as she could, still holding her phone in one hand, she removed the hand from his back and set it on top of his.

A flood of refreshing strength, like a cascading waterfall drenching arid soil, soaked into him, and the positive counter effects of the kickback swelled. Callie stared wide-eyed and questioning at his sudden ecstatic grin. "You just stay right there, sweetheart," he said excitedly, his voice now strong and clear.

Callie inhaled in surprise at his words. "It's helping?" Her hopeful smile made her green eyes shine.

"Yes, a lot!" he confirmed, and Ben's heart overflowed with pleasure at her reaction as he wasn't sure he'd ever seen Callie look more overjoyed. Doctor Navarro had been right. Callie was in this with him one hundred percent. She was indeed Succouri, too.

The draw felt the same, but the inflow of strength from Callie's touch eased the weakness resulting from it, allowing his hands to completely stop shaking.

"This whole thing is amazing!" Donovan observed, shaking his head. "How is she helping you?"

"That's a little complicated," Ben answered, glancing at Callie with another grin. "We haven't told you about all the perks of this Succouri thing yet."

Callie turned her attention to her phone as someone began speaking to her, and she soon informed Ben that they were two minutes out.

"Okay." Ben pleaded with his eyes as he stared at Donovan. "I don't want to let go of you, so you have to use your phone to drop the security and open the gate."

"No! Let's find another way. It's not a good idea…"

"Please, my friend. I'll let go and do it myself if I have to, but I don't want to do that until the paramedics are here, so please. It will only be for a few minutes." Ben begged him as he couldn't bear the thought of watching his friend suffer while he fumbled with his phone.

"Maybe I'm okay now. I mean, maybe it was just a quick head rush or…"

"Donovan! I can feel the draw. It's not gone. Please,

trust me. Even with Callie's assistance, I can't hold on for much longer, so we need to get you some permanent help."

A few seconds of tension filled the air as Donovan struggled to decide, but at last, with a look of horror on his face, he raised his phone and awkwardly, working with just one hand, began disarming the security system as they heard the sound of sirens in the distance.

Ben breathed a sigh of relief. "We'll be alright," he reassured. "I'll get it back up as soon as you're safely on your way to the hospital."

Donovan's phone buzzed, and he lifted it to his ear, speaking to someone for a moment before lowering it again. "Someone's on their way from the FBI office, but it may still be a while before they arrive. I guess they finally decided to take me seriously. The request probably got up the chain to Taylor, who likely ordered the help."

When the sound of sirens approached the house, Ben asked Callie to go and unlock the front door, cautioning her not to go outside. She was familiar enough with his home at this point to navigate easily, even without his assistance, so she moved quickly to oblige.

Surprised by how strong the effects of the draw felt without her help, Ben knew it wouldn't take long before he became dependent on having her with him whenever he was needed in this way. With Callie replenishing his strength in real time, he wondered how much longer he might be able to maintain the draw when helping someone in distress; the potential in the idea thrilled him and opened new doors of opportunity in his mind. As soon as she'd completed her task, she returned, and since she was no longer on the phone, she placed both hands on his. Ben took a deep, relieved breath at the comfort of having her safely back beside him and at the resumption of her aid.

When the paramedics entered the house and Ben released Donovan to their care, Callie and he watched with grave concern. Donovan's condition deteriorated quickly, and Ben was thankful he hadn't let go sooner to disarm the security. The medics worked diligently, but their serious tones and frantic motions as they tried to stabilize him heightened their alarm. At last, satisfied enough with his condition, they lifted him onto a stretcher and proceeded to the waiting ambulance.

"We have to go to the hospital," Callie urged as she walked with Ben behind the exiting group, supporting him in his weakened state. "Can you drive?"

"Yes, I think so," he answered, but his voice revealed his internal conflict about leaving. He wanted to be there for his friend, concerned that his condition may be precarious enough not to guarantee his survival through the night. But, on the other hand, his priority was Callie and her safety.

"Callie, I don't know if we should..."

"He might need us again. And anyway, it may not be as safe here as before since all of the security is down. We might as well let the FBI get here and check everything out and get it all back up and running while we go and be with him."

She had a point, but something in Ben's stomach began to churn.

As they followed the medics, heading out the front door and locking it behind them, the warning dread he'd experienced before began to creep up his spine. Ben closed the small gap between himself and Callie as they approached his car.

They watched as Donovan was loaded into the ambulance. When the lights and sirens faded, the night hung heavy and dark around them. The clouds were thick, blocking out the illumination of the stars and moon, making the blackness feel like a foreboding presence lurking ominously just beyond the reach of the house lights.

Ben rushed Callie to her door, but as he reached for the handle, the sensation of dread hit him like a physical blow, and he moved to cover her with his body just as a gunshot resounded through the night.

The bullet drove deep into his upper left arm, and the pain burned hot for several seconds. Callie screamed as he wrapped himself more tightly around her, forming an impenetrable shield with her between him and the steel of the car.

"Ben!" she cried, squirming as she tried to free herself, desperate panic and fear in her eyes. But even with his diminished strength, he easily held her petite body in place.

"Ben, no! Please, don't do this!" she begged, pushing at him with her arms. But he held firm.

"Callie," he whispered, an unnatural calm filling his whole being. "It's alright, sweetheart. I'm sorry, but maybe this is why I met you. Maybe this is my purpose, to protect you, to be sure you would be safe. I love you with all I am, so I won't move. I'm never going to move."

Her body shook violently and her heart broke with his as she began to weep in unbearable torment at the nightmare playing out around them, threatening to separate them forever.

For just a moment, Ben turned his head, letting the corner of his eye observe a figure slither, like a loathsome snake, out of the black hole of darkness. The ghostly shadow moved into the light, revealing the same dark, hollow eyes and evil smile that Ben had once obscurely observed through the windshield of an old Dodge just a few days after he'd met Callie.

He held a gun rigidly in front of him, aimed directly at Callie, and he stared, unwaveringly, into Ben's eyes.

"Ben Sawyer," he spat, hate oozing out in his raspy voice. "We finally meet. You keep getting in my way, but I'm about to end that permanently. I hear you're a hero." He chuckled mockingly. "I wonder how many bullets it will take to kill a hero."

Again, Callie pushed at him, nearly hyperventilating as she struggled to breathe through her sobs. "No! Please. No, Ben!"

Ben considered lunging at him or trying to quickly open Callie's door and push her into the car, but he knew the second he left any part of Callie exposed, this serpent would strike with no mercy, and he was close enough to kill her with one shot. If he stayed where he was, he might be able to take enough bullets to continue shielding her until the FBI arrived. He likely wouldn't survive, but she might, and that was all that mattered to him, as he cared nothing about living without her.

"What kind of demented coward has to kill an unarmed woman to prove himself," Ben seethed through clenched teeth.

Ruiz laughed, an utterly ugly sound that made Ben want to vomit with its inhumanity. "An eye for an eye, Mr. Sawyer. Her father robbed a member of my family of any kind of life, so I'm returning the favor, though with more dramatics, I proudly admit. I *am* going to kill her. I'm more than happy to go through you if you insist."

As he spoke, he inched closer, and Ben pushed tighter

into Callie. Though he had no desire whatsoever to continue talking to this devil, he thought that he might buy Callie a bit more time with the back and forth, so he spoke once more.

"All you'll accomplish here, Ruiz, is to join your cousin in rotting away for the rest of your life behind bars. Much too good of a fate for both of you." Ben's anger boiled inside of him.

"Ben, please, please," Callie begged through her sobs. "Don't do this; I can't… I can't watch you die and I don't want to live without you anyway. Please, Ben, just let me go. He might let you live. I want you to live. I need you to live."

Ben turned away from the approaching monster, knowing nothing would dissuade him until he did his worst. Pressing his cheek against hers, he allowed sweet memories to carry them both away as the bond connected their hearts.

Beautiful moments filled his mind, mingling joy and pain as they advanced. He saw Callie encircling her small hand around his arm for the first time and her radiant smile as she stood in her black gown. He watched himself lift her into his arms and carry her through the snow, and he saw the tears drip from his cheeks onto hers as he knelt over her, his bloody hands covering her wounds.

As he tuned into her thoughts, he saw her vision focus on his face for the first time, and he felt her heart break as she watched him struggle while reviving her dad. He saw images of her tenderly washing ash off his body and combing gentle strokes through his hair. And he watched them embrace and kiss in the park after she passionately convinced him she was his forever.

He had wanted so much more, hoped for years with her,

memories to fill perhaps a short but meaningful lifetime with happiness. As he heard Ruiz shouting curses, sensing the moment of his decision to act drawing near, Ben breathed in her scent and let it fill him up, transporting him to a place where all their hopes and dreams would come true, and this terrible long darkness would end.

Clinging desperately to him now, Callie no longer tried to escape. "I love you! You're my heart, my everything! I'll never let you go. Never!"

Sobs shook her whole body, and Ben knew, in that moment, that he'd had a love like no other. Why had he wasted so much time? Why had he let anything get in his way? He should have married her, never counting on life to offer him a single day more and never forgetting all he had to lose.

As Ruiz finished his rant and took his final step, raising the gun just a few feet from Ben's head, he turned to kiss her, a goodbye kiss that shattered the night's darkness with the light of pure and enduring love.

Ben heard two shots and Callie's scream of terror, and he waited for the blackness to close in around him. One second, then another, and Ben felt nothing except her warm tears dripping down his neck.

One more second, and he felt her breath on his face. And then a hand tugged at his shoulder.

"Ben." An anguished voice called his name.

He blinked, and Callie's face came into focus, still terrorized but also stunned. He turned his head toward the demon who had been taunting him and saw his lifeless body sprawled out awkwardly on the ground.

"It's over, Son. He's gone." the same voice reassured.

Ben turned back to Callie, and he saw the light dawn in her eyes just before she pushed her way out of his grip and enveloped him in a blur of cries and kisses filled with relief and joy. She buried her head in his chest, sobbing with abandon as the terror of the moment before washed over them.

Holding her tightly against him, he stroked her hair, at first, not allowing himself to believe it was true, that they'd survived, and he had a second chance at every beautiful possibility he'd watched fade away. He breathed in and out, again and again, until he could accept the truth: they were alive, and Ruiz was dead, no longer threatening them, hiding around every corner, casting a foggy haze over their future. He closed his eyes, wanting to remember that moment of immeasurable gratitude forever.

Finally, he leaned back and encircled her tear-stained, angelic face with his hands, speaking her name in a voice that contained the truest and most tested kind of love. They stared into each other, letting their eyes speak what was too deep and precious for words to adequately convey.

When at last their hearts felt whole again, and they'd convinced themselves that the danger had passed, Ben once again pulled her close to him as the weariness from the night's traumas began to hit him hard. He leaned against the car, letting his back slide down the side of it until he sat on the ground, the full impact of the last hour pulling him down like a millstone had been hung around his neck. Callie fell with him, collapsing in exhaustion in his lap, her head against his shoulder as she continued to cling to him and he to her.

"Ben." A man with dark brown hair streaked with gray, squatted in front of them, looking alarmed even as he smiled warmly at their display of love and relief. Something about his voice was familiar to Ben, and he focused through the weariness on his vivid blue eyes. As there was no one else in sight, Ben knew this had to be the man who shot their attacker and saved both of their lives.

"Thank you," Ben whispered with a sigh. "Who..." Ben started to ask, but the man held up his badge, halting Ben's question.

"I'm Agent Wes Taylor. I've been working with your man, Donovan, on this case."

Ben nodded, trying to get his mind to work as the weakness began to ease as Callie leaned against him. Even as it did, Ben felt a strange continuous draw, like he was assisting someone, but it wasn't coming from Callie. It was emptying his strength almost as fast as Callie was filling it.

"How did you get here so fast?" Ben questioned. Though he wasn't sure how much time had passed during the trauma, he didn't think it had been long enough for someone to get there from the FBI office.

"I was already on my way here when the call came in," he said, looking down at the ground nervously.

"Tracking him?" Ben asked, gesturing with a nod toward Ruiz's body.

"No. Well, yes, I've been continually tracking him, but that wasn't what originally compelled me to come here tonight." Taylor's voice was unsteady, and Ben saw the glistening of tears in his eyes. "When I arrived outside the gate, I saw the old Dodge Donovan had described parked along the side of the road. Then, I noticed the gate was open, so I parked my car and came on foot to investigate, sensing something was not right. Catching him here and ridding the world of him was great luck and timing, but I was headed here for a very different reason, Ben."

Callie turned her head, and they both stared at him in confusion.

Taking a deep breath, Agent Taylor reached into his

pocket, retrieving a folded piece of paper and holding it out for Ben. "I came here tonight because of this."

Perplexed, Ben slowly reached to take it, and he held it in front of him and Callie. The folded page said "T.T." in his handwriting on the outside, and when he unfolded it, Callie gasped and sat up, putting both of her hands over her mouth. "Ben, your letter!"

Ben looked back and forth from the letter to Agent Taylor, bewildered.

"You're T.T.?" Callie asked in shock and delight.

Nodding, he smiled. "Thomas Weston Taylor," he said very slowly, his smile becoming fuller with each word. He switched his gaze from Callie to Ben. "I've waited twenty-seven years to meet you, Son, and I wasn't about to let that monster kill you before I got the chance." His voice shook, and a tear escaped down his cheek. "I never imagined I'd be this proud on the first day, though. What you just did here tonight has to be one of the greatest acts of self-sacrifice and love I've ever witnessed." He shook his head in wonder.

Stunned, Ben sat staring in disbelief. "But... I only left this letter today, just a few hours ago."

Agent Taylor chuckled. "I'm an FBI agent, remember? I've had a standing request with that bank to notify me if anyone ever inquired about that box."

"But I thought," Ben stammered, "I thought you couldn't see me... I mean, be in contact with me, except secretly."

Agent Taylor nodded, then lowered his head, his face shadowing. "That was true until about two years ago. It's a long story, but suffice it to say, even when it became possible to openly connect with you, since I never heard from you, I didn't think you wanted contact with me, and...

Well, Ben, you've been very hard to find, even for an FBI agent."

Lifting his arm, Ben rubbed his forehead, trying to process and accept that his father was here, right in front of him, when he suddenly heard Agent Taylor sharply inhale. "Ben, were you hit?"

When he glanced at his arm, he saw the bloodstain on his shirt. Then he remembered. He'd been shot just after he moved to shield Callie. The pain had almost instantly ceased, but he guessed that the bullet, lodged in his arm, was the source of the mysterious draw.

Callie gasped, panic igniting again in her eyes. "Ben, you were. We need to get you to..." She stopped speaking and glanced over at Agent Taylor.

"Why aren't you bleeding?" Taylor asked with concern, coming closer and reaching for Ben's arm. "Let me have a look at that."

He examined the dried blood and the hole in Ben's shirt, and Ben didn't have the strength or inclination to protest. If this was his father, he needed to know the truth.

Pulling at the hole in Ben's shirt, Taylor ripped it in different directions, trying to get a good look at the wound. Callie stared wide-eyed at Ben as he watched Taylor. The injury was there, healing slower than usual in his weak condition but still much more quickly than humanly possible.

After a moment of silent examination, Taylor let go of Ben's shirt and shifted to look into his eyes, deep blue mirroring deep blue. Seconds of awkward silence hung thick in the air as they stared at one another, neither diverting their gaze.

At last, Agent Taylor spoke, his voice distressed and confounded. "Are you... Are you Succouri?"

Holding eye contact with his father, Ben took a deep, slow breath, letting the question hang in the air for a long moment.

"Since I was twelve," he finally whispered.

Agent Taylor's face went white with shock. He abruptly stood and stepped back, covering his face with his hands as Ben and Callie watched in confusion.

CHAPTER 17

THE EXPLANATION

When the police and FBI arrived, Ben and Callie retreated into the house, and Ben called Doctor Navarro to inquire about his arm. After bringing Ben a glass of water, Callie continued to cling to him, still shaken by how close she'd come to losing him and desiring to offer him as much aid as she could as he struggled to regain some strength, even as the bullet wound countered the effort.

Though the truth of Ruiz's death and the end to the threat he brought to their lives had registered in her mind, she knew it would take a while for her heart to relax into the peace of that reality.

Before they had time to process any of that, they also contended with the shock of Ben's father saving their lives and now being available and ready to engage in a relationship with Ben. Just before being pulled away by the arriving team of FBI agents to deal with the dead criminal in Ben's driveway, his father expressed surprise and dismay at the revelation that Ben was a Succouri and had been one since age twelve, though he evidently knew about the Succouri and the rapid healing provided by the gift. They needed answers, and Callie knew that until Ben could understand what his father had done and why, he'd never be able to move forward with any level of trust in him.

When he finished his call, Ben blew out a long breath and leaned over to kiss her hair and stroke her cheek, and Callie was certain she'd never take for granted the blessing of his presence with her, touching her, and loving her. After coming as close as they had to losing each other, neither was willing to let go of the other for more than a few seconds.

"Well, Miss LeVray," he said, smiling at her, enjoying the pleasure of touching her as well. "Are you up for another trip to Cape Cod?"

"What did he say?"

"The bullet must come out. It's draining me as my body continually tries to heal around it but recognizes that it shouldn't be there. He warned me that the procedure will make the blood draw seem like a pleasure cruise in comparison, but..."

"Oh, Ben!" Callie squirmed in fearful anticipation for them both as there was no way she could leave him alone to face the pain this time.

"It'll be alright," he promised, lifting her chin with his finger to kiss her softly on the lips. His eyes sparkled with life and love, causing her heart to overflow with happiness. "We've already experienced the worst pain we could ever endure today, and we came out alive. No way this could come close to that agony."

She ran her fingers slowly through his hair, suddenly taking on a stern expression. "Ben Sawyer," she said in all seriousness, "don't you ever, *ever* kiss me goodbye again."

He grinned, but the expression held deep conviction.

"Don't worry. I plan to keep kissing you hello for many, many years to come." Demonstrating his intentions, he offered several soft, unhurried kisses that both relaxed and excited her heart with the promises they carried.

As she helped him to his feet and Ben gulped a last mouthful of water, Agent Taylor entered the kitchen.

As she'd observed when he'd introduced himself to them outside, Callie was again struck by how closely Ben's father resembled him. Though she'd struggled to find common features between Ben and his mother, besides the evident distinction in age, nearly every feature and expression between the two was noticeably similar. Callie could, however, understand Rosa and Leo's statement that Taylor didn't have quite the same soul as Ben. Something in the eyes, the mannerisms, the gentleness of Ben's heart was distinct. Perhaps this was the Succouri in him, but Callie suspected it went deeper than that.

"We have to go to Cape Cod," Ben informed him, keeping his voice low, not wanting to share the information with the large group of agents and police officers that had descended on his former home.

"I'll drive you," he offered with no hesitation.

"Well, I…"

"Please, Ben." His father's eyes pleaded for the chance to make a situation right that had long been all wrong, and Callie's heart hoped Ben would allow it.

"Alright, thank you," Ben relented, apprehensive but sincerely appreciative of the needed assistance.

Ben made a quick follow-up call to Doctor Navarro, requesting permission to include Ben's father in their visit. Once he heard that Agent Taylor already knew about the Succouri and Ben's identity as one of them, he offered it freely.

When Ben had retrieved a clean shirt and instructed Agent Taylor on where they were headed, Callie and Ben settled in the backseat where she could stay close to him in an attempt to balance out the draw of strength being caused by his wound.

For the first few minutes, they were all quiet, each overwhelmed by the events and revelations of the last hour. Ben stroked Callie's arm and back as he held her close, and she breathed in the pleasing scent of him as she leaned against his neck.

"Ben." Taylor finally spoke up, pain and regret in his tone. "I didn't know. I'm so sorry. I didn't realize that you... I didn't think that was possible. I mean, I definitely didn't intend to..."

Ben put up a hand as Taylor watched in the rearview mirror. "I think you'd better start from the beginning," Ben suggested. "And don't assume I know anything because there's very little I know or understand in this situation."

Nodding, Taylor took a moment to gather his thoughts before he began. "When I met Addy, I was a foolish, troubled young man, lost and adrift. I had no idea your mother had become pregnant from our encounter, but to tell the truth, at that time, I was too drugged out and self-destructive to have cared or offered you anything good. It was a wise choice for Addy to keep you away from me. For the next five years, my life spiraled as I fell deeper and deeper into my addiction to drugs, eventually becoming a dealer myself and gaining some respected status in that dark and dangerous underworld."

He paused to deal with the anger rising in his voice as he described his former life. When he continued, his tone was notably softer. "When you would have been about five or six, I was nearly killed in the street one day; drug deal gone wrong. I was stabbed multiple times and left for dead, which was exactly what I deserved and earned with my terrible choices, but somehow, fate and a man named Owen Briggs had mercy on my soul."

He smiled affectionately at the memory as Callie and Ben waited for more. "Briggs found me and revived me with his touch. I remember staring at him, totally bewildered by the lack of any pain or cold as he held onto my arm."

"He was Succouri!" Callie exclaimed, unable to contain her emotions as she engaged with his story.

Taylor smiled. "Yes, he was, and the kindest man I've ever known." Taylor's voice cracked with deep affection and sorrow, and Callie guessed that Owen Briggs had died, perhaps recently.

"I begged him not to call the police or the paramedics since I was wanted and had a criminal record a mile long, and he didn't. He took me back to his home, and he and his compassionate wife cared for me. More than simply stitching me up and cleaning my wounds, they eventually helped me to change, get off drugs, turn my life around, and in return, I dedicated myself to repairing the damage caused by the world I had once promoted. Briggs worked for the FBI. His advantageous position helped him to protect the Succouri and the network that supports the phenomenon. I don't understand why he didn't turn me in immediately as he had done with many other criminals throughout his career without a second thought. I have no idea what he saw in me that gave him pause, but I'm eternally grateful to him for sparing me. Once I was clean and had gained his trust, Briggs worked out a deal for me: forgiveness of my past crimes in exchange for working undercover with the FBI. I was the perfect choice, as my reputation and scars earned me easy reentry into that world. It was dangerous, difficult work, but I felt I owed it to myself, those I'd hurt by my prior involvement, and to Briggs to do all I could to set things right."

He paused to look at Ben in the mirror. "When I found out about you, I was deep undercover, associating with the worst of the worst, and there was no way I was going to let any of that near you, Ben."

Ben nodded, and Callie could see in his eyes he was softening his heart toward his father as the story unfolded.

"How did you find out about me?" Ben inquired, almost in a whisper.

"Addy reached out to my parents. To this day, I have no idea what prompted the sudden contact, but she found them, and though I was careful not to have much association with them either so as not to endanger their lives, they did know how to reach me, and they got me word. I asked them to deliver the safety deposit box key along with a letter that offered a vague excuse for why I was unable to be a part of your life, but also gratitude for her willingness to keep some association with me and provide me with occasional pictures and basic information about you."

"That must be the letter we found," Callie suggested, and Taylor raised his eyebrows.

"We found two letters from T.T. in my mother's things just yesterday, and they ultimately led us to the box," Ben explained.

"Why only yesterday?" he asked. "I would have thought you'd found those years ago after she died."

Ben shook his head. "Now, that's my story to tell, but you first."

Taylor closed his eyes, trying to remember where he left off. "I spent the next several years getting educated and trained under Briggs while still working undercover. Eventually, I worked my way up the chain of evil until I was really in deep with some of the worst demons on the planet. My work saved many lives, but it was risky and disturbing, being so entrenched in such deep darkness. I was driven by guilt, not just for my past sins, but for abandoning the son I now knew about but could do nothing for. From the moment I found out about you, Ben, I've wanted to know you. I knew your basic needs were being met, well provided for by Addy and the family riches, but I also knew Addy. While I'm sure she kept you safe, she wasn't... well, let's just say she had difficulty warming up to people."

Ben smirked as he nodded in agreement.

"The pictures she gave me were always so stiff, and I wondered if she ever let you have fun, laugh, be a crazy, wild boy, as every boy needs the chance to be?" He spoke the sentence as a question, and Ben shook his head in response. Taylor's expression shifted to sorrow as he recognized with regret that his fears had been well founded.

"In the end," he sighed, "your life and safety meant more to me than my desire to know you and even provide for you in those ways. I'd already chosen a path, a lonely one, one I couldn't share with anyone outside of the agency. If I'd been discovered, none of the thugs I hung around with would hesitate for a single second to come after you for leverage or revenge, as I guess you and Callie understand quite well at this point."

They nodded at the painful truth in his words.

"I worked under the supervision and instruction of Briggs for years, and he taught me everything I know about the FBI and kindness and compassion. He helped me to stay grounded as I interacted with evil and depravity. He was like a father to me, and his wife like a mother. Though he was advanced in years and didn't do much field work anymore, there were times I'd call on him to use his gift to save a victim, and the wonder of it never failed to leave me awestruck. Briggs taught me about the Succouri, and I became quite enchanted with the whole thing." He paused to chuckle. "After all, it did save my life. Because of his kindness and generosity, I developed a passion for protecting this secret treasure, often working alongside him as he guarded those under suspicion or in trouble. Just weeks before I found out you were ill, I was shot in an undercover operation that went sideways, and though it seemed I was recovering well for a while, infection set in, and I found myself near death once more. That's when Briggs approached me and offered me his gift."

At this revelation, Ben audibly inhaled. "So, you *are* Succouri?"

Taylor shook his head. "I went through the training, was taught all about what it entailed, and was given the choice. It wasn't a tough choice for me. I had so much admiration and love for Briggs, and I imagined all that I could do in my work to help and protect others if I had the gift. I think that's a big reason Briggs chose me. He wanted someone to replace him at the agency who would carry on his legacy, preserving and protecting the Succouri." He paused to chuckle a little sarcastically. "And since I was dying and the change would save my life, it was hard to say no. So, I accepted, and Briggs gave me his blood, which healed my infection overnight. But two days later, before any of it had begun to manifest in any way, I heard about your leukemia. I don't know why Addy waited to tell me until you were nearly at the end of your fight, Ben, but she did. The letter she left me in the box was desperate and heartbreaking, and I almost quit my job and revealed myself to you right after reading it, but quitting wouldn't have freed me or you of the danger. It probably would have made it worse. You can't just walk away from that world."

"So, I don't understand," Ben stammered. "What did you do?"

Taylor shrugged. "I didn't know what to do. Being Succouri was brand new to me, and my touch wasn't yet manifesting any healing effects, so I couldn't help you by simply touching you. I had to help you, had to do something, so I went to the hospital and got tested for marrow and, shockingly, I matched. I guess the odds are like one in two hundred of a parent matching. I don't know if the Succouri aspect influenced the test or what exactly the factors were, but I matched nonetheless."

"But," Ben protested, "how did they get a sample? I mean, didn't they figure out that there was something not right with you?"

"Well," Taylor smiled, looking a little guilty. "For one thing, the gift was so new that my body wasn't healing nearly as rapidly yet as, well, as rapidly as yours does. As you probably know, it takes a while for all of it to set in, and I was in this in-between phase, which helped with the suspicion. In addition, Doctor Clemens had a son who was involved in some substantial criminal activity, and I knew about it, so, I..."

"You bribed him," Ben said flatly.

"In a manner of speaking, yes." His voice held no regret at the choice.

"No wonder he didn't like me and was angry about the whole thing," Ben reflected, shaking his head again.

"I was willing to do whatever I had to do to save your life. I'd done nothing for you, Ben, offered you nothing as a father or as a man, and I knew that I wouldn't be able to for years as the ramifications from my work would follow me long after I gave up working undercover. This was, I believed, maybe my only chance to offer you something meaningful. But I want you to understand, I had no notion whatsoever that you'd become Succouri. I thought the marrow would simply cure you. I'd been taught, and I understood that the only way to pass the gift was from an older Succouri who was in the right stage and, though I suppose I never asked directly, I didn't believe a child could ever become one."

Frowning, Ben nodded. "Yes, that seems to have been the general understanding of everyone until now," Ben's voice revealed exasperation at this now disproven perception.

"I only knew it worked; you got better, and your mother never informed me of the rest."

"We didn't know where it came from or what it was," Ben explained. "I didn't start showing signs for about a month afterward, and since I knew nothing about it, I didn't connect it to the transplant, nor did my mother."

"Of course," Taylor said softly, regret causing him to avoid looking in the mirror at his son's pained expression. "Addy never knew about me. I had no real reason to, so I never told her about the Succouri."

"So," Ben sighed, "somehow, perhaps because the gift was so new and not well-established, you lost it, passed it to me, and never became Succouri yourself." Ben spoke the truth, relief at the understanding resounding in his tone, yet also regret at the reality of a past, full of pain and confusion, that could never be undone.

"I assumed the marrow donation interrupted the reception process, caused it not to set in, but I was fine with that since it saved your life. Looking back on it now, I should have considered the possibility of transferring the gift but, again, I was absolutely convinced that that was impossible."

"What about Briggs? Did he know about me, about what you did?" Ben asked.

"No. I never told anyone about you, even Briggs. I didn't want the two worlds to overlap in any way out of protection. When I decided to donate the marrow, I knew Briggs wouldn't approve of my actions or my subtle threat toward the doctor, so I became even more cautious, not having much contact with your mother after that. But, Ben, if I had known that I passed along the gift rather than simply curing you, I would have told him; I guarantee you that. After all, it's Briggs's gift you possess. It wouldn't have been fair, not right, to keep you apart under those circumstances, to deny him the opportunity to teach you and you the opportunity to learn from him."

Ben's gaze dropped to the floor, and Callie knew he was contending with the regret of the missed opportunity.

"What did he think happened? He had to wonder why you never became Succouri."

"He did. It saddened him greatly," Taylor confirmed with a sigh. "It does happen, once in a great while, that the gift doesn't take. It's rare, but it happens often enough that no one investigated."

"And what happened to Briggs?" Ben asked somberly, anticipating the sad answer.

"He passed about a year ago," Taylor said quietly.

The pain of this truth weighed heavily on both men, and no one spoke for several minutes.

"And you continued working undercover for all these years?" Ben finally asked, his voice still strained with emotion.

"No. I quit doing that kind of work after Briggs retired

about seven years ago, but I still supervised those in the field. Even after I no longer worked undercover, the threat was still high as stepping out of that arena caused some strong suspicions about me among my former associates. It's only been in the last two years or so that I've felt like I was in the clear, no longer haunted by my connections to the darkness."

There was silence as each of them processed the new revelations. Callie tuned into Ben's breathing as she felt his heart reshaping to accommodate affection for a father he'd never known.

"Ben, I have many regrets about my life, too many to count, but by far, my greatest regret is not being in your life." Taylor's voice was a plea, a humble and sincere offering. "Despite my need to protect you, I'll never forgive myself for first, the pain you endured believing you weren't known or loved by your father, and second, the pain I caused you by leaving you in utter confusion and fear after the transplant; though admittedly that regret is new just today." He took a deep breath and let it out slowly before continuing. "I know these words will never fix the damage caused by my actions, but I need to speak them nonetheless. I'm sorry, Son, truly, deeply sorry."

A sweet kind of silence lingered as Callie and Ben's father waited to see what Ben would say, whether he would open his heart, offer forgiveness, and take a chance at building a new relationship. Knowing him as she did, Callie felt sure of his answer, but she waited for Ben's heart to respond in its own time.

At last, Ben sucked in a breath and let it out slowly, and Callie could hear him release all bitterness with the exhale.

He smiled, an exhausted, weak smile but a truly beautiful expression. "It's also unquestionably true that you have saved my life twice and probably Callie's today as well, so..."

Acceptance and peace settled in Ben's eyes, and Callie squeezed his arm and smiled, pride in his character and heart shining in her own eyes.

"Thank you," Taylor whispered hoarsely, overcome with gratitude at his son's kindness and grace.

Callie watched in the mirror as Ben's father's face relaxed and his blue eyes brightened, the resemblance to Ben undeniably evident in the expression. As she looked on in wonder, the forgiveness offered by his son changed his features, restoring youth to his face, smoothing the hardened lines and wrinkles etched by years of regret and hopelessness. She wasn't sure which was more profoundly beautiful, the offering of forgiveness or the reception of it, but both brought tears to her eyes.

"If you're comfortable sharing," Taylor said, still unable to speak normally as the emotions strained his voice, "I'd love to hear your story too, Ben; yours and Callie's. I've got a lot of catching up to do. It's obvious the two of you are well bonded and deeply in love, so I'm not just gaining a son today, but a lovely, kindhearted daughter as well." Taylor smiled as he looked at Callie in the rearview mirror, and she returned the smile.

Ben shared much of his past, being thoughtful about relaying the depth of pain caused by his confusion but not hiding it either, as it was an essential part of his story, explaining why he ran for so long. His father remained quiet as he listened, but his face reacted to each detail, both happy and sad. He smiled continually when Ben told the story of how he and Callie met and shared the progression of their relationship and bond.

Though his interest in every detail was evident, he

didn't ask many questions or poke into areas Ben wasn't ready or willing to divulge. Ben was careful not to mention the names of Ms. Essie, Louis, Raul, or Elena directly, respecting the privacy rules regarding disclosure of other Succouri's identities.

Callie shared the story of her father's stroke and how Ben had given her and Lee the chance to say goodbye, and Ben's father shed a few tears at the telling.

By the time they arrived at the Navarro home, significant progress had been made in establishing a foundation for trust between the three of them. As Callie still grieved the passing of her own father, witnessing the genesis of what promised to be a mutually nourishing bond forming between father and son brought healing to her heart.

CHAPTER 18
THE SUNRISE

It was nearly ten o'clock when Callie, Ben, and Agent Taylor entered the Navarro home and followed the doctor to his well-equipped, hidden medical lab. Callie's stomach hurt at the dread of Ben's impending suffering and the knowledge that the bullet lodged in his arm had been intended for her.

Though his recovery would be much quicker and easier than hers had been, the trade-off of having no anesthesia during the surgery was a terrible compromise. In the course of their relationship, she'd seen Ben weak and drained often but not in acute pain, and she had no desire to partake in that particular experience. But, considering he faced this trial because of his great love for her, there was no way she could abandon him to suffer this alone, so she reached deep for the strength to face it.

Doctor Navarro asked a few questions about what they'd uncovered that day regarding Ben's acquisition of the gift. Ben and his father gave him the updated facts on how it was accidentally and unknowingly transferred. The doctor's expression revealed how astonished he was at the story.

"That shouldn't have been possible," he said, shaking his head. "Not that anyone I've ever known has had the opportunity to do it. Since Succouri can't have children, rescuing their own isn't an issue, and even if they had children from their prior life, by the time the parent reached the ripening, those children would be too old to receive the gift. So, to my knowledge, this has never been attempted or even considered."

Taylor raised both hands. "I didn't intend to give him the gift. I just wanted to cure him, and since I was a match and he was dying, it would have been immoral, even evil, to withhold the help I could provide."

Doctor Navarro nodded in compassionate understanding, though perhaps not in full agreement or approval. He asked Ben's father if he would leave a blood sample for him to study alongside Ben's, and he willingly obliged.

Despite his curiosity and desire for more information about this mystery, Doctor Navarro quickly shifted to focus on helping Ben. He asked him, once again, to remove his shirt and stretch out on one of the medical beds, but before Ben complied, he turned to Callie. "Are you sure you want to stay?" He ran his thumb down her cheek. "I'll understand if you want to return when it's over."

"No!" she said emphatically. "You took this bullet for me, and I'm not leaving you alone to suffer the consequences."

Ben shook his head. "Sweetheart, believe me when I say that keeping you alive and with me was a fully selfish act, as there is no way I could live without you. If you want to stay, I'll gladly respect your decision, but if you change your mind mid-procedure, I *will* understand."

Callie squeezed his hand, answering his objection, and he smiled at her before moving to obey the doctor's requests.

Ben's father also remained in the room as Doctor Navarro requested his assistance. Callie's stomach churned, and Taylor's face dropped when the doctor informed them that part of that assistance might include holding Ben still, as his body would naturally want to pull away from the intense pain.

Though determined to stay, Callie's panic nearly overtook her when she saw the sharp instruments on a tray beside Ben.

"I'm going to try some local anesthetic," the doctor announced as he stood gloved and ready by Ben's left arm. "Because you used your gift tonight, and that's weakened your quick healing, the normally rapid dissipation of the medication might be slowed, thus providing a moment or two of benefit. The weaker state of being will also help with the procedure since every cut I make won't heal over quite as quickly, keeping me from having to make repeated cuts before I can extract the bullet. I'll still have to work fast to keep ahead of it, which means no break in the pain, Ben, but at least it should be over quickly. Small comforts, but comforts nonetheless."

Sucking in a breath of air, Ben nodded his head at the doctor, letting him know he was ready.

He gave Ben a shot, then waited for a few seconds before reaching for the scalpel. Taylor held Ben's wrist, and Callie noticed his pained expression. She imagined this was not what he'd envisioned doing on his first night with his son.

Holding Ben's right hand in hers, she stroked his face tenderly.

"Look at Callie, Ben. And, Callie, keep your eyes on his face," the doctor advised in a voice heavy with strain.

At the first cut, Ben's face contorted in pain, a look Callie had never seen on his face before, and her eyes filled with tears. The local anesthesia didn't seem to provide the moment of relief the doctor had hoped it would. She wiped his forehead gently with a cool cloth, keeping her eyes focused on his as he bit his lip, clenched his teeth, and sucked in halting gasps of air. For the second time that night, her heart broke in two as she helplessly witnessed Ben suffer indescribable agony resulting from his profound act of love for her, and she resolved never to forget his sacrifice.

As seconds ticked by like hours, pain-induced tears and sweat dripped down his face, and his jaw tightened along with the muscles in his arms and chest. He closed his eyes, concentrating all of his efforts on staying still despite his instinct to squirm and pull away.

"Okay," the doctor finally announced, "I see the bullet. Hang on, Ben. This will be the worst part, but then it's done."

In the next second, Ben let out an anguished groan that made Callie's tears flow freely as she lifted his hand and kissed it, feeling completely helpless. He clenched his teeth again and sucked air through them, the desperate sound piercing her heart. Through all the pain, he didn't move his left arm, somehow willing himself to stay in place and sparing his father the horror of having to restrain him.

"One more minute..." the doctor promised, and Callie held her breath.

Letting go of her hand, Ben formed a tight fist and drove it into the bed, bracing himself against the excruciating pain as the doctor dug out the bullet. Stabs of sharp pain ran through her whole body. Callie wasn't sure if it was their bond connecting her with his experience or simply her reaction to watching his suffering, but she put her hands over her stomach, feeling like she really might be sick.

"Done!" the doctor announced with a sigh of relief, stepping back and displaying the extracted bullet in small forceps.

Ben exhaled in relief as his whole body sank back into the bed, his muscles relaxing from the strain. Letting out a relieved breath and grabbing a fresh, cool towel, she lovingly wiped his sweaty face as her tears flowed.

"Ben, you're incredible!" the doctor praised, shaking his head as he wiped the wound with a sterile cloth. "There would have been absolutely no shame in crying out. I know that was excruciating!"

Ben offered another relieved exhale, confirming the truth in the doctor's words. Frozen in place, Ben's father stood silently, overcome with anxiety and pride at his son's continued display of unmatched courage.

After a few more deep breaths, Ben smiled weakly at her, but Callie had no doubt he'd just experienced the worst physical suffering of his life.

"Ben, I'm so sorry," she whispered, but he shook his head and tenderly wiped away each tear with his finger.

After the fire, Callie had thought about Ben's anonymous suffering as those he helped were unaware of the price he paid to save them. Now, here she was, seeing for herself the cost of her rescue. The truth of how sacrificial this life was sank deeply into her heart, making her all the more determined to lighten his burdens in any way she possibly could.

"Everything's good here," Doctor Navarro announced, removing his gloves and placing the tray of instruments on a nearby counter. "With Callie's help and that amazing Succouri healing, you'll return to normal in no time. So sorry for the torture. You guys, go home and get some sleep. I'll be in touch soon with my findings on the blood samples, and I definitely want to talk more when you all haven't just been through one of the worst days of your lives. Well, maybe worst and best." He smiled as he looked between Ben and his father.

"Thanks, Doc.," Ben managed as he sat up slowly and reached for his shirt.

Ben slept soundly on Callie's shoulder the whole way home. After helping Donovan, protecting her nearly to the point of giving up his own life, meeting his father, and undergoing surgery with no anesthetic, it was little wonder he was emotionally and physically spent. Though she was also exhausted, the flow of adrenaline and her frantic worry for Ben had her mind and heart racing, keeping her from sleep.

When they'd gotten into the car, Ben had removed his shirt again so Callie could place her hand over the deep, jagged wound on his arm, speeding the healing process. Gently, she moved her fingers back and forth over the wound, checking it continuously until it finally disappeared, letting her heart find peace at last.

She chatted quietly with Taylor a few times, but they both wanted to let Ben sleep, so they mostly drove silently. As there was no way Ben could have managed driving, Callie was grateful for Taylor's help, and she sensed his great pleasure at being able to offer it.

When they arrived back at the house, all was quiet. The FBI had removed Ruiz's body and vehicle and returned the home to full security. A single agent met them at the door, and after receiving Ben's approval, Agent Taylor relieved him to take over security for the night, again expressing gratitude for the opportunity to assist.

"I'm glad you were here today. Thank you for... for everything," Ben smiled wearily at his father as he leaned on Callie for support.

Ben's father looked him directly in the eyes. "I knew the day I met my son in person would be the best day of my life. From the pictures and stories your mother provided, I knew you were a kind soul, but I never imagined my son would overwhelm me with inexpressible pride. You are a great man, and I can say, with unwavering confidence, that Owen Briggs would be very satisfied at where his gift resides. You are so much like him and have the same soul. Perhaps that's why the gift passed from me to you. I'd be proud to know you, even if you weren't my son, but the fact that you are fills me with gratitude for the undeserved privilege I've been granted; the chance to be a part of your life and story. I love you, Son. Always have, always will."

The eyes of both men glistened with tears, and Taylor reached out to embrace Ben. Callie stepped back, smiling with great joy. She had once told Ben the same, that he was a good man, but it had been hard for him at the time to accept the praise. These precious words from his father would, no doubt, go far in progressing the healing of Ben's wounded heart.

Taylor warmly embraced Callie as well before helping Ben up the stairs and bidding them goodnight. Callie walked with Ben the rest of the way down the hall, smiling as he collapsed into bed. Though he was not unresponsive like he'd been the night of the fire, his weak, exhausted state reminded her of how she'd cared for him, and the memory was sweet, warming her heart.

"I love you, Ben Sawyer," she whispered near his ear as she leaned over him.

When he smiled back at her, there was more wholeness in the expression than she'd ever seen before. "And I you, Miss LeVray, forever and always."

Softly, she kissed his lips before retreating to quickly change her clothes. She lay down beside him and he, consciously this time, pulled her close to him. Before either of them had a chance to say goodnight, they fell contentedly and soundly asleep.

In the early morning hours, before the sun appeared on the horizon, Callie felt Ben's lips on hers and she opened her eyes. He sat on the edge of the bed, smiling lovingly at her and stroking her hair.

"Callie," he whispered, leaning over to kiss her again. "Come with me."

She thought she might be dreaming, but his lips were warm and soft, and the fire hot and fierce.

"Ben?" She sat up, rubbing her eyes, groggy and confused. "What are you doing up?"

"Come with me, sweetheart." He stood and held out his hand, and she took it wearily, struggling to her feet.

"Is everything alright?" She worried, still not understanding why Ben was up at this hour.

Nodding and smiling in response, he wrapped a thick coat around her shoulders and placed a wool hat on her head, pulling it down over her ears.

"Are we going for a walk?" she asked, yawning.

"Yes, a short one." He grinned, enjoying her dazed expression.

Slipping her feet into a pair of shoes, she retook his

hand as he led her down the stairs and out the front door. The air was cold but not frigid, and Ben wrapped his arm around her shoulders, his warmth keeping her from shivering. They walked around the side of the house and down a short trail that led to a private deck, which Callie had never seen before. Because of the threat to their lives, they'd spent little time outdoors, so she'd had no opportunity to see the property around the house.

Though it was dark, Ben's touch allowed her to see the shadowy river nestled between the dark, steep sides of the cliffs.

A wooden swing hung in the middle of the small deck, and Ben gestured for her to sit beside him. Unfolding a blanket, he wrapped them in it as he sheltered her with his arm, pulling her close.

"Ben, it's beautiful here, but couldn't we wait for the…"

After placing a finger over her lips, he pointed to the horizon, smiling as his eyes twinkled with excitement. "Just wait," he whispered.

She sat back and relaxed, feeling warm and satisfied next to the man she loved. *If he wants to sit in the dark, holding me all night, so be it*, she thought with a smile. She was incredibly grateful he was still here with her, alive, their lives and future full of wondrous possibilities.

Gradually, the horizon began to glow with the promise of dawn. The light grew and brightened until, in a moment of glorious, shimmering brilliance, rays of sunlight streaked over the horizon like a flower bud suddenly bursting into full bloom.

Callie gaped, awestruck at the beauty of a sunrise, something she'd never been able to clearly see before, and for a moment, she was unable to breathe or speak.

"Ben! It's beautiful!" she finally managed. "I've never seen…"

When she turned to look at him, she realized he'd moved. Though he still held her hand, he now knelt on the ground next to her, and she gasped as she recognized the intention in his posture.

"Callie LeVray, you are my sunrise. The moment I met you, the darkness in me vanished. You have filled every dark, hopeless place in my heart with the light of your unconditional love. When I met you, I woke up, came alive. You are the one I want to spend every sunrise and every sunset with for the rest of my days. I never dreamed, never hoped to win the heart of a woman so radiant, kind, and trusting. I gladly give you everything I am: my heart, body, and soul, my possessions, my name, and my promise. I guarantee that our lives together will continue to be an adventure, but I vow to be by your side, holding your hand through anything and everything that comes our way. I love you boundlessly and endlessly. Will you do me the honor of accepting all I am, and will you honor me by offering me all you are? Will you marry me, Callie?"

Before Ben could finish the last syllable of her name, Callie dropped to the ground in front of him and flung her arms around him, knocking him backward as they laughed with unrestrained joy.

"Yes, Ben Sawyer!" she exclaimed through the laughter, resting on top of him as he lay smiling on his back. "You already have my heart, but yes, it's all yours, forever."

Ben slowly sat up, holding her on his lap as she wrapped her right arm around his shoulders. He pulled a small box from his coat pocket and retrieved a sparkling diamond ring. The diamond was large but tasteful, and circling it were several layers of smaller diamonds as well as glowing green emeralds.

"I wanted it to match your stunning green eyes," He smiled as he watched her obvious delight at the ring's elegance.

Lifting her left hand, he slipped it onto her ring finger as they stared blissfully at the visible proof of their promised intentions.

"It's perfect!" Callie said as she exhaled in wonder, watching the diamond sparkle in the light of the emerging sun.

After a moment of admiration, she looked at him with a teasing smile. "The mysterious errand?"

He returned her smile, looking quite satisfied. "Yep. Now you know all my secrets."

Callie held her smile but pressed her lips together and tilted her head, the look playful. "I'm glad you had a ring this time."

Tilting his head, he wrinkled his brow, confused by her statement.

Callie laughed delightedly at his boyish expression. "You sort of asked me once before, but..."

"What? When?" Ben squinted his eyes, looking doubtful.

"After the fire. You were... quite out of it, and I told you I loved you, and you replied that you wanted to marry me. I think the exact words were, 'Very soon, I want to marry you.'" She giggled at the memory.

"I did?" Ben smiled tentatively, and she could see that he was desperately trying to remember.

"Yes, you did," she confirmed, enjoying the bewildered look on his face.

"What was your answer?" he inquired, surrendering to her version of events.

"Hm." She pressed her lips together like she wasn't going to tell him and Ben shifted his expression to an exaggerated frown.

"Not fair," he teased. "You know all my secrets now."

She drummed her fingers on her chin like she was trying to decide, and Ben's eyes pleaded with a look of mock distress.

"Okay." She laughed, unable to resist his plea. "If you'd still been awake, it would have been a yes but since you went to sleep before I could answer, I just sort of stood there stunned."

He smiled in satisfaction. "I'm glad I was awake for your answer this time, Miss... well, soon to be, Mrs. Sawyer," he said proudly, and Callie's heart soared at the idea of sharing Ben's name.

They laughed and embraced, wrapped in the joy of this precious moment they knew they would never forget and forever treasure. Ben guided her to sit back on the swing with him and then took her in his arms and kissed her slowly, letting all the happiness in his heart flow out in an expression of sincere love. Wrapping her hands around his neck, she then pushed her fingers through his hair as she returned the same affection. As the fire grew hotter and brighter, Ben breathlessly pulled away to speak, feverish desire making his eyes animated and brilliant blue. "Callie," he panted near her ear. "I want you to have the wedding of your dreams, whatever you wish. I'll ensure you have every resource and any help you want or need. But can you tell me... Well, how quickly do you think we might be able to arrange it?"

Callie smiled flirtatiously at the question, rapt in his

sincere longing for her as she comprehended and empathized with the urgency he expressed.

"I don't need or want a fancy wedding. I've found the man I want a life with, and that's the point of all of it anyway. I want my brother there, our friends, and... all our family: old, new, and adopted." She paused to laugh at how many people they considered family now, though they had no genetic relationship. "If you're alright with simple, I hope soon, Ben, very soon," she said, bringing back his words from the forgotten proposal.

"That suits me perfectly." He leaned in to whisper near her ear. "Weeks?" Ben softly kissed just above her collarbone. "Months?" He moved to kiss under her ear as he pleaded for clarification.

"Um," she stammered, having difficulty thinking with the distracting thrill in his kisses. "Weeks works for me."

He blew a soft breath of air on her neck, making her tremble. "Two weeks?" He kissed her neck. "Three weeks?" He kissed the corner of her mouth.

"You don't play fair, Ben Sawyer." She smiled, her eyes animated with her longing now. "But I'll make you a deal. I'll plan the wedding as quickly as possible if you plan the honeymoon."

Ben leaned away enough to let her see the elation in his eyes and smile.

"I enthusiastically accept that deal."

BEN AND CALLIE enjoyed an early breakfast with Rosa, Leo, and Agent Taylor. Upon hearing the news of their engagement, Rosa hugged them both, exclaiming with enthusiasm how delighted she was for them and pledging her and Leo's full support and assistance in wedding planning. Ben's father smiled broadly, offering Ben a firm handshake and a congratulatory pat on the back.

After breakfast, they placed several phone calls, joyfully sharing the news of their engagement and the demise of Callie's pursuer with all their family and friends. The announcement was received with wholehearted excitement and many additional offers to assist in any way needed.

Ms. Essie and Louis were particularly happy for them, relief evident in their voices as they'd been worried after what had transpired during their visit. Ben assured them that, though it was difficult to accept that he and Callie would never have children of their own, they were embracing their lives as Succouri and anticipating a very fulfilling future.

Lee had already started calling Ben "Brother Ben," consistent with his tradition of rotating nicknames.

Ben also checked on Donovan and was pleased to learn his condition had improved and stabilized. Though treatments were only temporarily effective, they bought him time, and he and Callie intended to take full advantage of that to pursue a more permanent cure for him. They hoped Doctor Navarro's extensive involvement in the Succouri network might prove helpful in connecting Donovan with a Succouri ready to transfer his gift, as they both believed Donovan would make an ideal candidate for this life of service and sacrifice.

After speaking to Grace about the engagement, Callie confirmed she and Donovan had been communicating, though his setback in health had caused Donovan to withdraw from that contact significantly. If their plan for Donovan proved possible, and if he was open to embracing it, Grace's life might also change in profound ways. Ben and

Callie hoped that their experience might be an encouragement as well as a guide for their friends should circumstances work out the way they hoped.

Late in the afternoon, while Callie and Rosa were chatting excitedly about wedding plans, Ben wandered back into his mother's bedroom. For a while, he stood staring at her portrait over the bed, trying to balance the good and the bad in the collection of memories filed away in his mind. She had loved him in her own way, and Ben would always love her. The fact that she fought so many of her own internal demons gave him pause in judging her inability to bond with him in a meaningful way.

Ben couldn't help but wonder how different things might have been for him if he'd known his father and had that balancing influence in his life. Though he also had a troubled past and had made poor decisions for years, Ben could already discern that he possessed far more likeness to his father in demeanor and appearance than his mother. Although he'd only just met him the day before, the genetic relationship was evident.

In his way, his father had lived a life of service and sacrifice, too, and though that service had separated him from Ben, he admired his father's desire to make up for his mistakes and do good in the world. Ben sensed that, when it came to his father's new relationship with him, he would do much the same, and that notion offered Ben a great deal of hope as he cautiously opened his heart.

He moved to the adjacent sitting room and sat on the couch, staring at the shelves of movies and books. This place held the most potent memories of his mother as it was where they spent hours watching musicals when she was trapped in her depression. This was where he'd helped her, one of the few places where he'd felt positive about his unique ability. Though neither he nor his mother understood it, and in every other regard, it had been a stumbling block for him during those years, in this space, it had been a gift, a soothing salve for his mother's troubled soul. As Ben's life moved forward into a new and wonderful future with Callie, he would hold on to this place in his heart, anchor his memories of his mother here, and, at long last, let the rest go.

"Ben?"

He was startled by Callie's melodic voice in the doorway. Rising quickly, he took her hand and led her back to the couch.

"Are you alright?" she asked, concern showing in the lines on her forehead.

"More than alright," he reassured, kissing her forehead and glancing down at the shining diamond on her hand.

Though not quite back to normal yet, the worst of the weakness from the day before had left him, and the happiness of his engagement to Callie filled him with such deep and abiding contentment that it was impossible to feel anything but whole and satisfied.

"Is this where you learned to sing?" she asked with a smile.

"Yes, I guess it is." He pondered, never having thought of it like that before. "I think my mother owned every musical ever made," he added, pointing at the shelves stocked with dozens of them.

"Which was her favorite?"

Ben thought for a moment, then moved to squat next to the shelf, looking through the titles.

"I think... probably, *Les Misérables*," he said, tugging the title from its sandwiched spot in the collection.

As he extracted it, an envelope dropped to the floor. Ben

set the movie down and reached for it, his heart pounding as he recognized the handwriting on the front.

"Ben?" Callie inquired, hearing the gasp that had escaped as he focused on his name written across the middle.

"I... I think this is from her," he stammered, unable to believe what he saw.

Callie's mouth fell open and she came to sit beside him on the floor. If his mother wanted to leave him a letter where no one else would find it, this was the right place. What she hadn't anticipated was that his broken heart six years before couldn't face the painful reminders of her.

Slowly, Ben tore open the envelope and retrieved the letter, taking a deep breath as he unfolded the page. Callie put her hand on his shoulder, supporting him as he faced this final ghost from his past, and he read the words aloud to her.

> My Darling Ben, I knew you would find this letter here in the special place we shared. Though I can no longer tolerate the darkness that presses in around me day after day, I want you to know that you were the one ray of light that always broke through. I know I wasn't much of a mother to you, lost as I've always been in my own sinking ship, but I am forever grateful you were sent to me, an unexpected gift I didn't deserve and couldn't embrace. The deficiency was mine, Ben, not yours. Forgive me for leaving you, but I know you will shine your radiant light into the world and make it a better

place. And I'm not leaving you alone. Below, you will find the location of a safety deposit box where you can connect with your father. Though he may not be able to offer you all you might hope for, it is my wish that someday he will be free to do so, and this might provide a good start. It was your father who saved your life many years ago when you were ill. I know you will, with that precious heart of yours, find a way to forgive him and me for our sins against you as inadequate parents. You've always deserved so much more. That gift you possess is wondrous, and though I know it has caused you great pain and confusion, it is my firm conviction that it grows straight out of your giving heart. The goodness inside of you simply can't be contained, so it overflows to others through your healing touch. Someday, you will come to understand how extraordinary and beautiful it is.

Goodbye, my son. Live a wonderful life filled with love and joy. And keep singing! I love you always. Your Mother, Adalynn Sawyer.

Though Ben made it through the whole letter without breaking down, the tears now came, and Callie reached for him, pulling him to her as her tears flowed with his. The letter left him conflicted, appreciative of his mother's assurances of love for him but heartbroken at her inability to embrace life's joys and the love he offered her. He regretted the years of emptiness he'd endured, realizing that if he'd found this letter sooner, he'd have at least enjoyed some connection with his father and perhaps a greater level of peace concerning his mother's terrible choice.

As Callie held him, his heart began to accept and understand how profoundly troubled his mother truly was and how out of reach curing her, through his efforts alone, also was. What happened to his mother wasn't his fault. He'd done what he could for her, loved her, and comforted her. Though he'd offered her the gift of his heart, a gift must be received, and that was something his mother couldn't do.

When he'd offered Callie his love, she, unlike his mother, had wholeheartedly accepted him, returning the same affection. His love, his gift, his heart wasn't poison after all. He hadn't destroyed his mother, her depression had. Sad as it was, this truth mended the remaining holes in his heart. The past was gone; Callie was his future.

Ben smiled as a new, abiding peace settled deep inside him. He leaned back and grasped her hands in his, gazing into her exotic green eyes and seeing forever there.

"Callie," he said, his smile full and satisfied. "Let's go home."

Nodding, she smiled back at him in understanding.

EPILOGUE

Doctor Navarro sat at his desk, staring at the numbers and images on his computer screen. He'd performed a full analysis on Ben's blood and compared it with previous samples from other Succouri, as well as the blood left by Ben's father. What he now knew baffled him.

This can't be right, he kept repeating to himself, but the images didn't lie.

His wife had talked with him about Callie's observations and concerns regarding the merging of the Succouri and human characteristics in Ben, but he hadn't paid it much mind, not believing that was possible. Now, he shook his head, recognizing that he should have known better than to so quickly dismiss the instincts of a bonded partner, especially one from this unique and extraordinary pair.

In his mind, he ran through all he knew about this case, trying to fathom how this could have happened. Ben's father had received the Succouri gift first, but it hadn't firmly established in his body before he donated marrow to his son. The donation transferred the gift but also some of

Thomas Taylor's own blood, blood that had remarkable genetic similarities to Ben's. Perhaps this close compatibility with Ben's own chemical makeup affected the way the Succouri additive interacted and was absorbed inside his body.

Then there was Ben's age. He was young and not mature. As his body grew and completed its development, it would have to work and grow in coordination with the Succouri additive. So, the Succouri grew with the man, or maybe the man grew with the Succouri. As he stared at the images, it was impossible to say which statement was more accurate, which was the problem. Ben was indeed Succouri, but in a way that did not compare to anyone who had ever claimed that identity.

He had to call them, but what he had to tell them was so unbelievable that, though he didn't know all the ramifications yet, it unquestionably would impact their lives and futures forever.

Acknowledgments

A special word of thanks to those who helped with the editing and designing of this book.

In particular:

Melanie Underwood (editor)

and

Hannah Linder (cover design)

And my numerous beta readers who offered me valuable feedback during the book's development.

THANK YOU ALL!

About the Author

As an Adjunct Professor of Human Communication for more than two decades, writing has always been a part of Meridith's life and career. Her novels combine her love for romance and storytelling with her communication and writing background. Legally blind since birth, Meridith's unique point of view and experiences bring intriguing and fresh perspectives to her storylines and characters. Beyond simple romance novels, Meridith writes unforgettable, epic love stories that sweep readers off their feet.

Meridith resides in Kansas with her husband, Jason, and her two sons.